# When the
# Lyrebird Calls

# KIM KANE

# When the Lyrebird Calls

ALLEN&UNWIN
SYDNEY·MELBOURNE·AUCKLAND·LONDON

**Australian Government**

This project has been assisted by the Australian Government through the Australia Council for the Arts, its arts funding and advisory body.

Readings Foundation

This project was also assisted by a Glenfern Fellowship supported by the Readings Foundation.

Allen & Unwin
83 Alexander Street, Crows Nest NSW 2065, Australia
Phone: (61 2) 8425 0100, Email: info@allenandunwin.com, Web: www.allenandunwin.com

A Cataloguing-in-Publication entry is available from the National Library of Australia, www.trove.nla.gov.au

ISBN 978 1 74175 852 8

Teachers' notes available from www.allenandunwin.com

The excerpt from the poem 'Lyrebirds' on page vi is by Judith Wright, *Collected Poems 1942–1985*, 4th Estate, HarperCollins Publishers, 2016, p164, © The Estate of Judith Wright 1994. First published in *Birds: Poems*, 1962. Used by permission of HarperCollins Australia.

'*Ye women of Australia, arise in all your might!*' on page 78 is excerpted from a poem signed 'C.E.C.', presumed to be the work of Caroline Emily Clark of South Australia, from *Worker* (New South Wales), 11 January 1896

The poem 'Mr Sludge, "The Medium"' on page 225 is from Robert Browning's collection *Dramatis Personae*, 1864

'*Latere semper patere, quod latuit diu*' on page 297 – Latin for 'Leave in concealment what has long been concealed' – is from Lucius Annaeus Seneca's *Oedipus*, 826.

'White for purity in public as well as private life; purple for dignity and self-respect; and green for hope and new life' on page 299 was reportedly a description by Emmeline Pankhurst, founder of the Women's Social and Political Union (WSPU), of the suffrage colours she chose for the group.
From: maas.museum/magazine/2015/10/purple-green-and-white-an-australian-history/

Cover and text design by Debra Billson

Cover images: Gert (photographer unknown, circa 1926, from National photographer's studio, Atelier National, Helsinki) and Charlie (photographer unknown, Kidderminster, UK) supplied by the Wishpom Vintage Image Collection: www.wishpom.com; Imo (by Adelaide Photographic Company, circa 1855–1900) and Bea (by Grut, T.A., circa 1910–1940) via State Library Victoria, slv.vic.gov.au; lyrebird (© Yulia Avgustinovich), dome (© Евгений Косцов), trees (© andreiuc88) & rough texture (© Nupean Pruprong) from 123RF.com; back cover frame (© Milen Stankov), shoe (by Firmin-Didot et Cie, France, 1897, photo © Lynen) & coin (© Fat Jackey) from Shutterstock.com

Set in 12.5/16 pt Fournier by Midland Typesetters, Australia
Printed in Australia by McPherson's Printing Group, www.mcphersonsprinting.com.au

10 9 8 7 6 5 4 3 2 1

For my grandmother Nen,
who is so old she has seen the olden days firsthand.
And to her step-great-granddaughter, Madeleine —
not only because she is an utter delight, but because
she has the courage to blaze her own trail.
A wise woman and a young woman,
bookending our family.
With much love, thanks and admiration. X
K.K.

Some things ought to be left secret, alone;
some things – birds like walking fables –
ought to inhabit nowhere but the
reverence of the heart.

'Lyrebirds'
Judith Wright

# Author's note

Parts of this novel are historical, and consequently the characters' language and behaviour is at times dated and completely unacceptable today – for example, it is often overtly sexist.

Similarly, the language and characters' behaviour in the historical parts of this book are also sometimes racist, because sadly so is our past and, quite frankly, our present. I think that to depict our history in any other way does yet another disservice to those who suffered and continue to suffer in Australia at the hands of racist policies – in particular, Aboriginal and Torres Strait Islander people as well as people from non-Anglo minority groups, such as Chinese people.

As Anglo Australia must own its sexism, so too must it own its racism and the consequences it had and continues to have for so many people.

Readers should be aware that the following racist terms appearing in the historical part of this novel must never be used today: 'half-caste', 'Chinamen' and, in the context in which they are found in this book, 'blackfella' and 'native' (see the AIATSIS 'Guidelines for Ethical Publishing' referenced in the Acknowledgements for more information).

While I am exceedingly uncomfortable with the words and actions of some of my characters, during the course of the research for this novel, I found countless examples of such overt sexism and racism in Australia's past, and while it may be more palatable to a contemporary reader to exclude this, I think that to do so would be dishonest. I also think that falsely recreating our history makes it harder for young Australians to learn from past wrongs.

In my mind this novel is set in the Mount Macedon area shared by the Wurundjeri, Dja Dja Wurrung and Taungurung people, as well as on Wurundjeri land in Melbourne. I wish to acknowledge this country and these people, together with others of the Kulin nation, and pay my respects to their Elders past and present.

It was important to me to include an Aboriginal character, Percy, in the story to acknowledge the role Indigenous Australians played in the suffrage story – the fight for all Australians to obtain the right to vote.

Percy is a made-up character, but the place where he grew up, Coranderrk Station, is real. The political activism undertaken by those on Coranderrk as they fought for justice – which is touched on very briefly in this novel – is an important story with which I hope all Australians will become familiar. I urge you to explore it further. (See Acknowledgements for some links.)

Tremendous thanks to Aunty Joy Murphy and the Wandoon Estate Aboriginal Corporation for giving me permission to include cultural references in the book; what an honour to have someone of Aunty Joy's standing, as a Senior Wurundjeri Elder, community leader, and the great-great-niece of William Barak, support this project. Sincere thanks also to Lisa Fuller, Gabrielle Wang and Rebecca Lim for their advice on how to most appropriately go about including historical racism in the story; this required a great deal of thought, and I was exceptionally grateful to have access to their suggestions and guidance as I struggled with these questions. Big thanks to Yolanda Walker-Finette for her generous on-the-spot assistance. Finally, thanks to the Dja Dja Wurrung Clans Aboriginal Corporation and the Taungurung Clans Aboriginal Corporation for confirming spellings for me.

Kim Kane, 2016

*Three girls were bunched together in a circle. At their feet lay a doll, nestled in a box filled with tissue paper. Its ankles, wrists and neck were shackled by silky cord. A white terrier rooted about in a pile of scrunched-up brown paper and fraying string. One of the girls tipped the box upwards with her foot and then allowed it to slap back onto the ground.*

*The doll stared.* Mama. Mama.

*The doll's eyes were big and purple-blue, like pansies. They were rimmed with feathery lashes, top and bottom.*

*'But she's just so beautiful.' The second girl leant down and pushed a sticky finger into a celluloid dimple.*

*'Her costume really is quite elegant.' The first girl sat with a dull thud and ran a finger across grey velvet so thick her finger left a smoky trail.*

*'Is that real ermine on her bonnet?' asked the third, kneeling to stroke the milky down that edged the doll's curls.*

*'Er-min, not er-mine,' corrected the first. 'Yes, I suppose it is.'*

*On the grass was a card, written in perfect copperplate, stamped with a muddy boot print.*

I am so very sorry.

*'Sorry?' The third girl looked around to check that nobody was watching and then pulled at one stout little doll-leg. The cord harnessing it to the box stretched taut and gave.* Ping. *'I'll show you sorry.'*

*'Careful,' said the first girl in a headmistress voice. 'She's precious.'*

*'She's not. She's modern, not china. She's cold and hard the whole way through.'*

The second girl pulled the doll's hips away from the box until just its neck was pinned back against the card. Purple-blue eyes stared.

Mama. Mama, *the doll bleated as the girl tugged.*

'You're destroying her,' *the first girl said. But she didn't reach forward to stop it, even though she could have.*

*The third girl snatched the doll. She stood and spun the box away from the circle, pushing and pulling, yanking the doll free from the last of its cords. Tissue paper fell from the emancipated toy in ribbons, drifting as gently as blossom across the lawn. The girl turned to face the others, clutching the doll by its neck. The others stood too. The doll dangled between them, as stiff as a hunt-duck.*

'Give her back,' *said the first girl in a wobbly voice. She took a breath.* 'She's not just yours.' *She snatched the doll and threw it, thwack, down on the lawn.*

Mama. Marr. Marr.

*The third girl gasped. She dipped into a crouch and drew a penknife from inside her boot. She flicked it open and raised the blade above her head, her wrist trembling.*

*The others watched on, mouths slack. The knife glinted in the afternoon light.*

*The girl wrenched off the velvet coat, its buttons spraying like pellets. Then she plunged the penknife into the doll's chest. There was silence as the girls studied the perfect part the knife had rendered in the spotted silk. Through the slit they could see the doll's flesh, thick and ample.*

'Oh,' *whispered the first girl, taking a step back.*

'Oh,' whispered the second, squatting beside the doll to pinch its chubby wrist. She picked up the doll's bonnet and hurled it into the air. It glided up in an arc towards the sun and disappeared for a second in the glare before landing. The stocky white dog bounded after it. Rruf, rruf, rruf. The doll's parasol followed, spinning all the way into some white azaleas.

The first girl was still another moment, poised, then she gave the doll a good sharp kick. Mama. Marr. Marr. The doll thumped across the grass. The girl reached down and ran her finger over the doll's fraying skirt. 'It's silk velvet.' She looked back towards the house, then turned, grabbed the doll's head and yanked it right off. The girl's face was as tight as a butcher's tearing the guts from a chicken, as tight as ice. 'Ghastly cousin,' she spat, grinding the head into the grass with her boot. There were tiny beads of sweat above her lip.

The second girl wiped the knife on her apron as if it were covered in real blood and guts, then crushed her own hat back onto her hair. She picked up the doll's torso and threw it straight and hard at the camellias. 'I hope the foxes find it and maul it.' The girls all watched as the flowers swallowed shredded coat, stockings and kidskin boots.

The first girl roared, a pained cry, deep and ancient. Then she blinked and walked across the lawn, smoothing her hair, each step punctilious, elegant, controlled. The other girls followed, the puppy scrabbling behind them.

Somewhere, from someplace deep in the garden, a lyrebird called.

3

# At Mum Crum's

M adeleine woke, her limbs loose, the bleat of the doll still raw. *Mama. Marr. Marr.* Her eyes swept across the room, sorting through shadows. Twisted in the sheets, she was breathless, tangled. Inky light streaked through the window at the foot of the bed and across the floor. The room swayed and creaked.

And then Madeleine remembered. She was not with three angry girls. Nothing had happened. She was at Mum Crum's. At Mum Crum's while her mum sweated over her final exams and her dad sweated through a cycling tour somewhere in Italy. She was at Mum Crum's and there was no doll; there were no girls.

Mum Crum was Madeleine's Grandmother Crumpton, and she currently lived in Elf Cottage – a small wooden house bogged in an English garden on the edge of a scone-and-tea town just outside Melbourne.

At Mum Crum's everything always smelt like dust and turpentine. Mum Crum was always renovating; she renovated properties herself and then moved on, collecting houses like kids collect footy cards – only instead of just tucking them away in a property portfolio, she let people like nurses and teachers stay in them for free while they saved for their own places. 'Property has got too damn expensive in this country,' said Mum Crum, 'and the government is doing nothing about it.'

Mum Crum watched renovating programs on telly and then rushed out to stock up on tools. This was why she currently had white floorboards that looked floury, and a green fake marble paint covering most of the furniture, created with a sponge and vinegar. The effect, Madeleine thought, was like mould.

Given the choice – and she was not, because Madeleine was never given a choice in anything – Madeleine would have stayed with Nandi. Nandi was her best friend and they were in the same class, the same cricket team and even did nippers at the same surf club, but Nandi's mum had just had a make-up baby with Nandi's dad, so the timing wasn't right.

'I'm sorry, Moo,' her mum had said from her study stacked with books and plastered with post-its, 'but you'll have to stay at Mum Crum's. If I can just get through these exams, things will be so much better for us, darling. To do that, I need to concentrate.'

'And what about staying at Dad's? Why doesn't anything *ever* get between Dad and a bike?'

'His bike pants do.' Madeleine's mum smiled.

'Gross.'

'Oh come on, Moo, you're not being fair. You know perfectly well your father's been saving for this trip for years, and cost aside, the tour's just not set up for kids.'

'But why doesn't Teddy have to come to Mum Crum's? You know she's easier to deal with if her attention's divided.'

'Madeleine, it's just for the winter holidays! Anyway, it's better if Teddy stays with Raj up here. He's got band practice most days, and Uma doesn't mind. Besides, he's Year Ten now, and at least Uma will make sure the boys actually *do* their maths homework instead of spending the entire time *talking about* doing maths from the PlayStation.'

'PlayStation? I wish! Painting and Pilates are more likely to get in the way of homework at Mum Crum's.'

Madeleine pulled her nightie down and fished around for her bedsocks, flipping the hot water bottle and pushing it against her stomach to try to squeeze out the last of its warmth. She breathed in the smell of rubber and cotton and damp under her sheet and lay quietly as the room shifted around her. How did Teddy always get his way? How did he manage to land his best friend and endless computer games while Madeleine got . . . sawdust and turps?

*Cock-a-doodle-dooo. Cock-a-doodle-doo. Cock-a-doodle-dooo. Cock-a-doodle-doo.*

Madeleine sat up. It was Mum Crum's alarm clock, crowing like a rooster through the wall.

'Morning, Maddie Moo,' said Mum Crum, swinging into the room and flicking on the light, every bit as chirpy as she had been when she went to bed. Her hair was curly like

Maggi Noodles and sprouted from her head in a wild woolly bun. Madeleine caught a glimpse of her grandmother's velour tracksuit pants (in tangerine) and buried her head in her sheets. Mum Crum claimed she only wore colours as bright as her personality, which excluded anything normal like navy or grey. Mum Crum was determined that old age would not leave *her* invisible.

'I'm going to meditate and then we'll head off to the pool.'

Madeleine cowered under the covers.

'Come on. I thought you were a wriggly girl like your grandmother. You brought your togs, didn't you?'

Madeleine tried to answer but her voice wasn't working yet. She *was* wriggly – at home she never stopped moving; she loved sports of all kinds – but even Madeleine didn't do swimming at this hour, and this close to the Antarctic.

'Scrunch and hold, two, three, four, five, six, seven, eight, nine, ten and out.'

Madeleine peeked at Mum Crum, who was now lying on the rug doing her pelvic floor exercises, fingers curling as she concentrated.

'Why couldn't I get a grandmother who retires to Noosa?' she asked.

'Better than having a prolapsed uterus like some of my friends, Moo. Stand up and you have to check you haven't left your gizzards on the seat. Millions and millions of dollars a year spent on medical research in this country and nobody has looked into *that* for women, have they?'

Madeleine rolled over to face the wall. It was too early for politics. 'Isn't this *my* room?'

'Virginia Woolf knew how important it was to have *a room of one's own*, but no, this one is still mine!'

Madeleine put her head under her pillow. She lay in bed and ignored her grandmother roaring 'I am Woman' in the shower; she ignored her grandmother while she waded waist-deep in laundry, swearing as she tried to find two clean socks; and she ignored her grandmother while she juiced seven types of vegetables. Madeleine found that she could not, however, ignore Mum Crum when she hauled back the doona and waved a glass in front of her face.

'C'mon, Moo darling. Mixed veg with kale *and* chia seeds.'

Madeleine sipped at the lumpy juice, which was disturbingly green in colour and tasted like mowing the lawn. Mum Crum patted her on the arm. 'Get into your togs, Moo. You'll feel so much better after a swim. It's invigorating.'

'I don't care about invigorating. Is it heated?'

Madeleine imagined Teddy tucked up at the Raos' while Mrs Rao tiptoed around downstairs preparing French toast, seasoning the house with the smell of butter, cardamom and burnt sugar.

Mum Crum looked at her granddaughter and her voice softened. 'Given it's your first morning, why don't we drive?'

*Why don't we drive? Why don't you bake? How the flying heck did you think I was going to get there?* thought Madeleine.

They got to the pool just as the doors opened. The pool attendants were still crusty-eyed, rugged in layers of pilled fleece. 'Morning, Mum Crum,' they croaked.

'Morning, Bruce. Morning, Emily,' Mum Crum called through her Carlton scarf. 'This is my granddaughter, Madeleine-from-Sydney.'

Bruce winked. 'You must be thrilled to be in a state where you can get a decent coffee, even in the country.' Madeleine smiled the polite half smile that she reserved for adults who were trying to be funny and failing: not wide enough to encourage further banter, but big enough not to be rude.

Madeleine followed Mum Crum into the changing rooms. Everything was still clean. Madeleine usually hated public pools because she hated the grot – the discarded shampoo bottles, the knots of other people's hair in the shower. You learnt far more about strangers in public pools than was necessary. And they learnt far too much about you.

Madeleine picked up her school bathers. She had to wear two pairs because they were both starting to go see-through, gnawed by the chlorine, and Mum said it was a waste to give almost perfectly good bathers to the poor. Madeleine looked up at Mum Crum. Mum Crum, it seemed, wasn't so thrifty. Or modest. 'You're wearing a bikini?'

'If you're an octogenarian like me you don't waste time in trainers, not when you've got the body of a fifty-year-old,' said Mum Crum and winked. The bikini was this season's – white with a palm tree design in turquoise. Madeleine pushed her towel towards her grandmother. 'Please, Mum Crum, just until we get in.'

The pool was freezing. It was so cold that it was hard to breathe. In the next lane, Mum Crum dived straight in and grunted as she swam in flippers. She whooped to herself at the end of each lap. The pool was filling with men in triathlon caps. Madeleine kept her eyes on the line of black tiles down the middle of the fast swimmers' lane and tried to ignore her grandmother's grunting and the aggression of the men slugging at the white water around her. Madeleine hid behind her goggles, the lines of her arms softened in the misty haze, the colour of her skin muted, like she'd been gently rubbed out.

⁓

After the swim, Madeleine followed Mum Crum to the changing room. Her grandmother looked fragile out of the pool. Madeleine could see stripes of fake tan on the back of her legs.

Madeleine stood in her bathers under the communal shower, water running over her shoulders and down her back. Mum Crum walked out of one of the changing cubicles lining the wall. Her bikini bottoms were strung between her hip bones like a hammock, and on her ankle a tiny tattoo of a tomato, greenish and smudgy, had sunk deep into the skin. Mum Crum's hands were behind her back, fumbling with the straps of her bikini.

'Excuse me.' Mum Crum's bather top shifted across small sacks of white breast as she headed for a thick-armed woman pushing her ponytail up under a blue cap. There was no sound in the change room but the marshy slap of Mum Crum's thongs against the concrete floor.

'You'd like me to help?' asked the woman, perplexed.

Mum Crum nodded. 'I can't undo the knot.' Her voice was brusque, impatient.

'Of course,' said the woman, a little too brightly. 'Turn around.' She took the straps and picked at them, puckering the freckled skin on Mum Crum's back. 'Okay then, there you go.' The woman picked up her goggles, and Madeleine tried to catch her eye in the mirror to thank her, but she was talking to another woman as they walked out of the changing room, her voice skimming the concrete floor. 'It's terrible when they get like that.'

Madeleine wanted the woman to know that Mum Crum wasn't *senile* – that Mum Crum had been like *that* for as long as her own mother could remember. She wanted the woman to know there was heaps that was great about Mum Crum, even if she was a bit much sometimes – especially for people who maybe just wanted Coco Pops, telly and a sleep-in on their school holidays.

But the woman was gone.

# A cupboard with a hole

~~~~~

**B**y the time they got back to the cottage, Madeleine did feel better, despite herself.

Mum Crum set about cutting up a mound of oranges and flipping egg-white omelettes, which she sprinkled with hairy sprouts scooped from a jar on the counter. 'Literally bursting with nutrients, these are.'

'I'd rather raspberry jam on toast.' Madeleine looked hopefully in the cupboard.

'Jam on toast is special-occasion food. Not for breakfast.'

Madeleine sighed a sigh deep and powerful enough to blow out a hundred birthday candles. She cut an egg-white omelette into eight pieces, distributing them around her plate; they were white and clear and bubbly in places, like frozen saliva.

'I thought you could help me with the cupboard today,' said Mum Crum.

Madeleine yawned; she'd been hoping to sneak in another hour or so in bed. 'Which cupboard?'

'The one in your room. I was going to get rid of it, but I'm not sure how I'd get it out the door. It's so enormous I suspect that the walls of Elf Cottage were built around it.'

Madeleine loved the cottage's name. It made her feel like a pixie. And the cottage was so small; it couldn't have been better named. Besides, with her bushy bun, mismatched socks and wiry limbs, Madeleine's grandmother did always look a bit like she'd just popped out of the ground.

Mum Crum ushered Madeleine towards her room and the old cupboard. The cupboard was a great box of a thing, which took up the entire right wall. It was covered in chipped yellow paint, with a peeling strawberry sticker halfway up the left-hand side. The cupboard didn't have a key, so there was a corner of a skirt poking out through the gap between the doors to jam them shut. Madeleine pulled them open and two mothballs rolled out onto the floor. She took out the skirt.

'That's an old one. I used to wear it with a black turtleneck. You should see if it fits you.' Mum Crum laid the skirt out on the bed.

Madeleine flipped through the other clothes hanging in the cupboard. There was, indeed, a black turtleneck jumper with three gold buttons, as well as a grey coat and several suits.

Mum Crum smelt one of the jackets and sighed. 'Pete looked so handsome in this.'

'What do you want to do with it?'

'The jacket? I'll keep it.' Mum Crum shut the cupboard door.

'I meant the cupboard.'

Mum Crum's voice slid from wistful back to businesslike. 'It really needs to be totally stripped down, but it'll have well over a hundred years' worth of paint on it. I thought that for now you could give it a light sand and then we can paint it white. Just to freshen it up. Come on, let's put this tarp down on the floor. The cupboard's far too heavy for us to try to move from the wall.'

'Sure.' Madeleine swallowed. It was the very last thing she felt like doing. Holidays were for hitting the cricket nets with Nandi or poring over clothes in shops or cutting chocolate fudge, thick with glacé fruit, into squares for the neighbours. Holidays were not for renovating.

Mum Crum thrust a block of cork wrapped in coarse sandpaper at Madeleine. 'You get going with the sanding. Just lightly – enough to scratch up the surface, so the paint will stick. Let me see those glorious muscles in action! Here, throw these on.'

Mum Crum passed her granddaughter a pair of overalls. There was a cloth badge tacked onto the front: *Adam was a rough draft*.

Mum Crum laughed. 'Do you get it? Eve was the final product! Isn't that clever!'

Madeleine rolled her eyes and turned to the corner to unzip her fleece.

'What are you turning around for? We've all got bosoms. Of course I didn't have them at your age and certainly not *those whoppers*, but you've only got the junk you consume to blame, or at least the plastic it's wrapped in. I've always said the trouble with youth today isn't sex, drugs and rock'n'roll; it's sex, drugs and coffee scrolls. Anyway, you've heard it all before; I'm going to get back to putting up a clothes rack in the laundry.'

'They're not that big,' said Madeleine, hot-pink and hunched over.

Madeleine started at the bottom of the cupboard and worked her way up. She rubbed and rubbed until her shoulder pinched. The rubbing, although painful, was mechanical and soothing in a way. All Madeleine had to do was concentrate on the next patch of cupboard, without having to think too much.

She paused for a rest, then opened the cupboard door. It was very deep, with a faceted timber face. It was the kind of cupboard that, if she had been younger, she might have hoped led to another world, with Turkish delight, fur coats and an enormous lion; another world with families whole and rosy, brimming with children and mums and dads, laughter and snowball fights.

At the bottom of the cupboard were two drawers with big brass rings, like those threaded through a bull's nose. Madeleine tugged one of the drawers open. It creaked a bit and then jammed. It was full of Mum Crum's receipts; so was the second one. Madeleine shut the drawers and stared at the shelf of wood that ran all the way along the top of them, flush with the cupboard walls at each side.

*That's funny*, thought Madeleine. *The drawers don't go all the way to the sides, but the wooden shelf above them does.* This left a small gap on each end – a little more than the length of a ruler in size – covered by the shelf and boxed in by the front panel. Madeleine ran her fingers along the edge of the timber where it met the cupboard wall on the left. She tapped. It sounded hollow, but the wood refused to budge. Madeleine moved to the right-hand side of the cupboard and felt along the timber shelf. It wobbled. She inched her fingernails down the small crack and pulled. A panel of timber flipped up.

A secret compartment! Madeleine took a breath and dipped her hand into the hole she'd just discovered, taking in the sweet smell of dust and old timber. 'Hey, Mum Crum, Mum Crum, check this out. The cupboard's got a secret compartment!' she called.

'What was that, darling?' Mum Crum walked into the room with a hammer in one hand.

'Look!' said Madeleine.

'*Wunderbar*,' said Mum Crum. 'Anything in it?'

'Hopefully not spiders.'

'Pfffft! Let me.'

In her excitement, Mum Crum tried to elbow Madeleine out of the way, but Madeleine resisted, groping around in the hole. Her fingers landed on a smooth piece of timber.

'There's something down here! I think!' Madeleine stroked the object with the tip of her finger.

'Grab it, then. Let's see what you've got.'

From the secret hole, Madeleine withdrew a box. It was made of plain wood, with metal hinges baked brown by time. On its front was a red enamel shield with a black stripe and three black clovers.

'The Williamson family crest,' said Mum Crum.

'What do you think's inside?'

'Crown jewels?'

'I hope so,' said Madeleine. 'But it could be a genie.'

'Genies tend to arrive in bottles, but if it is a genie, I hope he's hunky.'

'Gross,' said Madeleine.

The box creaked as Madeleine opened it. It was filled with creamy tissue paper so old it had lost its crunch. Wrapped in the paper was a pair of shoes.

'Just shoes. What a funny thing to hide in a cupboard.' Mum Crum did little to conceal her disappointment.

Madeleine unwrapped them. They may have been *just* shoes, but they were beautiful: long, fine court shoes with a Mary Poppins heel, all covered in creamy silk and alive with jewelled beads. The silk was so raw you could see the grains in it. The insides of the shoes were lined with ivory leather. Madeleine ran a finger along the instep. 'They look like they've barely been worn.'

Mum Crum turned one over to study the sole. 'They have, but probably only once or twice. See the way the leather's scratched? Must have belonged to some grand dame.'

'Can I try them on?' Madeleine didn't wait for an answer – she was already peeling off her boots.

The shoes looked funny popping out of the ragged ends of her overalls. Madeleine thought they were elegant, though. She took out her phone and snapped a picture of them.

'Why are you doing that?'

'I'll send it to Nandi.'

'And I thought our generation was vain.'

'It's not as if I spend the whole time taking photos of myself like some of the girls in my class. Being cool's a full-time job. This is more like a visual diary – a record.' Madeleine took a deep bow. 'Now I just need a dress, a ballroom and some dance lessons.'

'All those preening girls and they don't offer dance lessons at that school of yours?'

'Dance lessons? We don't even have a library, or an oval with grass.'

Mum Crum shook her head. 'Sometimes I wonder what we bothered fighting for. All those rallies and burnt bras, and the states blame the commonwealth and the commonwealth blames the states and your mother can't find you a local school with a library. It's ridiculous.'

Politics. If it wasn't selfies or scrolls Mum Crum was railing against, it was politics. Madeleine shook her head. What was the point? You couldn't change anything. Everyone was just knocked about like seaweed in the surf.

Madeleine went back to the box. 'Hey! Look at this.' She pulled out a yellowed card about the size of an A4 sheet that had been poking out from under the box's droopy tissue paper. It was covered in rows of neat handwriting. 'It's a list of names. Names and addresses!'

Mum Crum peered at the card. There were about twenty names and addresses, all in brown spidery writing.

*Amelia Morris, 6 Surrey Road, Prahran.*

*Polly Wilson, c/- Como House, South Yarra.*

*Nell Wentworth, 12 Little Charles Street, Fitzroy.*

'What a funny find,' said Mum Crum. 'Addresses for a tennis club? A cake-bake fundraiser? War widows? Let's take it down to the Muse with the shoes later on. They might be interested in them for their museum.'

Lyrebird Muse, as Madeleine knew from previous visits to Mum Crum's, was one of the old remaining homes at the edge of town. It had been a summer retreat for a wealthy Melbourne family in the previous century, when the big-bustled and high-hatted used to take to the cool of the hills to escape the heat and stench of a town then known as *Smelbourne*. Bits and bobs from the house and the area were exhibited in glass cases throughout the rooms.

Madeleine kneaded her shoulder and stood back to survey her handiwork on the cupboard.

'*Lyrebird Muse*. Were there lyrebirds here?'

'Absolutely. Here and in the Dandenongs. Sadly they've all died out around these parts, though; victims of farming and urbanisation.'

Madeleine sat down on the bed. 'I don't think I've seen a real lyrebird. Not even at the zoo.'

'They're extraordinary creatures, lyrebirds – birds of many voices. I wish we still had them here. Do you know they record sounds, copy them exactly, and then they pass those sounds on to their young? Lyrebird chicks will repeat things in their song that they've actually never heard – the click of an old-fashioned camera shutter; the crack of an axe. In a funny way, those birds are the keepers of our history.'

'What a shame they're gone.' Madeleine stood.

Mum Crum nodded and ran her hand down the cupboard. 'This feels wonderful, Moo, darling. Next up: paint. There is nothing more magical than a lick of paint. Quite transformative.'

Madeleine found herself smiling. DIY was as contagious as tinea. 'Do you mind if I go down to the Muse now?' she said, kneading her arm. 'I'm sore and I could do with a break.'

Mum Crum laughed. 'Watch the new woman in charge down there. She's an odd one, clinging to the grandeur of a world that no longer exists, yearning for its money and power, but inheriting nothing but airs – antiquated manners that might once have pleased King George.'

'I thought you admired manners.' Madeleine shook her head at her grandmother's topsy-turvy ideas: fake tan and overalls, burnt bras and push-up bras, dance lessons and libraries. It was hard to make sense of it.

'I think everybody appreciates good manners, but I don't like them when they're used as a sword.'

⟪⟫

After a shower, Madeleine put on a black T-shirt and then pulled Mum Crum's old turtleneck over the top. It smelt of dust and camphor, but its shape compelled her to hold her neck high and her back straight. She pulled the woolly skirt up over her tights and slipped on the glittery shoes again.

Madeleine tucked her boots into the wooden box, on top of the page of signatures. She stood. The skirt swished around her legs. She wasn't used to long skirts, since her school uniform was short – one iPhone's length above the knee, as the school rules required.

'Oooh, *bella*, *bella*,' said Mum Crum. 'Don't you look finer than Georgian iced fancy cake. You can have those clothes if you'd like – I won't miss them.'

Madeleine curtseyed. 'Thank you. They'll come in handy. The newspapers always seem more interested in sports-women's lipsticks than their hockey sticks.'

Mum Crum arched her back in a stretch. 'Nothing has changed, has it? Just remember, Maddy Moo, as my great-aunt used to say, *You won't change anything from the parlour.*'

'Parlour?'

'Couch is probably a better translation now, I suppose. Yes, you won't change anything from the couch. Don't forget the box, and make sure you take your own boots so you'll have something to wear—'

'Got them!'

'Good girl. And have a look at the view while you're there, Moo! It's beautiful. The Wurundjeri people were onto this place thousands of years before we stuck our thieving flagpoles in.'

Madeleine took out her phone, flicked her finger along the screen and smiled: Nandi had sent photos of her cats, her tiny baby sister, and her tiny baby sister's tinier Dunlop Volleys.

'Madeleine, honestly,' said Mum Crum. 'You kids are never actually in the moment – you're always somewhere else.'

*That*, thought Madeleine, *is the point*. 'Just checking the cricket score,' she said.

Madeleine tried to find a pocket in her skirt for her phone, but there was none. She tucked the box under one arm and balanced the mobile on top, but quicker than a kid could pinch a Smartie from a birthday cake, Mum Crum grabbed the phone.

'Mum Crum. It's mine!'

'Easy, sister. Watch your tone. Park it on the charger until you get back.'

'Oh, come on, Mum Crum. I just—'

'You'll only be half an hour, and you'll survive. I promise.'

Madeleine glowered at her grandmother and headed for the front door.

# Teeth and pearls,
# a child with curls

Once Madeleine was outside, her anger dissolved in the chilly mountain air. She wandered up the rough path outside Mum Crum's cottage and out onto the street. The shoes made her take neater, tenser steps as she had to clench them on with her toes. Madeleine was very extra-curricular and, apart from sport, her favourite subject was drama. There was something magic about walking backstage and breathing in the thick, chalky silence. Sport was no different – as much teamwork, as many bright lights, just more grass stains and fewer choc-tops. Traversing the hill in these shoes now, Madeleine had the sudden sense that she was on a stage; that the world was somehow watching.

At the end of Mum Crum's street, Madeleine turned left and headed up the steep hill. Lyrebird Muse loomed above her. Even the back of it, the higgledy-piggledy outbuildings, were far grander than any of the other homes in the area, many of which had been razed by bushfire and modestly rebuilt a century later.

The Muse was tall and built of stone, with a slate roof and huge windows blooming with jewel-coloured glass. It stood on the edge of the mountain, its chest thrust out like the figurehead on the bow of a ship, face to the wind, surveying the patchwork of farms that stretched towards Melbourne. A muddy lake curved in a bow at its feet a little way down the hill, home to a flock of bossy orange-billed geese.

Madeleine reached the stone fence separating the property's eastern border from the road. Just inside the tall iron gates were two flags beating against their own poles – one the Australian flag, with its Union Jack and starry Southern Cross; the other the Aboriginal flag, with its black peoples, red earth and a powerful yellow sun at the centre like a punch.

Attached to one gate, quivering in the wind, was a metal sign advertising a café that had been set up in the old stables to quench the thirst of tourists more interested in snacks than history. *Devonshire teas daily*, it said.

Madeleine had smuggled some coins into her left boot earlier at Mum Crum's, hoping the café might just be open. She danced onto the property, buoyed at the prospect of decent food and the accolades she might receive for the secret-hole shoes. *Kindly bequeathed by Madeleine Barnett*, a sign might say. Who knew, they may even want her photograph for the local paper, to run above a little caption about how she'd come to find them.

As soon as she was inside the gates, Madeleine stopped. The garden was as damp and mysterious as ever. The trees were so tall and so thick in some parts that the light that filtered down to the stony paths was as green as the moss that lined them. On the other side of the property, out along the western border, Madeleine could just see a small stream glinting in the afternoon light, marking the point at which the English garden gave way to the edge of the mountain and an army of tall, straight gums. On the far side of the stream, the grey tree trunks were bare, a tatty canopy of gum leaves arranged metres and metres above the ferns and scrub.

Madeleine followed the drive across to the house and walked up the stone steps and into the lobby. She was standing in a large timber entrance hall with a high roof and doorways leading in several directions, each cordoned off with dusty velvet rope. The walls were covered in dark-brown wallpaper that was curling up near the roof. The enormous floor was covered in pretty blue, green and terracotta tiles that were chipped in places.

On one wall was a large, glossy oil painting in a golden frame, showing a woman with a brown coat and a curly striped feather on her hat. The light in the hall reflected onto the subject's face, obscuring it completely.

A woman with a frozen bob peered over the edge of the counter. She wore a badge saying *Volunteer* pinned to her blouse, and an Alice band in her hair. She looked at Madeleine in her sparkly dance shoes and immediately pushed her thick pink lips together. 'I am sorry, but we're not open on Mondays.'

'Oh, but I just wanted to drop in—'

'I am sorry, but we are not open to the *public* on Mondays.' The woman tightened the knot on the printed silk scarf at her neck. 'That door really ought to be locked. Now, be a good girl and be off.'

The women said the word *off* like it had an *r* in it. *Orrrf.*

Madeleine stood her ground. 'But don't you have a museum? I thought you did, and I found—'

'We are *closed* on Mondays. You will have to come back tomorrow.' The woman put her head down, cauterising the conversation.

Madeleine spun and walked out of the lobby, closing the door sharply enough for the glass panes in it to rattle. She clutched the box under her arm.

*Uppity otter. I can't imagine any place I'd rather* not *put these beautiful shoes.*

Madeleine walked back down the hill to the park, which lay like a hem between the mansion above and the edge of the tiny town below. Mum Crum said that the park had once belonged to the Muse estate but had been sold off with all the land below it in a subdivision years before Mum Crum's time – around about the time Australia had become a federation.

At the entrance to the park was a barbecue and an old metal slide. A line of oaks ran across the hill, like soldiers standing guard. A helicopter chopped overhead, sending the birds flapping as it whizzed weekend bankers back to their banks. Madeleine walked across the hill, away from the noise, following the knobbly path of the oaks. Acorn caps crunched under her feet.

At the very end of the park was an old, torn woolshed.

Madeleine trailed her hand along its corrugated-iron wall. She let out a low, steady '*Ahhhhhh*' as she walked, listening to the undulations under her hand in the rattle of her call. On the other side of the woolshed was a lane edged in stone and lined with grass and rubbish. Somewhere beyond the lane, Madeleine could hear the creek.

Madeleine stepped into the lane and turned left, following it downhill. She had never been down this lane before. It was, she figured, the kind of lane she might have been down with a dog, because dogs were more likely to explore that sort of thing – well, more likely than grandmothers, even curious ones who collected property.

Madeleine reached the end of the lane and understood why Mum Crum had never bothered: it was a dead end, damp and musty and filled with shadows. It smelt of hay, lanolin and rust. The old-fashioned shoes pinched Madeleine's feet on the uneven ground, and she stopped and pitched, rocking from one foot to the other. She looked about for a bench, but there was nothing – it was not the sort of place to rest.

Madeleine hopped over to a small heap of stones with old chip packets and faded cans jammed between them and sat down, wiggling her achy toes. The glittering shoes slashed the shadows. They reminded her of the tiny phosphorous mites she had once seen with her father as they'd fished. The phosphorescence had glowed from the water and the stars above them had cut the salted air, and Madeleine had felt weightless, giddy, suspended in a briny Milky Way.

She had pressed against his woollen sleeve to stop herself tumbling away.

Madeleine looked around her at the stones on which she sat. *Maddison 4 Kai* was carved into one of them – carved deep, finger deep. A person no doubt needed true love to make that much effort, thought Madeleine. She pushed her nail into the *K* of *Kai* and wobbled the rock, trying to imagine what sort of hand had carved it. Then she pushed some more. The *Maddison 4 Kai* rock tilted on its point and flipped.

Cemented onto its other side was a photo in a copper frame. It was an oval-shaped photograph in sepia, partially obscured by grime, of a small child with a big bow in her light curls and cheeks lit with dimples. Madeleine ran her fingers around the frame, trying to work out what it was doing attached to the rock and how on earth it had got there. It was a bit like the photographs attached to graves in the cemetery, but this wasn't a gravesite, and while the photo was old, really old, it obviously wasn't of an old person. Madeleine examined the rock. There was no name, no cross, no indication that it was a tombstone.

She flipped up another piece of stone. A couple of slaters curled into balls and rooted in the moss underneath, but there were no more photos. Madeleine knocked the rock back and hauled up a third. While this one did not hold a photo, it was studded with wonky, creamy-coloured beads. Madeleine traced them with her finger; they ran in a loose ring around the stone. She pressed down on one. Its tip was sharp. It wobbled and then, with a puff of dust, fell into the palm of her hand. Madeleine dusted the bead off and held it up to the light. It was only then that she realised she held a tooth.

'Now *that* is gross.' Madeleine almost dropped it. The tooth was disgusting, completely disgusting, but it was also intriguing. It was an eyetooth, a milk tooth, which, like paper, had yellowed with age. Madeleine tried to push it back into its socket, but the glue had crumbled to powder. She put the rock down and balanced the tooth carefully on top. *I wonder if the tooth fairy brings money for other people's teeth*, she thought.

Madeleine heard a rustle and looked up. Then she heard a laugh – a high-pitched, musical laugh, which leapt up from the ground and did *pas de chats* against the sides of the stones and the tips of the trees. It was coming from the mouth of the lane, but the lane was empty.

Madeleine grabbed her wooden box and stood up. 'Hello?' She stared down at the framed photograph at her feet. The little girl smiled back at her through a slick of mud and silver insect trails. Madeleine bent to wipe the glass with a finger, and then she pushed the rock back over. *Maddison 4 Kai*. She felt awful leaving the photo facedown like that – it was like burying the girl alive – but Madeleine didn't want to leave her exposed either.

There was a rustle from a patch of browning bracken on the other side of the lane. Madeleine stood and peered over to see a bird stomping on a damp soil mound. It had stocky legs, short rounded wings, and a long, white, feathery tail, shaped like the fern fronds that ringed it. The bird raised its tail up in an arch and lowered it down over its back gently, like a fan. The two feathers that edged the tail were heftier, as cream-and-brown as a Burmese cat, with squarish crenellations of colour like the gappy bricks at the top of a castle. The bird cocked its head and warbled, looking at Madeleine with a stony eye, the feathers on its neck jiggling. But rather than a bird call – well, a normal bird call – the deep, brassy *boooonnnng* of a gong sounded from its beak instead. It looked at Madeleine and blinked. Then the same noise sounded again, only from somewhere else, further up the hill.

*A lyrebird? It must be!*

The bird twitched and ducked further behind the bracken. Madeleine wobbled. She had to get back to Mum Crum, to let her know that lyrebirds were still here! If only she'd had her phone, she could have taken a video.

Madeleine picked a path that avoided the stones, the damp spots, and began to walk back across the hill towards the park's entrance on her tippy-toes. She almost tripped, but steadied herself. Looking up, she found that she was disoriented.

A tall band of gums traversed a part of the park Madeleine had never visited before. There was no slide, barbecue or tall soldier-oaks. There were no acorn caps. To her left ran a line of waist-high saplings. Madeleine reached out and snapped one of the soft branches absentmindedly.

'What *are* you doing?'

Madeleine looked up. A girl with a face as round and red as a Christmas ham stood before her. Madeleine started. 'Sorry, I wasn't thinking. I . . . I just sort of reached out and snapped a bit off. I hope I haven't damaged it.'

The girl scowled from under the brim of a hat. Madeleine looked from the red face to the grass, taking in a volley of dark skirts and puffed sleeves. There was something about the girl's patchy freckles and wide forehead that was frustratingly familiar, and yet her accent, her clothes and really her face were strange. Madeleine twitched, trying to work out whether she had seen the girl before. She might have been from Sydney. That happened sometimes, when you saw people out of context and didn't recognise them – like seeing a famous actor holding a bowser at the petrol station.

The sun had sneaked out from behind the clouds, and sparkles from the shoes bounded about the grass. Madeleine looked back up. The girl crossed her arms. 'I was not enquiring after the shrubs,' she said imperiously. 'I want to know what you are doing in Bea's dress slippers.'

# Meeting Gert

'Bea's dress slippers? I don't think they belong to a Bea. I found them hidden in a cupboard.'

'They are Bea's dress slippers. Not surprisingly, they were made to go with a dress – the first she wore during her season.'

Madeleine took a step back. She felt her face shuffle in confusion.

'Take one off and look inside. The cobbler always stitches our initials.'

Madeleine wobbled on one foot and handed a shoe to the girl, who flipped back the tongue. *B.C.W.*

'Beatrice Cecilia Williamson. I told you so. You've a cheek, waltzing in here and stealing. Have you taken her feathers too? I ought to . . . to . . . to turn you over to Percy. I'll get him to fix you – he can pop you on the train to Melbourne, throw you into the river and let you fester amongst the horse carcasses.'

Madeleine tried not to look startled. 'Horse carcasses?'

'From the tannery. By the time they get to the city they're curdled and swollen. Daddy doesn't call it the fetid river of death for nothing, you know.'

In all the years Madeleine had come to Victoria to stay with Mum Crum, in all the houses Mum Crum had owned down here, she had never heard of the Yarra containing horse carcasses and she had never heard of it described as *the fetid river of death*. Muddy, sure. Rowers, sure. Shopping trolleys even – but this sounded like a very different waterway from the iced-coffee-coloured river she had once chugged along in a tourist boat.

'I think you're exaggerating, but I hadn't reali—'

'You'd better give me the other slipper now.'

Madeleine shrugged. She slipped off the shoe and handed it to the girl. 'I was going to deliver them to the museum. We could still donate them, if you'd like – together, I mean.'

'The museum?' The girl laughed, but it wasn't a laugh between friends. 'What would the museum want with Bea's left slipper? Museums have things like stuffed kangaroos and gruesome masks from Oceania, and shrunken heads no larger than oranges with sewn lips – which my father says come from *real* cannibals. Bea's dress slippers would look quite daft amongst that lot.'

Madeleine tried not to snap back. 'I actually wanted to keep the shoes, but Mum Crum, my grandmother, suggested it.' She eyed a row of tiny hand-stitches in the kidskin. 'You don't get craftsmanship like that anymore.'

'It's just a shoe.' The girl rolled the shoes into her apron and the fierce look on her face faded. 'Not that my sister doesn't have a number of pairs.'

'Your sister?' exclaimed Madeleine with a start. She had assumed Bea was an old, powdery lady – the girl's great-aunt or something. 'How did Bea's shoes end up in my cupboard?'

'I don't know what you're talking about. We can ask Anna, but I suspect you're fibbing. Bea's terribly careful, you know. Me? *I* might leave my slippers in somebody's cupboard, but Bea never would, and certainly not the dress slippers from her season.'

Madeleine's feet were cold and damp in the grass. She opened the box to pull out her Docs. She couldn't understand why the girl kept going on about the season. It was clearly winter.

'What on earth have you got those boots for?' The girl looked appalled. 'Did you pilfer them from one of the servants? What sort of strange shoe-filching curio are you?' The girl's currant-eyes leapfrogged from Madeleine's feet to her woolly skirt and then up to her turtleneck. As they skipped, they narrowed. She blinked. 'You're not from here, are you?'

Madeleine wobbled on one leg as she tied a shoelace. 'No. I'm down from Sydney.'

'New South Wales? How exciting. I've only been there once, but Daddy travels often. My grandparents have a property there.'

Madeleine tied up her second boot. 'Are you from the country? I thought you were from England. Your accent is weir—' Madeleine swallowed. 'Unusual'.

She'd just been trying to make polite conversation, but the girl's face fired to a hivey red. 'You are *impertinent*. My mother

34

is actually from Germany, if you must know – and your own accent is frightful, only I was far too decent to comment.'

Madeleine looked at the girl's clothes. The country girls she knew all wore jodhpurs or grubby jeans, flannel shirts and caps. None of them wore pinafores or old-fashioned skirts. Maybe this girl was Amish, or from some other religion, a cult even – one of those weirdo sects that made the women bake bread, grow their hair long and marry old-man cousins.

Whatever she was, this girl was definitely a capital-F freak – and a bossy one at that. Madeleine shrugged. 'Well, I'm sorry your sister's shoes ended up in Mum Crum's cupboard, but I should get going,' she said, doing her best to sound class-captain. 'Can you point me in the direction of Reginald Road?'

'Reginald Road? I'm certain there's no road of that name here.'

'Well, what about the entrance to Lyrebird Muse?'

'That's my home, and you are here, as I have already noted, trespassing.'

Madeleine looked around. Up the hill, the muddy lake still curved in a bow, but the houses and roads below had gone – instead, square-bottomed sheep with black faces and thick woolly legs grazed in a paddock. The air was so still that she could hear the silence. Madeleine sat with a thud. Sticks crackled under her bottom. She felt woozy and her mouth was thick. 'Where . . . where have the houses gone? Where *am* I?'

'Why, you're in the Colony of Victoria, of course. Are you mad? Have you taken ill?' The girl stepped back and slapped both hands over her mouth and nose.

Madeleine rubbed the soft skin between her eyes. 'It's all right,' she said weakly. 'I don't think it's catching.'

The girl took a further step back. 'You can't always be sure – it could be measles, scarlet fever, influenza, *plague*. My mother is forever putting together baskets for the servants' families, and there are dozens of rats here. Not as horrid as in New South Wales, though, where Hen Pen says men are being paid to bring them in dead.'

'Servants' families?' Madeleine whispered. '*Plague?*' Her voice caught in her throat. Her heart was beating so strongly that she was quite sure it could be seen thumping against her turtleneck. 'W . . . w . . . *when* am I? What year is it? Please?'

The girl took a third step back. 'You *are* ill. It's nineteen hundred. Only six months to go until we're a proper, stamped federation. Daddy's been working ever so hard on it.'

Light pressed in on Madeleine from every direction. Her breath constricted. She could feel sweat oozing from her pores and taste bile bubbling in her throat. Everything was bleached and lined with ragged lace. With each breath she took, the ham-faced girl moved in and then out of her vision, until the girl dissolved into the pale background, her apron and boots spinning like a windmill.

Madeleine fell – back, back, until that vast, lacy whiteness swallowed her whole.

# *Something old, something new*

M adeleine woke to find a face blooming so close to her own that its edges were fuzzy. It was a fine, angular face, dusty with dirt, with very blue eyes, which seemed lit from behind. A straw hat was propped on the back of a thatch of yellow hair running in a series of short tufts and cowlicks, beaded with grass seeds. The face scowled and its owner, a girl who looked around eight, removed a small leather notebook no thicker than a box of matches from her boot. She tapped her yellow pencil twice on a clean sheet of paper and said, 'Where did you find the enemy lurking, Gert?'

The ham-faced girl loomed suddenly into view, a hand-kerchief bound across her face in a way that was more cowboy than surgical mask; then she retreated until all Madeleine could see was the herringbone lines in the fabric of the girl's skirts. Everything smelt of new grass and washed cotton.

'I found her just here,' said the ham-faced girl – Gert. 'She was wandering about in Bea's dress slippers – and not terribly much else.'

'Oh God, I'm still here,' said Madeleine.

'Don't take the Lord's name in vain!' said Gert. 'You're running a dreadful fever, and if one thing's certain, we're going to require Him on our side.' She struggled out of her pinafore and sent it billowing up then brought it down to settle across Madeleine like a bedsheet. She then untangled her hat and crunched it under Madeleine's head. The hat was still warm, which made the gesture uncomfortably intimate. 'There, that should do for now.'

'What has she done to these slippers?' the other girl exclaimed, examining the pretty shoes. 'They look like they've been weed on.' She sniffed at one of the slippers and scrunched up her nose. 'And they reek like the dead aunts.'

'Charlie,' snapped Gert, 'you know you're not to rummage through the dead aunts' possessions. If Nanny catches you wearing their specs again, she'll lock you under the stairs for so long you'll actually need spectacles to see.'

The girl called Charlie was still studying the shoes. 'Apart from being warped and yellow, there are no other peculiar markings. Have you managed to obtain any vital information from the enemy? Where is she from?'

'She's from New South Wales, although why she's in such a state of undress I'm not sure.'

Charlie picked up Madeleine's turtleneck with a stick. She swung it by its label, holding it out from her body as if it were toxic. Madeleine felt dizzy. She couldn't remember taking it off. This whole experience was like watching clothes in a dryer – just when she thought she spotted one of her socks, it would be swallowed by something vast and foreign, like a beach towel.

Gert put her hands on her hips. 'Charlie, don't touch anything. You know what Daddy said about the bubonic plague being all over Sydney at the moment. Over a hundred deaths! Do something rash and we could all end up in quarantine.'

'But I must check thoroughly for clues.'

Gert didn't respond. They all watched the turtleneck swing above them, lynched.

Madeleine closed her eyes. This place, the clothes, the girls – sisters. They rocked about her head, just out of reach.

Her eyes snapped open again.

'I've dreamt about you girls!' she exclaimed. 'I can't really remember it anymore, it's blurry – but I'm fairly certain there was a . . . yes . . . there was a doll. In a garden. Do you know it? The doll with unblinking eyes? The one that says *Mama Mama* like it's possessed?'

The two girls stared at Madeleine as if she'd spoken in tongues. Then Charlie shook her head and turned her attention back to the turtleneck. It dangled, helpless. Three gold buttons ran down one shoulder – coin buttons, featuring deer antlers and edelweiss. Charlie brought the garment closer to read the label: *Handgestrickt in Deutschland*.

'Deutschland, Gert. Hand-knitted *in Deutschland*.'

'Deutschland?' Gert looked confused.

'*Deutsches Reich*. Germany,' Charlie spat right out the side of her mouth, as if telling the punchline to a dirty joke. 'Ger-many.'

Gert looked shocked. 'Oh my!' She took Charlie by the arm and marched her to the other side of the saplings, her face knuckle-white. She didn't quite march her far enough to be out of hearing, though. 'Do you think she's our cousin?' she hissed.

Charlie held a pencil to her cheek. 'Well, Mummy's cousin *is* German. And she's been staying in New South Wales.'

Gert looked over at Madeleine and smiled. And nodded. And smiled. 'But she doesn't have any luggage. She wouldn't arrive clutching Bea's soiled slippers with little else – and she telegrammed to say that she would be here on Tuesday.'

'Perhaps she's early? The coaches aren't always reliable, and it would explain her accent.'

Charlie smiled like she'd found twenty dollars on the footpath and returned to Madeleine. 'Do you mind if I ask some questions?' she whispered. 'I've never met a real German before, you see. I'm one-quarter German, but I'd like to be properly German when I'm grown up. I just require some tips. Do all Germans wear those funny tight jerseys? Do they all dress, well, a little like nuns?' Charlie flipped back the cover on her notebook like a journalist. She cocked her head to one side and looked at Madeleine as fixedly as a dog eyeing a chop on a barbecue.

Madeleine pulled her turtleneck back on and shut her eyes. She had studied one year of German at school, and her mother's first boyfriend had been a German exchange student called Horst. It was not a lot to go on. Thankfully,

Madeleine was saved from needing to decide whether or not she should pose as a nineteenth-century non-German-speaking German because Gert had begun rooting about in Madeleine's shoebox and had discovered the piece of paper with the signatures.

When Gert turned to Madeleine, her eyebrows were hitched up into question marks, and her voice was as sharp as mustard. 'You're not Mummy's cousin, are you?'

Madeleine looked straight at Gert. 'No. I'm not, and I never said I was. I'm Madeleine Barnett. I know you both think I'm a thief, but honestly, I was *returning* the shoes. They *hurt*. They're not my thing at all – I spend half my life playing cricket, so I'm always in runners, and you've seen the boots I brought with me.' Madeleine motioned at her Docs.

'And this? Where did you get *this*?' Gert flapped the page of signatures in Madeleine's face.

'I found it in the cupboard with the shoes. I don't even know what that is, and I certainly don't want it.'

'It's a page of signatures.'

'Even I worked that out!'

'They're signatures for one of my aunt's petitions. Charlie spied more of them in her room, didn't you, Charlie? She's like that – forever sneaking about. Our father says she's our own little blackfella, always on her tummy in the long grass.'

Charlie nodded.

Madeleine kept waiting for one of them – for both of them – to be shocked by Gert's racism. *Our own little blackfella? Seriously?* But neither said anything. Apparently they found wearing Doc Martins or your grandmother's hand-me-downs far more scandalous.

'I've come across pages of signatures like these a number of times,' said Charlie. 'Aunt Hen usually stores them in a trunk under her bed.'

Madeleine looked from one girl to the other. 'My grandmother just handed the page to me and told me to bring it here. Pinky promise.'

Gert's voice softened. 'Your grandmother?' She looked at Charlie. 'Is she a friend of Aunt Hen's, then?'

'Aunt Hen's a spinster,' said Charlie to Madeleine in a whisper.

'Charlie, that's unfair.' Gert looked cross. Then to Madeleine, she said: 'Does your grandmother really know our aunt?'

'Quite possibly; I don't know. She's sort of wacky, my grandmother, and she does know heaps of people.'

'Wacky!' Charlie giggled. 'That's a funny word.'

Gert knelt down on the grass next to Madeleine. 'Aunt Hen is currently on her constitutional, but we'll make enquiries as soon as she returns. I wish you'd shown me this earlier – it would have avoided a tremendous amount of fuss.' She went to pat Madeleine's forehead and stopped. 'I'm sorry you're unwell. Mummy and Daddy are in town. Don't worry, though, because Nanny will know exactly what to do. She's at her best in a crisis.'

Madeleine looked up at the girl's soft face and felt

exceptionally grateful. 'Thank you,' she said. 'Thank you, very much.'

'Charlie, don't look so vexed,' said Gert. 'If you leave your mouth that wide open you'll catch flies. Please fetch Nanny now.'

'But Nanny's taken Imo for a walk,' protested Charlie.

Gert sighed. 'Well . . . Percy then.'

'Percy Hops? You know as well as I do that neither Mummy nor Nanny will approve of that.'

'Charlie, we need to get Madeleine up into bed; then she can talk to Nanny and Aunt Hen when they return. We'll require Percy's strength.'

Charlie pulled up her sleeves and flexed her muscles. 'As the strongman of the family, I should probably attempt to carry Madeleine myself.'

'That would be even less appropriate! We still don't know if Madeleine's contagious, so I really don't think we should go near her. Percy can do it. Go and find him – now!'

# *The hired help*

'ercy Hops, Percy Hops,' Charlie chanted.
'Well, look what the cat's dragged in.'

Charlie laughed.

Madeleine closed her eyes tighter and pretended to sleep. A kind voice, deep and measured, spoke above her.

'She fainted in the garden,' said Charlie.

'Percy, could you help us get Madeleine up to the house?' said Gert. 'Nanny's out.'

Two arms scooped Madeleine up. She could smell sweat and horses and tobacco. The man's breathing was rhythmic as he carried her snug against his chest up the hill. Gert and Charlie whispered at his heels.

'There you go, miss.'

A chair creaked as Madeleine was gently lowered into it. The room, with its heavy liver-coloured curtains, was cold. So was the chair. Madeleine looked up into big brown eyes. With his dark skin and his curly hair, Percy was a handsome Aboriginal man.

'Oh, thank you. Thanks very much,' Madeleine whispered. She smiled the shy, polite smile she gave to her school principal.

'Percy, hat! You know Mummy's rules,' said Gert. Charlie seemed to have vanished.

Percy didn't look at Gert, but he pulled his hat down from his head.

Of course Madeleine had seen Aboriginal people before on telly, playing footy or on the news, and she'd seen re-runs of Cathy Freeman flickering across the finish line at the Olympics – a green streak with a golden medal and a grin to fit the nation's pride. But Madeleine had never spoken to an Aboriginal person before, not up close, not in her normal life. And while nothing about *this* was *normal*, it dawned on Madeleine just how weird that was. It was even weirder that it had never occurred to her before today.

Percy stood holding his dented hat. He looked unsure of what to do next. 'Shall I ask Anna to send word to Nanny, Miss Gertrude?'

'We can manage,' said Gert primly. 'You can get back to the stables.'

Madeleine stared at him. 'Are you from here? Has your family lived here for, well, forever?' she asked, interested and earnest. 'Are they Wurundjeri?'

Percy's eyes flicked from Madeleine to Gert and then back to Madeleine. He narrowed them and shook his head. 'I'm from Coranderrk. Grew up on the station there before they—' He shrugged, then turned and left.

'Thanks, Percy,' Madeleine called after him.

Gert shook her head. 'Do sit here while I try to find Nanny. I'll send Anna in.'

Madeleine watched the ribbon in the back of Gert's hair swing as she left the room, hating her prim step, her erect back.

Madeleine looked around the room and shivered. There was a small fire hissing in the grate, but the room was huge and felt moist as well as cold. There was a great deal of dark, dumpy furniture squatting on an enormous rug. Even the wallpaper was decorated, in slushy swirls all gilded and rich. It was like sitting in a fruitcake – a fruitcake jam-packed with curly vases and pictures of wild horses and stormy seas hung in golden frames.

The door creaked and a girl wearing a black dress under a long, white apron with a heart-shaped bodice arrived, carrying a tray. She looked like someone delivering room service at a big hotel. 'Are you quite comfortable? Would you care for a little tea?'

Madeleine blinked. 'Tea would be great as long as it's milky, thanks. I'm freezing!'

The girl smiled.

'What's your name?' asked Madeleine.

'Anna, miss,' said the girl. She was one of those people who was quite pretty until she opened her mouth, and then her teeth were so big and so wildly crowded that she had to curl her lips over them when she talked. Anna blushed and turned to poke the fire. It flared red and billowed out heat.

'Do you fancy a late luncheon, too? The family has dined, but I could bring you something if you'd care for it.'

Madeleine's stomach rumbled. She was starving. 'What would the something be?'

Anna smiled around her teeth. 'Whatever takes your fancy!' She tucked a wisp of hair up into her bun.

Madeleine had been brought up in a household where people did their own chores – where cleaning ladies were considered unnecessary and exploitative (although the family budget couldn't have stretched to one anyway). That was her family's values, their moral code – as indelible as the little tomato tattoo on Mum Crum's ankle. It was clear that her own moral code had been written in chalk. 'Biscuits and tea would be delicious, thank you.'

Anna brought the tea in on a tray. The pot and the little cup were as pink as fairy floss. Anna poured the tea – it was dark and strong.

'Milk, miss?'

'Yes, please!'

Madeleine watched as milk spiralled white within her cup. The cup was so delicate that it was like cradling the ribs of a small bird, warm in her hands.

Now that Anna was up close, Madeleine could really look at her. Despite the pockmarks in the skin on her face, Anna was surprisingly young. 'How old are you?' asked Madeleine.

Anna blushed again. 'Thirteen.'

'Only just older than me!' Madeleine was about to ask how on earth she'd come to be at work in the middle of a school day, but then again Gert wasn't at school either, and Anna looked so uncomfortable that Madeleine decided to can that idea. She got the distinct feeling she wasn't meant to chat to Anna and Percy.

Anna held out a plate with a dainty pile of biscuits on it, as long and thin as nailfiles. 'Cat's tongues. Cook made them this morning.'

Madeleine helped herself to a biscuit and it dissolved on her tongue in a buttery stream. 'Oooh, it *is* good,' she said, taking another. Anna turned around to bind the curtains open. By the time she returned to the chair, Madeleine had finished the entire plate.

'My,' said Anna, looking shocked. 'You were hungry.'

'I'm sorry,' said Madeleine. She suddenly felt very greedy. She wondered if it was unladylike to devour an entire plate of biscuits, crumbs and all.

'I'll have Cook send in some more,' said Anna. 'It's rare we have a guest with an appetite! Particularly a girl.'

*So it* was *unladylike*, thought Madeleine. *Great.*

Madeleine did like her food – she ate like she talked and thought and ran: fast. And she was definitely not 'ladylike'. Madeleine and Nandi were the kind of girls to count batting averages rather than boys on the bus, and to save their pocket money for cricket pads rather than padded bras. Madeleine yearned for clothes as much as the next kid – especially theatrical dress-ups – but she didn't care enough to talk about them. She wore chapstick instead of lip gloss, zinc instead of fake tan, and if her hair had a wave, it was because it had been scrunched under a bike helmet.

Anna picked up a bellows and used it to pump air at the fire. The coals sprayed and sparked deep orange. They looked like they were alive, breathing. Anna set the bellows down gently and left the room.

Madeleine sat watching shadowy patterns cast by the fire bobbing on the ceiling, trying to work out what on earth to do next. She had no idea how to get back to Mum Crum and Elf Cottage. She had no idea how she'd got here; how any of this was even possible. Above all, she had no idea how to behave like a lady – no idea at all.

# Federation fibs

M adeleine heard a scraping noise. She turned and found herself looking straight into a bright eye spying on her from behind one of the liver-coloured curtains. Out tumbled Charlie, with her notebook in hand and a little white terrier at her heels.

'Don't tell anyone, not Nanny, not Gert. They'll slaughter me. I'm not to bother guests, you see.'

Charlie grabbed at the dog's collar. 'Sit, Millie,' she said, and the little dog sat.

Millie had one ear up and one down, which gave her a wonky, lopsided look. Charlie also looked a bit wonky. Without her hat, her hair looked even choppier, as short and bristly as an old toothbrush. Her pinafore was tucked into a strange pair of long, white linen shorts, out the bottom of which shot two skinny shins sheathed in thick black tights and covered in mud and bits of grass.

'Master Charles Williamson,' said Charlie, putting out her hand. 'I'm not sure we've been formally introduced. How do you do. While my father is away, I am the man of the house.'

Charlie smelt a bit earthy, not unlike beetroot fresh from the ground. Madeleine shook her hand.

'And this is Millie.'

'You can sit down if you want.' Madeleine gestured towards a couch and Charlie sat on it. Millie tried to leap up next to her but couldn't clear the seat. She bounced around on her hind legs with her tongue hanging out until Madeleine scooped her up. Millie snuffled and snorted and licked Madeleine's hand.

'Millie, Nanny will eat you *alive* if she sees you on a chair in the drawing room.' Charlie scowled at the dog, who leapt over the back of the couch and down – *clack* – onto the wooden floor.

Charlie sat forward on the very edge of the sofa, suddenly quite prim. Just as she opened her mouth and took a breath, presumably to start asking more questions, Gert burst in, glowering at her sister. 'What are you doing in here?'

Charlie ignored Gert and scribbled in her book. Madeleine could see fine blue veins in the skin near her temple.

'Would you cease your note-taking and hide these soiled shoes somewhere Bea will never look before she chances upon them? Bea will throttle us if she discovers them in this state – even if we had nothing to do with it.' Gert tossed Madeleine a pointed look as she thrust the sparkly shoes at her sister. 'You know how particular Bea is, and I'd hate this to mar her complexion.'

Charlie rolled her eyes, licked her finger and flicked through the pages of her book.

'*Things that have supposedly marred Bea's complexion: ashes from the summer fires (last year); the sound of possums fighting in the roof; foregoing Clarissa A'Beckett's party because of the storm; the sight of native ladies' bosoms in the museum* . . . Which leads me to the conclusion that it is much easier to mar Bea's complexion than everyone supposes.' Charlie smacked her notebook shut.

*Native?* Madeleine suddenly missed her brother. Unlike these girls, Teddy was not racist, and he was also good at science and maths and interested in all things peculiar. He subscribed to a magazine called *The Unexplained*, which he and Raj read in the backyard in the tent they set up to get away from her. Madeleine would sit outside the filmy wall of the tent spying on them while the boys talked and read, watching the yellow bullseyes from their torches flash about, listening to the flick of pages and their murmurs about time and the afterlife and sink holes. Teddy and Raj would know how Madeleine had got wherever she was, and, more importantly, how to get back.

Gert puffed up her chest. 'Charlie, Nanny should be back shortly, and she will not be happy to find you and Millie in here.'

'You can't scold me, Gert. You're not Nanny.' Charlie picked at a scab on her elbow.

'I may not be able to scold you, but I can ask you to leave, and return those shoes while you're at it. I can also warn you that if you don't, I shall tell Nanny you sneaked Millie into our bedroom last night and had her in your bed.'

'You wouldn't.'

Gert raised one eyebrow.

'You are a beast.' Charlie ran out of the room, Millie clacking behind her.

Gert waited until the thump of leather on wood could no longer be heard. Then she said, 'Well, that should keep Charlie occupied. Let's find you something warmer to wear. That way, you will not have expired from the cold by the time Hen Pen returns from her constitutional.'

Madeleine found Gert's language hard, and her old-fashioned accent was like a wall. Madeleine could really only comprehend Gert when she stopped trying to understand each word and let the sentences wash over her.

Gert passed Madeleine a pale-blue shawl. 'Put this on.'

The shawl was made out of a spidery wool, the threads fine as hairs, and it was sewn along its edges in nimble yet not machine-neat stitches, just like Bea's shoes.

Madeleine wrapped herself in the shawl and huddled in the chair. She suddenly felt terribly grown-up and responsible and desperately sorry for herself all at the same time.

Gert sat down on the couch, which still bore tiny ripples from Charlie's bottom, and looked at Madeleine more closely. 'Are you all right?'

Madeleine pressed her index fingers into her eyes to dam the tears. 'I just, well, I just feel a long way from home.'

Gert sighed. 'Whenever I'm feeling sad at school, Hen Pen always says to look at the moon and remember it's the very same moon our family is under. I always look at it and think of Imo waiting for me in the drive with her chubby, outstretched arms. She is always thrilled to see me come home.'

'Come home from where?'

'From school. The little ones have a governess – well, they currently have Nanny – and Bea's completed her lessons with a tutor, but I attend a proper school in East Melbourne, and now that we've moved into the Muse full-time because of . . . well, because of Mummy, I am a boarder. Of course I come home for the hols, but sometimes I feel so homesick that I actually get ill. The taste of the plum cakes Cook sends makes me feel better. Mummy asked that I only get one a term, but Cook sends extra. Aunt Hen urges her to.'

'Does Bea get them too?' asked Madeleine.

'Bea's too grown-up to be greedy. She's become a lady and a bore ever since she moved out of the nursery and started eating luncheon and dinner with the adults.'

'And Charlie and Imo? Who *is* Imo?'

'Imogen's the baby. She gets cake whenever she feels like it. That's the problem with being a child, you see – an in-between. All the adults love babies, and they love each other, but adults don't like children, not really – and that makes it hard for children to be heard.'

The room was still.

'Gert, do you think you can help me?'

'Well, I'm not sure I can, but Aunt Hen is bound to, given that she's an acquaintance of your grandmother's.'

'I do need help, Gert. I *need* to get home, and I have no idea how.' Madeleine started to cry again.

Gert leapt up and held her arm. 'Don't cry. Please don't cry. Here.' She pulled a napkin from her skirt and unwrapped it. Inside was a piece of white fondant about the size of one of those bouncy balls from a vending machine. The fondant looked slightly grubby. 'It's peppermint. Not as good as Jacksons, but Cook keeps it in the safe to make sweets with.'

Madeleine broke off a bit. It was soft and rubbery and tasted like toothpaste. She smiled. 'Thank you.'

Gert sat down again. 'Peppermint and plum cake can solve almost any problem. Have you been to Jacksons? It's in town and it's my very favourite sweet shop—'

'Gert!' Madeleine interrupted, making a sudden decision. 'I'm not sure how to say this . . .'

Madeleine was silent, trawling for the right words.

'You can confide in me,' said Gert. 'I shan't tell. Charlie, on the other hand, is a frightful blabber.'

'Well,' Madeleine said at last, taking a deep breath, 'I *am* from Sydney, but I was staying with my grandmother, and I dreamt about you – about all of you – here at the Muse, and then somehow . . . I somehow . . . Gert, I tumbled back in time.'

It was a very difficult thing to tell someone you were from the future, and apparently it was a very difficult thing to hear, too.

'You're what?' Gert's face crinkled like a pug's.

'I'm not from here, Gert, from now. I'm from the next century.'

'Don't be daft.'

'I wish I were being daft, Gert, but I'm not. One moment I was walking along with a pair of shoes I'd found in an ancient cupboard, and the next moment, I bumped into you and Charlie in the grass and you were accusing me of stealing slippers I never stole.'

Gert shook her head.

'It's *true*, Gert. We don't have servants to bring in tea, or polished silver, and we don't wear knickerbockers. We have central heating and too many cars, and Australia is a nation of states, not colonies – for so long, in fact, that we forget it wasn't always like that.'

'How many states?'

'I'm not sure.'

'You're not sure? Molly McGolly, you're from the *future* – how can you not know?' Gert's voice had dropped to almost a whisper, and her hands were clenched.

'Well, let me count them. There's the Northern Territory and the ACT – they're not really states but territories. Then there's South Australia, New South Wales, Victoria and Queensland, Tasmania, of course, and Western Australia.'

'Western Australia?'

'Of course.'

'If only that were true, Daddy would be so pleased to know. Western Australia will just not make up their mind.

First they said no, but now the miners have demanded the vote, so it could all change.'

Madeleine thought about an Australia without Western Australia, with its mining and crayfish and beaches. It would be weird to have that state as another country. Western Australians would need a passport to come and see the footy in Melbourne. 'But it's part of the same continent,' she protested to Gert.

'Yes, but it's further away from Victoria than New Zealand is, and John Hall said the twelve hundred miles of Tasman Sea are twelve hundred arguments against New Zealand joining. So . . . did they?'

'What?'

'Did New Zealand join?'

Madeleine shook her head. 'No, New Zealand is another country altogether.'

'Daddy will be disappointed. He was happy to include a clause which might allow them to join at some stage. What about Fiji? Did Fiji join?'

'No! Fiji is where people go for cocktails in pineapples, coconut oil and hair braids with beads.'

'I was fooling. Fiji hasn't been included for years, and they never did want to be involved.' Gert sat back and stuffed the last of the fondant in her mouth. 'Fooling like you. You know, you really are a fibber, Madeleine Barnett. First you steal Bea's slippers, then you wheedle your way into our home for tea, pretending you're faint, and now you're trying to tell me that you're from the future. That's preposterous. I'm off to find Percy, and he can drag you kicking and screaming to the police. Then you might start telling the truth.'

And with that, Gert marched out of the room.

# Lyrebird

M adeleine sat alone in the drawing room for another
few seconds, her breathing shallow and panicked,
and then she bolted out of the room after Gert.

She found herself in the grand entrance hall, with its
blue, green and terracotta mosaic tiles and its high dark
walls lined with paintings of stern-looking men hanging
from a rail. Gert saw Madeleine following and ducked
into a doorway to her right, just past the sweeping staircase. The slap of her boots echoed about the hall, and the
painted men stared. Madeleine ran into the room after
Gert. She had to stop her.

Gert ran around a very long shiny dining table, on top
of which sat an enormous centrepiece made of silver clam-
shells, with a big silver pineapple on top. She disappeared
through a smaller door on the left-hand side of the fireplace, into a narrow corridor where Anna stood leaning
against a bench, polishing spoons. Madeleine followed.

To the right was a tiny set of white-painted wooden
stairs leading upwards. To the left was a heavy door with
a big brass lock. Gert opened it and flew outside, onto a

covered pathway paved with great slabs of stone, which hedged two sides of a square courtyard. A number of low doors ran off the courtyard, and a strong smell leached from somewhere – a bleach or permanent-marker sort of a pong, but different.

One of the doors across the way was open, and inside a woman stirred a deep pot on a long, cream enamel stove, which pumped the sweet smell of burnt butter into the air.

'Keep the eggs outside in this weather, Miss Gertrude, and you'll never get a cake to rise – I've seen doorstops with more air than these drop scones!' The woman spoke very quickly and in a very high pitch. Madeleine thought it sounded lovely, quite lyrical. The woman held up a plate of floury scones as the girls tore past. 'Take 'em off my hands to make me less grumpy?'

But Gert had already shot off to her right, along the opposite side of the courtyard to the kitchen, leading Madeleine past a steamy laundry in which a purple-cheeked woman was squeezing sheets through two rollers, then past an open set of big doors on enormous brass hinges that looked weirdly exaggerated, like the type you found on kids' diaries or pirate chests. Madeleine caught a glimpse inside what appeared to be a garage – the floor swept bald; various carriages lined up in a row.

Gert bolted around the side of the garage, running all the way around the house in a loop, past some stables and two long-lashed cows chomping at the grass, their pink udders dangling low and thick. Gert ran over the front drive, past a clipped grass tennis court, and then she turned left along a wobbly stone path, out beyond a low-walled garden and a well.

Gert ran and ran, right to the edge of the mountain. The sky was greying and the air was sharp. The ground was so cold that Madeleine could feel it hardening the soles of her boots and getting in through the weave in her tights. The olden days had never looked this freezing in photos.

The girls leapt a small stream at the garden's edge and crashed uphill through fern and bracken. Great gums with bark hanging in careless strips muttered above them.

'Gert, Gert, stop, please!' gasped Madeleine. She reached out and grabbed Gert's arm. Gert jerked away and tripped over a log. Her boot cracked against the hard timber.

'Are you all right?' Madeleine knelt beside her. There was a noise: the crack of Gert's boot on the log. Again.

Gert nodded, panting softly, and put a finger to her lips. There was a rustle in the bushes next to them. She parted some bracken, and behind it was a bird, just like the one Madeleine had seen earlier. It too was stomping on a soil mound. The bird cocked its head and warbled, looking straight at the girls with one eye. First, from its beak, came the crack of Gert's boot on the log, then the thud as she'd landed.

Gert giggled. 'Isn't it clever?'

The bird made a call that sounded like a gong, just as the other bird had done earlier that day – *booooong*.

'He's imitating sounds to woo his lady,' whispered Gert.

'He's quite a pants man,' said Madeleine. The bird broke into the sound of a kookaburra. 'That's some repertoire.'

'It is. Charlie says the female looks after the chicks and the male just dances and prances. They're terribly active in winter.'

There was another rustle in the background and another, plainer bird hopped into sight and then ducked away again, but not before the male bird had folded its tail down in a how-do-you-do bow.

'They're lyrebirds, aren't they?' said Madeleine.

Gert crossed her legs and nodded.

'I thought so. I spotted one earlier. Lyrebird Muse. Mum Crum was right – they really were here!'

'Did you see the stuffed one in the hall? In the bell jar? Mummy gave it to Daddy for his last birthday. It was the perfect present for him.' The lyrebird's feathers fluttered like a fan. 'He's so elegant.'

'He's incredible,' Madeleine agreed, and then added, 'I see them all the time at home.'

Gert rolled her eyes. 'Don't tell tales. Where do you see them?' Her voice was runny with sarcasm.

'Hang on and I'll show you!' Madeleine pulled off her boot.

'Whatever are you up to now?' asked Gert.

'The Devonshire-tea money. I stuck it under the inner-sole in my shoe to hide it from Mum Crum.' Madeleine lifted the flap and, sure enough, there were the cream-tea coins still warm in the bottom of her boot.

'What are they?' Gert was peering into Madeleine's boot.

'Coins,' said Madeleine.

'No, they're not. Not any coins that I know.'

'They are. From my time, the future, just like I've been telling you. Look!'

Madeleine held out a ten-cent coin. It was silver and worn down on the sides. On the front was a lyrebird – the bird barely visible under its extravagant tail.

'There, I knew it!'

Gert took the coin in her fingers. 'It's funny. They always draw them like that – with their tails high and curly – but you never actually see them like that. Well, not in the garden. Only on pictures and under Daddy's bell jar!'

Gert turned the coin over. On the back was the Queen. She was a young queen, with soft curls and a pretty crown. 'Who's that?'

'Queen Elizabeth, but she's just a figurehead – not our real queen or anything.'

'But our queen's Victoria.'

Madeleine took the coin back. 'Look. *Elizabeth II, Australia 1987* – and that coin's old. I'm from the century after that.'

Madeleine flipped over a shiny fifty-cent coin. On the back, the Queen was much older: there were lines on her forehead and around her eyes, and the skin on her neck was sagging. It was dated two thousand and ten. She kept flipping. One twenty-cent coin said *Australia's volunteers, making a difference*; it was dated two thousand and three.

Another fifty-cent coin said *Centenary of Federation, 1901, 2001* and depicted a funny coat of arms with two women in robes either side of it. Madeleine's last fifty-cent coin was dated two thousand and said *Millennium year*.

Gert was staring at Madeleine. 'I . . . you . . . you weren't making it up.'

'I wish I were,' said Madeleine.

Gert flipped over a tiny five-cent coin with an echidna on its back. '*Australia 1972*,' she read. 'So it's true, then. The colonies really do federate? Daddy's been so worried about England saying no.'

'Yes, they do federate. That's what I've been trying to tell you.'

Gert ran a fingertip over the coin and then passed it back to Madeleine. 'Put them back in your boot, Madeleine. We will get in terrible trouble if anybody else discovers them. People around here are not used to schoolgirls tumbling in from the future.'

The lyrebird gonged from somewhere further away.

Gert smiled, a little hesitant suddenly. 'So . . . if you're really from the future, then you must tell me more. What happens to us, to my family? What happens to *me*?'

'I have no idea, I'm sorry,' said Madeleine, feeling very strange as she realised that by her time, Gert would be dead and buried.

'Oh,' Gert said, disappointed. 'Then . . . how about this house? What happens to it?'

'That one I can answer!' Madeleine pulled her bootlaces

tight. 'The house is still here, but it's a sort of museum. Tourists come to see the garden. The Muse's land is much smaller, and it's not so isolated. Down there, for example, there's a park and a lane, and then there are more houses below that.'

'I can scarcely believe you have learnt of that! Daddy has just had plans for some new homes drawn up a fortnight ago. It hasn't yet been announced. I only know because Charlie found them in his study. Nobody tells us *anything*.'

'My grandmother owns one of them. In the future.'

'How wonderful! What else?'

'Well, upstairs – the room at the top of the stairs? There's a window, and one of you girls will have a terrible tantrum and cut the glass with your mother's diamond ring.'

Gert laughed. 'Like Queen Elizabeth the First when she was imprisoned at Woodstock!'

Madeleine nodded, even though she had no idea what Gert was talking about. All her history classes at school had been about the Eureka Stockade.

'I suppose this explains why your clothing is so peculiar,' Gert said.

Madeleine nodded. 'What will I do, Gert? How will I get back?'

'Well, first we've got to come up with a story for *them* to explain where you came from.' Gert motioned towards the house. 'And I've no idea how we'll do that. But before we even begin, come to think of it . . . Charlie? Charlie, are you there? Millie?' Gert hopped up and peered into the bushes around them. 'You can't be too careful with Charlie. She gets in everywhere, like weevils in flour—'

All of a sudden, Gert let out an almighty scream.

There, on a log, the one Gert had tripped over, was a rat the size of a possum. The whiskers quivering on its nose were as thick as violin strings.

Madeleine thought of every historical story she'd ever read about the black plague and screamed too. She looked at Gert and they both ran.

The girls raced through the bracken and soon set upon a path, which led them downhill and then forked at some fruit trees. Madeleine could hear Gert puffing. She was so plump that her legs pressed together, grabbing her skirts until they kicked out just under her knees. As she ran, her shoes flicked petticoats, twigs and stones out to the sides.

They took the left fork and came to another vast lawn area edged by brown stones much like those in the fence and rimmed with a number of large trees. The biggest tree of them all had a small opening in its trunk at ground level. Gert dipped inside.

'This is the empty tree,' she puffed.

It was wonderful – a completely hollow tree. Madeleine leant back and looked up the trunk, which led to the sky like a knobbly chimney flue. 'It's so peaceful.'

'I know. I used to play with my dolls here. It would be the perfect hiding spot if only we didn't all know about it.'

Madeleine slid down the bark. Little fibres speared her

back. They sat in a silence that was comfortable, only their running-breath echoing up the knobbly chamber.

'We need a story,' said Gert.

'We do.'

'We can't go back to the house until we have one – and nothing too clever or too tricksy or they'll march you straight off to Constable O'Hanlon.'

Madeleine stared at Gert.

'For being from the future?'

'No,' said Gert, quite seriously, 'for being mad. If you try to tell any of the grown-ups the truth, I have no doubt that they shall lock you up.'

Didn't they have the death penalty in the nineteen hundreds? Wasn't Ned Kelly hanged? Madeleine had definitely seen his death mask at the Old Melbourne Gaol.

'I hear that once one's condemned, it's almost impossible to remove oneself from the madhouse,' Gert went on.

Madeleine tried to use the whole-body breaths they did in meditation at school.

'I don't think we said anything to Percy other than that you're ill, and he won't say anything. Charlie thinks your grandmother knows Aunt Hen, so perhaps we could elaborate on that story.'

'What about Anna?'

'The housemaid? I didn't tell her anything, and she hardly matters. It's Nanny we have to worry about. If we get Nanny onside we'll be fine, because Nanny runs the family, but that's the hard bit. Charlie and I sent word to her earlier, asking her to come home, but we only said that we had an unexpected guest from New South Wales, who had taken ill. Let me think.'

Gert put her head in her hands and tapped her nails on her forehead.

'I know. We'll tell them you're a friend of mine from school, whose mother is unwell.'

'Like with the plague?'

'No. They'd ship you straight down to quarantine. If Nanny had been here to see you faint she'd have had you down there before you could have said *Doctor Purves*. You were fortunate nobody was home.' Gert frowned. 'Hmm, your family is from Sydney, and you are a boarder at my school.'

'Aren't there schools up there?'

'That's a decent point, but you need to go to school down here for us to be acquainted, and if we made you from Melbourne, our parents would be bound to be known to each other – they would probably attend the same concerts and parties. Our fathers would have luncheon together at the club, and our mothers would sit on the same charitable boards. Besides, we've already sent word to Nanny that our guest has just arrived from New South Wales.'

'Hmm.' Madeleine rubbed the back of her head against the tree. 'Okay. I'm boarding down here because the education's better?'

Gert looked at her strangely. 'A family would never do that for a daughter. It took an awful lot of convincing to let me go to school at all. Perhaps your mother went to school down here?'

Although she hadn't been here for long, Madeleine could already imagine that family tradition was going to be a language Gert's parents spoke. She nodded.

'That ought to work. We'll tell Mummy she won't know your mother because she was only here for a few years and then moved to New South Wales. Oh, and your father is dead.'

'That's complicated.'

'Not as complicated as telling them that you're from the future.'

Madeleine couldn't argue with that logic.

'I shall tell Charlie we concocted the whole tease about us not knowing each other and Bea's slippers being stolen so that she had something to write in her silly notebook. And we shall write a letter.'

'We'll what?'

'We shall write a letter to Mummy, setting out the circumstances and requesting that you stay. Perhaps it's best we say your mother is away, not ill.' Gert stood and cupped her hands to her mouth and spoke through them in a stern voice.

'*Dear Mrs Williamson, I understand from Miss Fraser*—'

'Who's Miss Fraser?'

'The lady superintendant.'

'Lady superintendant? It sounds like a prison rather than a school.'

'Shhh. *I understand from Miss Fraser that you have offered to host Madeleine for the fortnight while I am returning from abroad. I am very grateful, as I hadn't expected our ship to be delayed and the school is unwilling to have girls stay over the winter break – dreadfully inconvenient and leaving me in quite a spot. Please let me know if there are any expenses for which I can reimburse you.*

'*I had the good fortune to meet Gertrude the last time I was in Melbourne and I couldn't help but notice what a kind and bright young girl she is – so well mannered. I am hoping some of her fine breeding might rub off on Madeleine.*'

Gert's face was gathered in an exaggerated frown.

'Are you serious?'

'Yes. Mummy will love that bit. Any compliment paid to us is a compliment paid to her. And to Nanny. *Yours, Mrs* . . . What's your mother's name?'

'Isy. Well, Isabelle Barnett.'

'Isabelle is Mummy's name too, only Mummy's called Bella for short! But I meant what do we call her – what are your father's Christian and middle names?'

'David, um, John.'

'*Mrs D. J. Barnett.*' Gert jumped up. 'Let's go and write it down before we forget. Mummy and Daddy are due home tomorrow, and if we backdate our letter and slip it into Daddy's post, we can pretend it's been misfiled. He's been away, so he'll never know.'

'Ingenious.'

'But we'll have to find Aunt Hen and explain it to her today – before we run into Nanny. Nanny is more likely to believe the story if it comes from a grown-up, and Aunt Hen is adept at holding herself against an opponent, even an older, bossier one.'

'Thanks.' Madeleine found herself feeling very grateful.

'I wonder if Aunt Hen has returned from her walk. I don't know how we're going to get you back, but at least this should allow you to stay while we try to resolve the dilemma. Elfriede – our *real* German cousin – arrives tomorrow morning, and with the *derangement* her arrival shall entail, we ought to be able to make ourselves scarce.'

Madeleine ran this information over in her mind and nodded. 'Okay, it's a plan. And by the way, Gert?'

'Yes?'

'How old are you?'

'Twelve.'

'Me too.' Madeleine was surprised. Gert was clearly competent, but still, she seemed so much younger than Madeleine. She'd barely developed physically; Madeleine felt sure she wouldn't have had her period yet.

'Are you really twelve?' Gert looked surprised. 'I assumed you were at least fifteen. Are all girls from your time so ... tall?' Gert's eye fell to the pillow that Madeleine's breasts squished under her turtleneck.

'A lot of girls my age wear bras, yes,' Madeleine said evenly. 'I've had mine since Grade Four.'

Gert's face had turned beet red, in turn making Madeleine feel uncomfortable. 'What grade are we in, then?' she asked in an attempt to change the subject. 'At school?'

Gert tugged at her pinafore and then crossed her arms. 'Class Two. Now hurry. Nanny will be back any minute, fussing about an unexpected visitor, and we need to catch Aunt Hen before they bump into each other.'

Madeleine ran the names over her tongue. There was so much to learn, but she was relieved – she had Gert on her side. If this were a computer game, she wouldn't have won yet, but she'd definitely have made it through the first level. Madeleine just didn't know what the next level would entail.

# Convincing Aunt Hen

The girls found Aunt Hen back up at the house, in the drawing room waiting for them with Anna. Madeleine spotted her shadow against the hallway wall first: dark and hooked and bumpy. When Madeleine followed Gert into the drawing room, however, she was surprised to see a tall, broad woman shuffling from one foot to the other.

The woman saw Madeleine and brought a handkerchief to her nose.

'How do you do. I am Henrietta Williamson.' Through the white handkerchief, Henrietta's voice was muffly, but it was still much spikier than Madeleine expected of a woman with a frizzy greying bun.

Madeleine dropped her head and bobbed as she had seen Anna do. 'How do you do.'

Henrietta looked over to Anna and then back to the girls again. 'I do apologise, but Charlie explained that you are in ill health, so we shall need to keep you isolated in another of our rooms until you're cleared. I was just about to send for Doctor Purves. Anna has already cleaned all the surfaces in here thoroughly with carbolic.'

'Carbolic?'

'Carbolic soap. Surely you have that in New South Wales?'

Madeleine had noticed the strong smell as soon as she walked into the room; it was the same chemical stench she'd smelt in the courtyard earlier. She tried to breathe through her mouth. She looked over at Anna, but the girl had her head down and her eyes averted.

'There's been another outbreak in Sydney this week,' Henrietta went on, 'and boats from New South Wales are arriving in Melbourne practically on the hour, all teeming with rats. They're burning the Sydney slums, but it won't be long until we're overrun with it down here as well – not if it's travelling on the back of fleas as they're suggesting. Or on Chinamen. Hopefully carbolic shall help. Are there any boils?'

'It's all right, Hen Pen!' Gert exclaimed, completely ignoring Henrietta's racism. 'Madeleine is not unwell. She just fainted – it was fatigue. There's no need to notify anybody.'

'I'm sorry, Gertrude, but I'm not taking any chances. I have change to effect, and I shan't be affecting much from a coffin.'

Although Henrietta's hair was greying, her skin was unlined. She wore a long, white dress that hung comfortably in cotton and white buttoned boots with wooden heels shaped like eggcups. Her feet, Madeleine couldn't help but notice, were particularly large.

Henrietta caught her staring at them. 'I am very firmly rooted in the ground,' she said crisply and bustled across to the window, her bottom marching from left to right under her skirts.

Madeleine blushed. 'I . . . I came on a train, not a ship.'

Gert shot Madeleine a look. 'Hen Pen, I need to explain. This is my school chum, Madeleine Barnett. Madeleine, you have already been introduced to my Aunt Henrietta, Miss Williamson. We call her Aunt Hen or Hen Pen.'

Madeleine smiled.

'Madeleine brought you something,' Gert went on hurriedly, and she pulled the page of signatures from a pocket in her pinafore and handed it to Aunt Hen. '*Something I think you should see.*'

Aunt Hen took a pair of steel-framed glasses from her dress with long, pincer-like fingers and popped them on her nose. It was a long, fine nose with a bump on it. She looked up at Madeleine sharply. 'Where did you get this?'

'It's from my grandmother. I was to return it,' said Madeleine.

'It looks like it's a page from an old petition – one of the ones procured well before I got back from England. There were thousands of signatures – they sewed them onto a monstrously long linen roll. How funny. Thank you, and please thank your grandmother for me. What is her name?'

'Alexandra. Alexandra Atkinson.'

'Alexandra *Atkinson*. She must be Sybilla's cousin. You know, I think I do remember an Alexandra in the family.

Who would have guessed she would become part of the shrieking sisterhood? Well, as I say, it takes all types because it affects all types! Please thank her. Is she a member of the W.C.T.U.?'

Madeleine nodded. It was a lie as instinctive as a kid pulling her hand from a boiling bath.

Aunt Hen picked up a book resting on a table beside her and slipped the sheet inside its pages. 'I'll tuck this in here to stop it being spotted by *certain* people. Provocation in one's own home is fatiguing.'

Gert looked at Madeleine and smiled. 'Nanny is not mad on Hen Pen,' she explained. 'And I am not always mad on Nanny.'

Aunt Hen walked towards the door.

'That's not all, though!' Gert cried. 'Madeleine is staying with us for the hols – her mother has written to Mummy, as she's a widow and has been delayed abroad.'

'Oh, I'm terribly sorry about your father,' said Aunt Hen. 'And what a blow – you must have been looking forward to seeing your mother.' She cocked her head to the side. 'Gertie bounds home whenever she can!'

Gert rolled her eyes. 'You make me sound like Millie.'

Aunt Hen laughed. 'You girls are so much better off at the Presbyterian Ladies' College, with proper teachers, rather than being stuck at home with a governess. The only school with a mandate to educate young ladies as well as any young man – and attended by Vida herself. An institution that produces a woman of that mettle is the school for you.'

Gert smiled. 'As Mummy and Daddy aren't home yet, could you please inform Nanny? You know what she's like with change and it will be much better coming from a grown-up.'

'Ah, yes, Nanny is not one to embrace any sort of change – even change that might see her station improve.' Aunt Hen blinked curtly and sighed. 'I'll speak to Nanny. You see Madeleine up to the nursery. We'll sort it out – nothing is impossible in this world, if one puts in enough thought and elbow grease.'

'Splendid,' said Gert gratefully. 'And as Madeleine's trunks haven't turned up, could you—'

'Alert Anna to that fact and ask her to procure some appropriate clothing for Madeleine to wear until her own arrives?'

Gert smiled at her aunt, who in turn looked to Anna. Anna nodded curtly and left the room.

'Although that mourning skirt does appear extremely comfortable, and I am not one to sniff at comfort,' said Aunt Hen, looking at Madeleine.

'Hen likes to wear pantaloons,' whispered Gert to Madeleine, 'but Daddy has forbidden it on any of his properties.'

'The loon in pantaloons!' Aunt Hen laughed. 'Most fitting. I was a member of the Rational Dress Society as a student in England. Now, what's the time, what's the time?'

She pulled a watch on a thick silver chain out of her pocket – just like the white rabbit in *Alice in Wonderland* –

and brought it up to her face, squinting at it through her glasses.

'Good afternoon, girls. I have colonies to emancipate. But first the battle with Nanny, and mark my words, it will be a battle.' Aunt Hen turned to go, her skirts swirling about her legs like a treble clef. 'Oh, I do love a good fight! *Ye women of Australia, arise in all your might!*'

And with one last swish, Aunt Hen was gone.

# Nanny

The nursery was right up the top of the stairs, tucked in under the roof of the right-hand wing of the Muse. It comprised four rooms, each joined to the next like a paper chain. Two were used by the children and connected by a set of double doors, the third was used by Nanny as her bedroom, and at the very back was a schoolroom.

The nursery room Gert led Madeleine to had a low sloping roof covered in wallpaper patterned with little forget-me-nots, which looked like flyspots. The window looked out across the property and down to the gates. There was a small fire burning in the corner and a washstand near the door. The room was smaller and much less grand than any of the downstairs rooms, the rug worn – almost a bit shabby – but it was extremely cosy.

Just as Aunt Hen had promised, there was clothing waiting for Madeleine to change into, laid out on a small, smooth bed.

'Play clothes,' said Anna from behind a pile of sheets. 'I'm terribly sorry but we're not able to accommodate mourning. The Misses Williamsons have nothing appropriate in your size.'

'Oh, that should be fine, shouldn't it, Madeleine? It has been a good deal of time now.' Gert kicked at Madeleine with her boot, and Madeleine nodded.

'Sing out if you need help – I shall be in Nanny's room.' Anna left, still holding her pile of linen.

'Do kids here wear mourning clothes – everything in black?' Madeleine asked Gert.

Gert nodded. 'You have to wear them for a year.'

'Nobody wears black in Sydney except goths – although everyone in Melbourne does. Well, everyone except my grandmother!'

Madeleine sighed and got undressed. When Gert saw Madeleine's sports bra, she went to speak, paused, turned red and passed Madeleine layers of cotton without comment.

Instead of undies, there was a pair of shorts like the ones Madeleine had seen on Charlie earlier. Gert called them drawers and blushed.

Gert then passed Madeleine a thick cotton vest to pull on, and over that a thicker, tighter woollen vest, which was stiff and a bit fleecy and had buttons running in a line down the front and some other odd buttons along its bottom edge. It had hard bands sewn inside its two front panels.

'I don't think the liberty bodice is going to do up,' said Gert, pulling the two fleecy sides of the stiff bodice closer together in an attempt to do the long row of buttons up. 'It's an old one of Bea's.'

'I'll just wear my sports bra,' whispered Madeleine, mortified.

'That? I thought it was a stayband. Either way, we don't want Nanny to see it.' Gert yanked at the bodice again. 'Breathe out.'

'Out? Shouldn't it be in?'

'No, that makes your lungs bigger.'

After much tugging, they got Madeleine and her sports bra into the liberty bodice. It turned out that the buttons punctuating the bottom of the bodice were for buttoning on extra layers of underwear – they buttoned on a flannel petticoat, and then attached some garters to hold up a thick, black pair of longer woollen stockings to keep Madeleine's knees and thighs warm. Gert pulled a brown dress that did up at the back over Madeleine's head, followed by a white pinafore, which slipped over the top and tied together at the sides with tape ties.

The buttons pulled the dress's fabric tight across Madeleine's back, and the fabric felt tight around her wrists, too. There was no stretch in it at all. The ruffle of the apron ballooned off her shoulders like the sails of the Opera House. Madeleine looked at her reflection in the window and saw an oversized Holly Hobbie doll.

'Do you seriously go through this every morning? There are more layers than a lasagne. And the *buttons*!'

'Oh, there are heaps more buttons if it's a *good* outfit. You'll see.'

*These girls would love a Bonds T-shirt and a onesie*, thought Madeleine. *Or even just velcro.* She sat up very straight on the little bed. She had to.

'I'm not sure where we're going to find boots for you,' said Gert. 'Your feet are bigger than ours, too.'

The *too* sat at the end of the sentence like bosoms. Madeleine looked down at her broad, black-stockinged feet splayed on the rug. They were usually in runners, and actually pretty big by any measure. 'I can wear my boots. They're not ideal, but they're better than nothing.' Madeleine couldn't get over how tiny and narrow Gert's feet looked in her own boots – like they'd been popped into the oven with a chip packet at two hundred degrees Celsius and left to shrink.

Anna returned with a small mirror and helped Madeleine bind her hair into two plaits, tying them up with heavy ribbons. Her hands smelt of lavender and carbolic. The plaits were so tight that Madeleine's eyes were pulled sideways and she could hear the *click* of each blink.

Anna nodded at Madeleine. 'Much smarter. Are you really feeling better?' She passed Madeleine a bundle of nut-brown wool. 'Here, you'll need a woollen jersey outside.'

Madeleine took the jersey, and Anna knelt by the fire, picked up a pair of brass tongs and fed the flames lumps of coal.

Madeleine was finding it hard to breathe. The bodice made her sweaty and the stockings itched. 'Is it always this uncomfortable?' she asked Gert. She stood up and walked about the nursery, wriggling her shoulders, trying to shift the prickles from her chest.

'Uncomfortable? Corsets and bodices assist ladies in supporting the weight of their own backs. Bea wears a proper corset, much to Aunt Hen's chagrin! But both bodices and corsets are frightfully good for keeping the kidneys warm, and they are windproof.'

'What does Hen wear, then?' asked Madeleine.

Gert laughed. 'Well, it's said servants wear liberty bodices, so *of course* Aunt Hen does too. She would like all women to win the vote, you know – not just ladies of property as Daddy proposes, but the servants, too. So she feels a certain level of solidarity with them. Daddy says it's ridiculous as liberty vests were invented to emancipate women but only served to emancipate servants to do *more* work, and that Aunt Hen just hasn't thought it through yet. He says her solidarity is flawed.'

Gert was more animated than usual, Madeleine noticed. 'Do you think I could borrow one of Hen's bodices?' she asked. 'This one is quite tight.' Madeleine wasn't actually sure they were going to get the thing off. She could feel it cutting up under her arms. 'They might have to get Doctor Purves in with his surgical knives to remove it.'

Gert raised one eyebrow. 'That's not such a daft idea. We shall sneak into Aunt Hen's room as soon as we're able. But for now, we have to get rid of *these* before Nanny finds them.' Gert held up the bundle of Madeleine's clothes.

Just then there was the heavy batter of heels in the hallway. Gert shoved the bundle behind the doll's house seconds before a woman with a bossy bun and clipped lips surged into the room. She wore a grey dress and a rigid apron and stood with her hands on her hips. Madeleine jumped up.

'Really, Miss Gertrude, it is entirely improper to impose a guest on the family like this. You ought to have warned me, or at the very least to have asked for permission,' the woman said in an English accent. Charlie was at her heels, along with Millie the dog and a very small child who immediately hid behind one of the beds. The woman placed a thick hand on Madeleine's forehead. Her palm was the colour of unbaked biscuit.

'I didn't know either, Nanny – nobody did. Madeleine's mother was delayed abroad, and she was unable to stay on at school. Madeleine had nowhere else to go, and her mother *did* write,' Gert protested.

'I certainly never received a letter.'

'I'm sure it was addressed to Mummy or Daddy.'

Madeleine was impressed by Gert's spry mind.

'Well, it's a relief you're not unwell,' the woman said to Madeleine, ignoring Gert altogether. 'You do seem to be a picture of health. Allow me to introduce everybody. I am Nanny. You will come under my supervision while you are here, and needless to say I expect the same standard of behaviour from you as from the other children in this home. You know Miss Gertrude from school. This is Miss Charlotte.'

'*Master* Charles Williamson,' said Charlie and swung down into a bow. 'We are already acquainted.' Charlie looked accusingly at Gert. 'And I know all about the tease and I never fell for it!'

Nanny ignored her, just as she'd ignored her sister. 'And this here is Miss Imogen.'

A little face peeped around the edge of the bed. The girl looked to be around five years old, and Madeleine's mouth dropped open – it was the girl from the photo on the rock. Her curly hair was as tightly sprung as corkscrews, and she was as plump as a little partridge. Her cheeks were so pink they looked patched on, like thick circles of felt. Her face was strangely flat but was punctuated by very deep dimples when she smiled, and her teeth were as square and white as pieces of chewing gum.

'It's you!' gasped Madeleine. There was something so wonderfully comfortable about the girl's tiny face – it was like having to move house but discovering your old couch in one of the brand-new rooms.

The girl – Imogen – edged out from behind the bed. 'Who are you?' She was even sweeter in life than in the photo; no picture could capture the soft lilt in her voice.

'I'm Madeleine,' said Madeleine, wondering how Imogen would react if she knew that her photograph would end up cemented to the underbelly of a rock in a country lane well over a century from now. 'And . . . uh . . . I'm another boarder from Gert's school, but I'm actually from New South Wales.'

Nanny nodded.

'Thanks so much for letting me stay. I was in a huge pickle.' Madeleine smiled her most winsome smile.

The invisible thread in Nanny's lips tightened. At her feet, the little white terrior sat down with a thud and started licking its bottom. Nanny took one look at the dog and ruptured, releasing a round of orders as deftly as Madeleine potted tin ducks at the Easter Show.

'Miss Charlotte, please untuck your pinafore. It does not look like knickerbockers, it looks like you have your pinafore tucked into your unmentionables – in other words, improper and utterly ridiculous. And once you've done that, you can take Millie downstairs immediately; you know full well that animals are forbidden up here. That dog has no sense of decorum whatsoever, and she smells.

'Miss Imogen, please stop pestering our guest and go and fetch Bob-Bear from your father's study. You are well aware that you are forbidden to play in there, but if you are going to flout my rules I suggest you don't leave evidence lying about for the servants to find.

'Miss Madeleine, while you are here, you shall share this room with Miss Gertrude. I will have Anna make up the bed under the window. Miss Imogen and Miss Charlotte share the room next door – just through those double doors. I shall allow you to settle in now, but please do let me know if there is anything further you require.'

Nanny turned to the other girls.

'Miss Gertrude, run down and ask Cook to delay nursery

tea. In all this *unexpected* kerfuffle, we are running half an hour behind.' And with that, Nanny left.

'Man, she's terrifying,' said Madeleine.

'Terrifying?' said Charlie. 'Nanny *can* be utterly terrifying – even Daddy's a bit scared of her. That, however, was Nanny at her most charming. Just wait and see.'

# *Bea-utiful*

After Nanny had left, Madeleine found herself alone in the still room as the girls hurried off to perform their duties.

They dribbled back in a few minutes later. Imo was the last to return, clutching a large bear. She climbed up onto Madeleine's bed. Her chubby legs, encased in tights, looked as squidgy as sausage.

'I can whistle, you know,' she said to Madeleine. 'Listen.' She let out a sweet, merry sound. '*Toow wooooo.*'

'That is impressive.' Madeleine tried to lean back against the wall, but the bodice made it impossible. She sat up, rigid, instead. 'I only learnt to whistle last year. How old are you? Five?'

Imo giggled again. 'Did you travel here in a ship? Did it have dancing and music and *service à la russe* with blancmange?'

'Excuse me?' It was taking Madeleine a while to decipher Imo's baby lisp and English vowels.

'The ship. The ship from New South Wales.'

'I came on a train, and I've never heard of blancmange, but it sounds delicious – what is it?' asked Madeleine.

'A sort of custard. Mummy and Daddy went on a boat to England and it served blancmange. And *biscuits*!'

'Biscuits in the palest pinks and greens—' Gert stopped short as another, older girl wafted into the room; a girl who was as long, lean and beautiful as any Madeleine had ever seen, not in a beachy *Home and Away*-star kind of way, but rather in a delicate, cameo-brooch way, with her heart-shaped face, high cheekbones, curly mouth and thick, glossy hair loosely entwined in a bun.

'Bea!' Imo jumped off the bed and flung her arms around her. 'This is our biggest sister, Beatrice, but we call her Bea,' she said to Madeleine. '*She's* been on a boat with *service à la russe*; she's eaten jellies and pink cakes with silver baubles and lemonade and mounds of other grown-up foods. The jellies were—'

'Darling, too much! Too much!' Bea laughed a laugh to match a harp and drop-pearl earrings. 'How do you do, Madeleine. Nanny explained your situation. I am sorry to hear your mother is caught abroad.'

Madeleine smiled, feeling strangely shy, but before she could think of anything clever or gracious to say in return, Bea's eyes had swept past her and on to Gert.

'Gert?' Bea's voice had flipped like a weathervane, from *sunny-no-chance-of-rain* to *celestial storms* in one puff. 'Have you taken my looking glass?'

'No, Bea.' Gert was quiet.

'Gertrude, I know it was you. The one that matches Granny's manicure set. The one set in tortoiseshell and silver.'

'No, Bea.' Gert picked at the skin around her fingernails.

'Don't fib, Gertrude. It was in my room this morning, and it's not there now – and with a blemish as towering as *that*, I'm not surprised you needed it.' Bea flicked a long, pale finger at Gert's face.

Gert put her hand to her red cheeks, sweaty and ashamed. 'I didn't take it. Perhaps one of the servants took it?'

'You spend your life blaming the servants, Gertrude Williamson!'

Madeleine thought of *Alice Through the Looking Glass*. A mirror – a looking glass was a mirror!

'Anna fetched a . . . a looking glass earlier that sounded just like that so she could show me the back of my plaits,' Madeleine spoke up, a little more loudly than she'd intended. It felt great to tell the truth. For once.

'Oh, well, that's quite fair enough.' Bea laughed to wash away the acid, and nodded at Madeleine. 'Excuse me. I shall ask her for it.'

Imogen followed Bea to the door of the nursery. 'Bea, Bea, will you play with me?'

'Not now, darling. Perhaps later.' Bea breezed off so smoothly she seemed to hover on air.

'Thank you.' Gert nodded at Madeleine once Bea had gone. 'She'd never have believed me. I spend my entire life getting the blame. If anything goes wrong in this family, it is always my fault.'

'She's very beautiful.'

'Everyone says that.' Charlie flicked through the pages of her book.

'Charlie, your notebook is so daft.' Gert rolled her eyes.

'They do. Nanny says Bea's beauty is Mummy's greatest source of pride. And look here . . . *Third of August eighteen ninety-nine, Mr Bartlett to Mr Raymond: 'She's a lovely girl, that eldest Williamson. Lovely.* When people say *lovely* they really mean beautiful, don't they, Gert?'

'Charlie. This is dull. You are the most boring child in the colony. And when I say boring, I mean as boring as sago pudding.'

'It's not dull, Gert. You're just cross because nobody comments on you. Well, not favourably.'

'I can see I'm going to have to be very careful around you!' Madeleine exclaimed, feeling alarmed at the thought of what Charlie might read out about *her*. Fortunately, Charlie snapped the book shut. 'Bea thinks it would be terrible to be plain.'

'Molly McGolly by golly. You should stop spying and spend more time at the grotto like the lonely little cave-dweller you are.' Gert looked down, her face still red. Even though she'd attacked her sister, to Madeleine she looked, well, sad.

⤳

Madeleine was so exhausted that evening she could barely eat. Gert led her downstairs to a small, windowless room off the kitchen. A round table was layered with a white cloth and then another white drip cloth on top, like in a fancy restaurant. Although the room had very high ceilings, there was a small fire in the grate, and the room smelt cosy, like buttered toast.

The table was set for the three youngest Williamson girls, plus Madeleine and Nanny. Bea was nowhere to be seen.

After a dinner – or, as Nanny called it, *nursery tea* – of googy eggs and little brown smoky fish, Nanny ushered them all upstairs again, and while the others grumbled, Madeleine was relieved.

Gert helped Madeleine out of the tangle of clothes and undergarments she'd squeezed her into earlier, taking care to hide the sports bra from Nanny.

Nanny handed Madeleine a very long white robe made of fabric that was stiff and smelt of lollies, with a high lacy neck. She passed it to Madeleine as one might pass a tin of peaches for labelling on a production line, brusque and humourless. Madeleine pulled on the robe, climbed into the little bed heaped with pillows as cool as clouds seemed from the window of an aeroplane, and closed her eyes.

'Here is the chamber-pot, in case you require it,' said Nanny as she left the room, 'and do not forget your prayers.'

Madeleine opened her eyes. In the dim glow from the fire, she could see that Nanny had hoisted up the seat of a large, pale wooden chair about a metre from the bed. Inside was a blue-and-white china pot.

'Oh man,' said Madeleine. 'It's a toilet in a chair – a

massive potty.' She shuddered and vowed never to use it. It seemed unhygienic to sleep with wee in the room. 'Isn't there a toilet up here?'

'There's a bathroom on the first floor with a lav that we may use during the day, but we use chamber-pots at night. I'm sorry – I ought to have shown you the bathroom this afternoon.'

Directly opposite Madeleine's bed was the tall doll's house Gert had stuffed Madeleine's clothes behind earlier. Set into an alcove in one corner of the room, just visible from where she lay, was a bulky cupboard.

Madeleine sat up. 'I didn't notice that before,' she whispered.

Imogen was already making snuffling sleep-noises in her bed through the open double doorway.

'The doll's house? It was Bea's. Imo plays with it now,' Gert whispered back.

'Not the doll's house – although it is divine, especially that painted ivy on its walls. I was talking about the cupboard!'

Madeleine slipped out of bed and went to the cupboard, opening it with its little brass key. The wood was a lovely golden-brown, the colour of honey cake, and the clothing inside was hanging face-forward on hooks, rather than along a pole. Madeleine crouched down and slid her fingers along the bottom until she felt the lip of the secret compartment she'd found Bea's shoes in and pulled it open. Charlie snored a deep old-man's snore from the next room.

'This is where I found Bea's shoes.' Madeleine looked over at Gert.

'What? Are they in there now? Why would Bea keep them down there?'

'I have no idea why,' said Madeleine softly. 'They're not here now, but they will be – I promise you.'

Madeleine returned to her bed. 'All I know is that I'll be scrubbing this cupboard down in over a hundred years' time. Where I'm from, it's white; I'm about to give it a quick lick of paint.'

'And they let you do that – *paint*?'

'Yep.'

'Charlie would love the future.' Gert giggled.

A groggy murmur came from Charlie's bed in the next room. 'What would I love?'

'Charlie! Don't meddle – go back to sleep,' said Gert.

'But what would I love?' Charlie asked again. Madeleine could see through the doorway between the rooms that she was sitting up at the end of her bed, her eyes wide now.

'The place I'm from,' said Madeleine, reckless. 'Because you'd get to do things boys do, like scrub down cupboards and shoot people with paint guns. And fight with the army.'

'As a soldier? Victoria has its own army, of course, and our troops are fighting the Boers, but ladies don't fight, they nurse.'

Madeleine sat up. 'Of course I'm joking, but I think women *should* be able to fight, I really do. Wars run better that way, because female soldiers can do things like speak to civilian women, and women are meant to be good at strategising. Anyway, I'm stronger than most of the boys in my class.'

Gert was making choking sounds from her bed. 'That's just ... *silly*, Madeleine. Our sex may not be as feeble as Mummy thinks, but war is—'

The door to the nursery flew open.

'Girls, *silence*!' Nanny was silhouetted in the doorway, square and furious. 'One more word from *any* of you and I'll send Miss Madeleine straight back to New South Wales.'

'Yes, Nanny,' said Gert and Charlie quickly.

'Sorry,' mumbled Madeleine.

Nanny shut the door.

'Nanny No Nonsense,' whispered Charlie.

Madeleine sank back into her pillows and gazed at the cupboard in the shadows – the very same cupboard she would be staring at from her other bed a century from now. Or at least she hoped she would be; she really, really hoped.

# *The next day, about a hundred years ago*

W hen Madeleine woke, she could see nothing but white: a bright, clean, pitiless white. She opened her eyes wide. Then there was a rustle of movement to her left, the linen sheet was whipped from her head, and Madeleine found herself looking into Gert's freckled face.

'I thought I'd gone blind for a moment there. That really would be the last straw.'

'Well, I'm not sure about blind, but I've seen more life in a rice pudding.' Gert smiled. 'We'd better get dressed for breakfast.'

Gert poured some warm water into a bowl at the wash-stand and wiped a face washer across her face. Then she helped Madeleine do the same and shepherded her through the tedious task of getting into her outfit. Anna plumped pillows, emptied the water bowl, refilled the jug, folded nightgowns and ran around with the bellows, puffing all the fires in the upstairs rooms. A similar degree of industry was apparent when the girls went downstairs; the household was buzzing.

Gert led Madeleine back to the small room in which they had eaten supper the night before. It was gloomy in the half light of morning. Charlie, Imo and Nanny already sat at the table, bowls of porridge before them.

Madeleine sat down and took a scoop of porridge, only to nearly spit it out again. The oatmeal was creamy but as salty as the sea. At home, Madeleine made her own porridge from a sachet that came in flavours like creamy vanilla and only took ninety seconds in the microwave. Luckily, in her new tight underwear, she had very little appetite anyway.

'Why is everyone so busy?' whispered Madeleine to Gert as Anna shot by in the corridor again, this time with a tin bucket of soapy water in hand. It wasn't very relaxing sitting down while everyone flapped around them.

'Mummy's cousin is arriving today, and so Daddy and Mummy are returning – Daddy's been working in his chambers, trying to finalise something on the new Constitution with England, so they've been at Park Street.

'Park Street?'

'We still have a town house, as Daddy is frequently required there.' Gert turned to Nanny. 'Excuse me, Nanny, may I have please have a little cream?'

'No, Miss Gertrude. You know to wait until you are offered something, and there is no cream. Children do best with sensible, plain foods – I dislike the way Cook indulges you. Her tastes are far too decadent, but that's what one gets when one engages an RC.'

'RC?' asked Madeleine.

'Roman Catholic, Miss Madeleine, and do not interrupt. Regardless of what they might teach you at college, forthrightness is terribly unappealing in the female sex and intolerable in a child.'

Madeleine was so angry she felt her whole face and neck turning pink.

Nanny took a deep breath. 'No, plain and wholesome food is best for children; that's what my mother used to say. There are, however, stewed prunes if you would care for them, Miss Gertrude – stewed prunes are very good for digestion.'

She gestured towards a bowl of shiny black prunes in syrup at the centre of the table.

'Straight back, please – and Miss Imogen, do not whistle that incessant tune at the table – or any tune, for that matter. Excuse me.'

Nanny got up from the table and walked through the door into the hall.

'Well, *you* get cream,' whispered Gert to Nanny's retreating back. She leant over to Madeleine. 'When Mummy and Daddy are here, everyone gets to eat breakfast in the morning room together. It's a much merrier affair. Mummy finds it too glum in here, and she's very keen we learn dining etiquette.'

'This can be merry too.' Charlie winked. 'Master Charles Williamson has a plan.' She disappeared beneath the lip of the tablecloth momentarily, and re-emerged brandishing a long wooden peg.

'Yes, yes, yes! Oh, please, Charlie – musical porridge!' Imo clapped.

'Shhh, Imo.' Gert looked at the door.

Charlie and Gert each put both hands on the tablecloth, and together they slowly spun the table. Madeleine held her spoon and watched the bowls of porridge spin around twice, like they were sitting before a giant lazy Susan at a Chinese restaurant.

Imo giggled.

They heard the clod of Nanny's heels on the lino. Charlie stopped the table expertly and slipped the peg back in to hold it in place. 'You required cream, Miss Gertrude?' She stood and bowed like a butler.

'Yes!' Gert tucked into Nanny's porridge.

Nanny returned, none the wiser. 'I'd like you all outside to play in the garden after breakfast. There is nothing quite like fresh air and exercise. Percy will set out the *bicyclettes*.'

'All right,' said Gert, pushing out her chair, which screeched on the lino.

'All right? Is that what they're teaching you at school, Miss Gertrude?'

'Yes, Nanny.'

Nanny looked at Gert sharply. 'Just because your mother always says you're the clever, difficult one does not mean you can be rude. Not while I'm on guard.'

Gert blushed a deep red. 'Sorry, Nanny. I meant to say that there shan't be any nonsense.'

Madeleine felt sorry for Gert. She found Nanny too gruff – gruff but weirdly formal, with her *Miss Madeleine*s and her *Miss Gert*s. Madeleine's only experience of baby-sitters had been Year Eleven girls from school, who'd let her spoon Nutella into her mouth straight from the jar and stay up really late watching too much TV while they sent texts to their boyfriends from the couch – things her mother would *never* have allowed.

'Don't worry, Gert, I say *all right* all the time at home,' said Madeleine quietly. 'I didn't even know it was rude.'

Nanny took a bottomless breath. '*Miss Madeleine*,' she said in a whisper more biting than any shout, 'in this household, I answer to Mrs Williamson, and the children answer to *me*. As our guest, I expect you to show me the same respect. It appears there is very little to be said for the manners of children from a penal colony. I can't say that I wasn't warned.'

Nanny beat her bare palm on the edge of the table, then put down her napkin. Madeleine and the other girls jumped.

'I'm sorry, Nanny,' said Madeleine, not entirely sure what she was being accused of. 'That came out all wrong.'

Nanny spooned porridge into her mouth. If she noticed her own serving of porridge was uncreamed, she was too angry to comment.

After breakfast, Madeleine, Gert and Charlie spent hours playing outside. Gert and Madeleine rode a set of old bikes without any gears across the lawn and tennis court and down the hill towards the lake. The bikes were as wobbly as front teeth. Imo watched and cheered, her little legs too short to reach the pedals. The sun was bright, but the morning was cold, and there was a layer of white frost across the grass, crisscrossed with dark trails left by the bike tyres. It crunched as Madeleine rode over it, and the cold air bit her lungs.

She and Gert finally tired and returned to the house, sitting together on the stone steps that led up to the front door. Madeleine tried to pry the bodice away from her stomach. Her sweat had pooled and dried inside it, and the salt on her skin was itchy. She also stank. If there was deodorant here, it had not been offered.

'Those bikes are great fun,' said Madeleine. 'Much more fun than the bikes we have. Ours are so stable you don't need hands to ride them. I was freaked out!'

Gert smiled. 'Freaked out?'

'Terrified. You know what I mean.' Madeleine tried to get a finger up under the end of her bodice to scratch her ribs. Her finger wasn't long enough, though, and it was impossible to scratch effectively through all the material. 'Is there any chance we can sneak me one of Hen's chastity vests now? I'm *so* uncomfortable in this tight one. It is the worst thing *ever*.'

'Liberty bodice! And I'm afraid Aunt Hen hasn't left for the day yet, so no. She's always off somewhere, though, so it's only a matter of time. I'm not sure it's the *worst thing ever*. Your turn of phrase is terribly amusing.'

'So's yours.' Madeleine wriggled again. 'Even in this thing, I'm starving. What time's lunch?'

'*Dinner* should be in about an hour. We children still have dinner. Only Bea is allowed to join the adults for luncheon.' Gert looked put out.

'You call your lunch dinner?'

'Of course,' said Gert, 'Although we call the adults' evening meal dinner too. Children have nursery tea.'

Madeleine shook her head and looked up at the sky. An English flag – the Union Jack – snapped in the breeze from one of the two white flagpoles by the front gate, flying at full mast. Next to it, on the second pole, flew a white flag with a Union Jack in the corner, boxed in by a blue cross with stars.

'What flag is that?' asked Madeleine. 'I've never seen it before.'

'It's the flag for federation! *One people, one destiny, one flag!* Daddy doesn't usually fly it, as it's a little too close to the Eureka flag, but it's become so popular lately I think he's decided it would be churlish not to raise it occasionally.'

Gert smiled. 'And if that flag is flying, that means . . . *they're home!*' And she leapt up and flew into the house, Madeleine behind her.

The girls burst through the front door. A clump of men stood in the drawing room just off the entrance hall, a murmuring circle: backs straight, tipped towards the centre, bent slightly at the waist. It was a colosseum of white collars and whispers, *hmph*, *hmph*, *hmph*s. Their very presence demanded space be left around them, like a glob of oil in vinegar.

'It has to go through. There is no other practicable means by which the united Australian voice of the six colonies may be heard or made effective,' said one of the men.

He was taller, leaner and less hairy than the others. He had a flop of blond hair that fell down in front of his face, and he was golden. *Yes*, thought Madeleine, everything about him was golden – his skin, hair, eyes, all as golden as the crested ring on his pinky finger. Without the moustache, he'd have looked like a Bondi lifesaver – and yet he seemed to be the sort of person who spent most of his time buttoned-up in the study. He checked his fob watch and shook his head.

Gert grabbed Madeleine's elbow and pulled her sharply to the right to ensure that the girls kept a sizeable distance between them and the men as they passed them by.

'Sorry, Daddy,' she whispered to the golden man, removing her hat and avoiding eye contact.

A plump man with a large red nose and bushy beard said something Madeleine didn't catch, and the circle laughed.

'That's the Premier, Mr McLean,' whispered Gert. 'He has quite the parish pickaxe, doesn't he?'

'Quite the *what*?'

'A prominent nose!'

Madeleine laughed, quite loudly. Gert elbowed her in the side.

Gert's father gestured and the men exited the drawing room and crossed the hall, retreating into the musky warmth of a study lined with leather-bound books.

'Don't you want to go in and say a proper hello?' asked Madeleine, but Gert just frowned.

Charlie and Imo tumbled in through the front door with Nanny.

'Come on, let's follow Nanny and find Mummy,' said Gert, heading towards the stairs that led back up to the nursery.

The girls took the stairs two at a time. Madeleine's breaths were short and stiff within the liberty bodice as she strove to keep up with Charlie, but she still panted a lot less than Gert. As she climbed, Madeleine held up her itchy, slippery tights with one hand to prevent them from sliding down her legs, dragging the drawers with them.

Charlie was about to reach the top when a voice floated down the stairs from above them.

'Nanny,' called the voice, 'we're expecting Elfriede this afternoon. You will need to find something suitable for Gertrude's guest to wear if her trunks still haven't arrived.'

Madeleine looked up and was met by the sight of a solid woman ascending the staircase. Although her limbs were heavy, her skirts seemed to glide above the boards, her little shoes kicking out from beneath them.

'Mummy!' Gert and Imo cried in unison.

Mrs Williamson smiled loosely in the girls' direction. She wore a high-collared shirt with a pattern on the front and shoulders, and a high-waisted, dark-blue skirt that showed the curve of her stomach and hips.

Imo and Gert ran up to their mother and threw their arms around her, Charlie close behind them. Their hugs didn't dent her clothes. Mrs Williamson patted Gert's head limply, gave Charlie a squeeze and planted a big kiss on Imo's cheek. 'I was just going to the nursery to look for you. Oh, I have missed my girls!'

Then she turned to Madeleine and smiled. She held out her hand. Madeleine shook it vigorously, as her mother had shown her, and looked her straight in the eyes. 'Good afternoon, Bella. I remember that because it's the same name as my mum! I'm Madeleine.'

Gert stepped forward, her eyes shifting uncomfortably from her mother to Madeleine. 'I was just about to introduce you to my mother, Madeleine – *Mrs Williamson.*'

Gert could not have put more emphasis on the *Mrs Williamson* if she'd slashed it with a massive fluoro pink highlighter.

Mrs Williamson took back her hand and looked at Nanny. 'It's certainly a Teutonic handshake,' she said, raising her eyebrows. She turned to Madeleine again. 'You must be Madeleine Barnett. I'm terribly sorry but your mother's letter was swept up in Thomas's pile – he's only just unearthed it. I shall respond immediately, but of course you may stay, Madeleine dear. You must. Gert has spoken very warmly of you. Your poor mother will be frantic; I shall telegraph a response to her posthaste.'

'Thank you, *Mrs Williamson*.' Madeleine took a breath that came from somewhere deeper down than her knees. At home she called even her teachers by their first names or, sometimes, their nicknames – Margie, Sharon, Helen, Starky – but she could see that she was going to have to be careful around the adults here. Mrs Williamson, however, seemed to have moved on. She smiled and leant over to give Imo another kiss.

'Poor Nanny had no idea you were arriving, Madeleine, but you will soon discover she is very good at looking after us, very good indeed. Nanny, on that note, perhaps a lesson revisiting greetings would be useful for *all* the children.'

Nanny nodded gravely. Greetings were obviously something she took extremely seriously – as seriously as Mum Crum took carbohydrates and Madeleine's mother took Middle Eastern politics and knowledge of the periodic table.

'Well, I shall see you this afternoon, children, after your dinner,' said Mrs Williamson. 'I shall be in the garden and then the morning room if anyone needs me before then. I have some correspondence to attend to.'

She looked once more to Madeleine. 'Do you have other siblings, Madeleine, who may also require assistance?'

'Only my brother Ted . . . Edward, but he's staying with a friend in Sydney.'

'A brother. Well, your parents are fortunate.' Mrs Williamson's voice had gone soft. She looked down and blinked. 'I shall be off on my constitutional now, Nanny.'

'Yes, Mrs Williamson. It is a lovely day.' Nanny smiled, for the first time since Madeleine had met her, and it was a smile from the soul. She looked . . . well, she suddenly looked like a human being after all.

Gert grabbed Madeleine's hand once Mrs Williamson had passed them, and the girls ran the rest of the way up the stairs.

'With your father in his line of work, no wonder every-one's on *constitutionals* instead of walks in their spare time,' said Madeleine.

They both threw back their heads and laughed.

# Enter Elfriede

The four girls were spread across Gert and Madeleine's room in the nursery, playing with the doll's house. Winter sunlight shone through the window and onto the rug.

Imo and Gert were cross-legged by the doll's house, controlling the narrative. Charlie had lined all her tin soldiers up in rows on the floor under the window. 'Watch out, troops, it's a Trojan Dog!' she yelled, sending Millie into the scrum. The soldiers tumbled. 'Ahhh, casualities! Help me pick up my soldiers-bold.'

Madeleine sat up on her bed, changing the remaining dolls into various little outfits Bea had made, as directed by Imo. Imo was very bossy. Madeleine would have preferred to sit on the floor too, but the liberty bodice cut so solidly into her body that it made it too hard. She didn't know how the other girls coped without complaint.

Mrs Williamson knocked on the nursery door, Nanny at her side. 'Hello, darlings. Aren't you all terribly sweet, playing so quietly. Elfriede has arrived and is just getting refreshed in her room. Nanny, please ensure the girls are downstairs and dressed for tea in an hour.' She paused a moment and then added, 'I thought their muslins for this afternoon, Nanny? I would like them to look pretty.'

Mrs Williamson's instructions set Nanny into flurried work mode, which smashed the calm of the nursery like a piñata. Within ten minutes, all the girls were being washed and brushed down like spaniels for a dog show.

When the work was finally complete, Nanny did an inspection.

'You can stand there, Miss Madeleine. It's a becoming dress.' Nanny nodded at Bea, approving. Madeleine moved to the exact leaf on the rug to which Nanny had pointed.

The pale-yellow dress was hayseed light. It had a wide yoke and was then gathered across the chest in a series of pleats, with puffed sleeves, long, tightly buttoned wrists, and a sash. It was clearly a little girl's dress, but a beautiful one. Bea had brought it in for Madeleine earlier, on Nanny's direction. Madeleine had felt a little thrill as she'd taken the coathanger.

'I'll feel like a lemon-yellow angel in it!' she'd said. She was anxious to please Bea, and she wasn't quite sure why. There was something so assured and yet ethereal about her.

'That dress is an old one of mine,' Bea said to Madeleine now. 'Gertrude's such an awkward shape that Mummy doesn't care for her in my clothing.'

'Thank you,' Madeleine replied and then wished she'd said something to defend Gert instead.

Opposite Madeleine, Gert, Charlie and Imo were lined up in a row in front of Nanny like Charlie's soldiers.

While the three sisters' dresses were near identical except for their colours, the effect couldn't have been more different.

Charlie's dress was pale blue – some sort of concession, perhaps, to the fact that she had to wear a dress at all. Although Charlie was slight, the bodice was tight across her square chest, and her broad shoulders filled so much of the sleeve that there was little room for puff. She looked more like a lifeguard in a swimsuit than a little girl in a party frock. She looked like she'd make a good cricketer.

'At least it's blue and not pink,' said Madeleine.

'*Blue?* Blue is for *girls*. Why can't I wear pink?'

'Isn't pink for girls?' Madeleine was now very confused. 'Where I come from, it's almost impossible to buy clothes for little girls that aren't pink or purple. It drove my mum mad.'

'Blue is a daintier colour. Blue is always appropriate for girls,' said Nanny. 'Anyway, chin up, Miss Charlotte. At least it is as blue as your mood.'

'I want to wear a sailor suit like *normal* boys.' Charlie scowled deeper.

'You know how your mother feels about that,' said Nanny.

'She's scared you'll turn out like Aunt Hen.' Gert laughed.

'Have a look at your own reflection before you go sniping about Charlie,' said Bea.

Madeleine looked from Gert to Imo. Bea was right. Both were in pink versions of the dress, Imo's a pale pink and Gert's a deeper, fleshier shade, and while Imo was as pink and delicious as a sugar mouse, Gert looked as ridiculous as a bald baby in a headband.

'I can never get near the looking glass,' Gert retorted to Bea. 'Because *you're* always gazing into it.'

'Miss Gertrude Williamson, do not be nasty!' Nanny pulled the silver hairbrush she always seemed to carry from a pocket of her pinafore and raised the yellow bristles with just a hint of malice – either as a threat to start brushing Gert's hair again or to beat her bottom. Madeleine wasn't sure which, and she suspected that Nanny wasn't either.

Bea shook her head charmingly. Her hair was plaited and then coiled so that it lay like a snake at the nape of her neck, light and dark blondes running in shiny streaks like treacle. She stood behind Imo and retied the little girl's sash, haughty but calm.

Gert had told Madeleine that she and Bea were five years apart, but Madeleine could see that the gap between them was wider – as wide as the gap between Cook and the Williamson parents; between Madeleine's time and now. Somehow, Gert had been left behind.

It was because Madeleine was jiggling about in her dress that she was looking at the floor as they walked into the drawing room, and it was because she was looking at the floor that Madeleine smelt Elfriede before she actually saw her. Madeleine would always remember that smell: Elfriede von Fürstenburg smelt heavenly.

'Ah!' said Mrs Williamson and clapped her hands. 'How delightful, the children are here. Friede,' she tinkled, 'may I introduce you to my children: my eldest, Beatrice; then Gertrude, Charlotte and Imogen-the-baby. And this is Gertrude's schoolfriend, Madeleine Barnett. Girls, this is my cousin Elfriede von Fürstenburg.'

Elfriede glided towards them on a wave of smoke and cinnamon. She held out a slender hand; Madeleine was almost too nervous to take it. She suddenly wished that she didn't bite her fingernails.

Charlie was the first to break the silence. 'Do you spell that with a small *v*?' she asked, crooking her head and looking straight at Elfriede. Elfriede looked confused.

'You know – big *E*, little *v*, big *F*?' Charlie said.

'Why, yes,' said Elfriede as it dawned on her what Charlie was talking about. 'Aren't you clever.'

Charlie beamed. 'My middle name is Alexandra, and I want to spell it with a small *a* but Mummy says it's not done. The Germans are frightfully fond of big letters, you know. They capitalise their nouns.'

Now the children's mother looked confused. 'Remember, Charlie, that Friede *is* German,' she said and laughed.

'We're one-quarter German and three-quarters English,' said Charlie eagerly. 'Daddy says our German-ness is minute, two arms at best, but I think it's probably a bit more. There's no telling how German-ness would settle in the body. I like to think it's in the heart.'

'Darlings,' said Mrs Williamson in a voice like pudding. 'Why don't we let poor Friede sit down before we barrage her with conversation.'

'I'm actually learning German,' said Charlie, ignoring their mother and barraging away anyway. 'I'm teaching myself from a book. *Ohne Hast, ohne Rast. Without haste, without rest.* That's a quote by Goethe, and it's the motto for Gert's school. French is for girls and Latin is for old-fashioned men in sheets, but German is the language of fighters, of knights – of real men.'

'I have never heard anyone describe German as the language of men,' said Elfriede. She laughed, and her eyelashes flickered like the tail of a lyrebird.

Elfriede von Fürstenburg with the small *v* certainly did not sound like a man, and she certainly didn't look like one. In fact, she looked as heavenly as she smelt. She was, Madeleine guessed, older than Bea, but not by much. While her face didn't have the structure of Bea's, she was very striking. She was immaculately groomed, but she didn't look oily or powdery. Her lips were thick and red, and her eyes were as round as nutmegs. Her curls couldn't have looked more polished if they'd been slapped with varnish.

'Luscious, Elfriede is,' said Charlie later. 'Everything about her is quite luscious.'

Happily for Imo, Elfriede was not the only luscious thing in the room. 'Look!' she exclaimed, pointing out the food that had been laid out. 'It's a special-occasion tea.'

Madeleine looked over at the table. There were slices of cake stacked with glazed fruit; scones with yellow cream and raspberry jam; paper-fine sandwiches with curls of cucumber; and little shortbread biscuits. Every meal was an occasion here. Nobody ate like Madeleine's mother: standing at the fridge.

'Come, Elfriede,' said Mrs Williamson. 'You must be tired after your journey.'

Once they were seated, Mrs Williamson directed Anna to pour the tea. Madeleine couldn't help but notice how unembellished Mrs Williamson seemed next to her exotic cousin.

'Poor Mummy,' sighed Bea later. 'How dreadful to be so spongy, so drab.'

Spongy or not, Mrs Williamson had a lot of questions for Elfriede. She asked Elfriede about this cousin and that *Cousine* in Germany, this play and that *Novella*, slipping easily from English into German but looking self-conscious each time she strayed.

She punctuated her reminiscences about places and people with thick apologies. 'Oh, I am dreadfully sorry about the state of the house. Oh, I am dreadfully sorry about this dress – I have got so plump. Oh, I am dreadfully sorry about the girls' manners. Do sit up straight, Gertrude. Gert and Charlie are the ones I have to keep an eye on: like bunnies and blackberries, they're the most wont to turn wild in this clime.'

Madeleine couldn't help but notice that Imo wasn't particularly interested in manners, either. She was just as captivated by the treats as she was by her cousin; she climbed up onto Elfriede's lap, crumbs sprinkled around her mouth.

'Imogen, darling,' said her mother, 'I'm not sure Friede will like being climbed upon.' Imogen reached for another shortbread but stayed put.

'She's fine, Isabelle, really.' Elfriede stroked Imo's hair. She pulled a coil and it unrolled, doubling in length, before it sprang back against Imogen's head.

'There's no doubt which side of the family these come from!' Elfriede's own curls bobbed as she laughed again. It was a high-pitched, musical laugh that leapt up from the table and did *pas de chats* around the ceiling. Madeleine started – it was the exact laugh she'd heard in the lyrebird's call, back in the lane near Mum Crum's.

'They're from her crusts, most likely,' said Charlie, mesmerised. 'Imo gets through an awful lot of them.'

'Indeed?' Elfriede smiled.

'Why do you speak like that?' asked Imo.

Although Imo was the first to comment on it, Madeleine had certainly noticed. While Elfriede's English was flawless, her intonation was slightly out, her emphasis not always on the right syllable. Before anyone could scold

Imo, Mr Williamson swung into the room. Hen Pen came in behind him.

'Daddy!' yelled Imo and leapt off Elfriede's lap to run across the room and hug him. Gert, Charlie and Bea showed more restraint, but their eyes all lit up too. Their father had clearly bathed and changed since they'd seen him earlier; his hair was still wet on the back of his neck and Madeleine could see the comb-tracks running through it.

'Thomas, this is my cousin Elfriede von Fürstenburg,' said Mrs Williamson, prouder than punch.

Mr Williamson's tanned cheeks were split by dimples, and his golden hair flopped forward.

'How do you do.' He nodded. 'It's wonderful to meet you finally.' He strode across the room and Elfriede offered her hand; then he gestured over his shoulder at Aunt Hen. 'My sister, Henrietta.'

Aunt Hen offered her hand, straight and strong, to Elfriede, taking in every fold of fabric and shepherded curl. She nodded at Mrs Williamson, smiled at Anna and helped herself to a cup of tea.

'And now the whole family is here,' said Imo. She went on before anyone could comment: 'Did you know, Elfriede, that Daddy has O-legs, just like Charlie? Very bandy, but perfect for riding.'

'Do you ride, Elfriede?' asked their father, changing the subject while he accepted his tea.

'Not as often as my mother would like.'

'Charlie and I love to ride, don't we, Charlie? I'm teaching her to hunt, too.'

'That's Master Charles Williamson to you, Daddy.' Charlie winked at her father.

Mr Williamson laughed and ruffled Charlie's every-which-way hair.

'Oh, and this, darling,' said Mrs Williamson, 'is Gertrude's schoolfriend Madeleine Barnett, whom we discussed earlier today. I telegraphed her parents this afternoon.'

Madeleine channelled Elfriede and smiled up at Mr Williamson with her best how-do-you-do smile. Mr Williamson nodded in Madeleine's direction. 'Mrs Lüers stayed in Sydney then?' he asked Elfriede.

It wasn't really a question. Elfriede tilted her head and peeped at Mr Williamson over the lip of her own cup, taking every bit of him in.

*All that lipstick and none on the cup*, thought Madeleine. Not one smear.

'Yes, she did,' said Elfriede in her singsong intonation. 'She's still recuperating from a dreadful bug she picked up at a Pacific port. She tires easily, but the doctor doesn't think it's malaria.'

'Poor thing,' said Mrs Williamson.

'She insisted she'd travel on with me, but I had to put my foot down. I'm relieved she stayed behind, really; she was so unwell, and one probably ought not to say it, but she is rather advanced in years now.'

'A bit long in the tooth, is she?' Aunt Hen smiled into her tea dregs.

Mrs Williamson took in a sharp breath and glared at Aunt Hen.

'She felt infinitely better about it once I promised her my mother would never know,' Elfriede went on. 'I was a bit nervous at first, but travelling alone has been fabulous fun!' Her eyes sparkled. Mrs Williamson smiled.

Madeleine watched as Mr Williamson stirred sugar into his tea – two measured spoonfuls. He swallowed and his Adam's apple rolled. As he placed his teacup back on the saucer, he tipped it slightly and the blue cup's inside flashed white across the table. Madeleine wriggled.

'I must say,' said Elfriede, 'that I had never expected Melbourne to be so far away.'

'Mel-*bin*,' corrected Imo. 'We say Mel-*bin*, not Mel-*bourne*.'

'One has to admit, however,' said her mother, smoothing things over, 'that Mel-*bourne* sounds somewhat urbane. Infinitely more appealing.'

'Oh, Mel-*bin* is not such a backwater,' said Aunt Hen. 'There's quite a lot going on, really, if one has a jolly good poke around.'

'Well, Mel-*bourne* does sound like the sort of place that might at least have a symphony orchestra!' Elfriede laughed.

Hen Pen smiled politely. The other adults laughed too. Bea giggled along with them, teeth blinking. Imo looked at the adults and joined in. She held her stomach like a too-full man, spurting crumbs as a whale spurts water. 'That is terribly funny, Mummy.'

Gert picked up her cake fork. 'If I'd laughed with a

mouth full of cake, I would have been sent to the nursery before you could say Molly McGolly,' she said out of the side of her mouth.

Madeleine looked around. Nobody acknowledged either her or Gert. It was funny to be present but completely ignored. It made Madeleine feel as if she were dissolving, like a last shard of soap in the bath.

While Charlie hadn't dissolved, she had disappeared, possibly under the table. Nobody appeared to have noticed. The other adults and Bea, however, were all giving Imo chocolate looks and laughing some more. The laughter bound them.

Mr Williamson glanced at his watch and stood up. 'I'm sorry, but I really must tend to some business.' He scattered more dimples around the table and checked his fob watch again. Madeleine was pretty sure he didn't really *see* the time. She watched as Mr Williamson gave Mrs Williamson a vague pat on her back. Then he strode out of the room, flicking his hair and tucking his watch back into his pocket as he did so. When he had gone, the room was still for a moment, like the point at the very end of a breath. Even Anna, scuttling about the fringes of the room, muted her clearing.

Madeleine sat up straight and took a gulp of milky tea. She put the teacup carefully back in its saucer. Aunt Hen winked.

Mrs Williamson smiled, nodded and sat back, content. 'Well,' she said with Girl Guide enthusiasm, 'who would care for a little more tea?'

‹‹‹‹‹

The girls wandered back up to the nursery in some sort of trance – all except Bea, who was allowed to remain sitting with Mrs Williamson and Elfriede. Aunt Hen also remained but she wasn't chatting, she was reading the newspaper quite seriously in the corner.

'Your family is so lovely,' said Madeleine as she lay back onto her little bed. And they were – they were like a *real* family, the sort that you saw in car ads or in oil paintings from the olden days, all lolling around together under willow trees, or playing with hoops; families in which gas bills and maths test results and Lean Cuisine and single parents would never figure. Families full of pretty, happy people in pretty (if uncomfy) clothes.

Gert had been as dreamily quiet as the other girls since they'd left the table, but this seemed to snap her into an unhappy mood. 'I just don't understand why Bea always gets treated like she's an adult while I'm always lumped in with Charlie and Imo. I mean, surely if there was going to be a line, the obvious place to draw it would be below me.' She kicked at a wooden cradle on the floor stuffed with dolls and knitted animals. 'What happens in your family?'

'I only have a brother,' said Madeleine. 'So it's more like the kids versus the adults; I get thrown in with Teddy. And now . . .'

'What's it like to have a brother?' Charlie's voice was high with excitement.

Madeleine sighed and suddenly felt flooded with nostalgia. 'Well, he has cheesy feet, especially after he's worn his Air Jordans to basketball – they make his whole room stink. And he leaves the milk carton in the fridge when it's empty. Drives me mad.'

The girls all looked as blank as a squash-court wall. Madeleine searched for better examples. How did you explain the concept of a carton of milk in the fridge to people who had a cow in their backyard? 'His boots reek and he's always taking the last piece of cake.'

'Like Gert,' said Charlie.

Gert pinched her. Charlie didn't scream. She just rubbed her arm. 'Get off, Gert,' she said, frowning. 'It was only a tease.'

Gert flicked Charlie's leg with a hair ribbon and Charlie danced back, laughing. *That*, thought Madeleine, *is more like it.*

Gert caught sight of something on her front and stopped, holding out her dress. Down the bodice was a great dollop of raspberry jam. She rubbed it until it smeared and looked even worse. 'And I wonder why I'm sent back to the nursery. Bea would never do that.'

'Then Bea should help herself to bigger spoonfuls of jam,' said Madeleine. 'Mum Crum always says that kids who are neat aren't being kids.'

'I'd like your Mum Crum,' said Gert. 'Perhaps she'd be interested in replacing Nanny.'

'You'd like parts of her,' said Madeleine. 'And so do I.'

Madeleine went over to Gert's bed and picked up Gert's teddy. Although it was meant to be a bear, it had hard, strong limbs. *Mum Crum would approve of a teddy like that*, she thought. It was like a bear that had done a lot of Pilates.

Madeleine bent the bear's legs and sat it next to two dolls on the windowsill. Beyond them was a pale moon, as wispy as a ghost in the afternoon sky – a shadow moon, a moon made of winter cloud. Somewhere, sometime, under that very same moon was Mum Crum – Mum Crum and her crazy ideas, just so far away.

# Stockings in clumps

The next afternoon, the girls crowded around Elfriede in the dining room after lunch. Bea had eaten with the adults, while the others – the *littlies*, as Nanny insultingly called them – had eaten in the poky room off the kitchen again.

Madeleine, as the old visitor, had lost her new-girl status and was now just lumped in with the family. That always happened with new kids at school – they were celebrities for a week or so, until everyone realised they ate salami sandwiches and listened to the top-twenty hits too.

'Do you want to come and see the garden, Elfriede?' Gert asked. Madeleine noted Gert hadn't used *Friede* as Mrs Williamson had, and she agreed with the decision. *Elfriede* felt better. Even in the warm glow of Elfriede's beauty, there was a coolness to the girls' cousin that Madeleine thought was probably European. It was funny, though, because it seemed everybody else's name here was shortened or changed: Bea, Imo, Charlie, Hen.

'Oh, you must see the garden, you just must,' said Imo, taking Elfriede by the hand.

'Leave poor Friede alone,' said their mother. 'She's still adjusting.'

'I'm fine, thank you, Isabelle.' Elfriede smiled. 'And I should love to see the garden.'

'I shall let the children escort you, then. Don't forget your hats.' Mrs Williamson turned to Elfriede. 'This sun is so strong here, even in winter. Gert and Charlie are already as speckled as Dalmatians.'

It was a perfect time of day, Madeleine's favourite hour. Although it was winter, the sky outside was clear. The sun was high, and the garden was fresh and sparkly. Oranges hung bloated on branches in a small orchard down near the empty tree. Gert pulled at one and offered it to Elfriede. The tree juddered and another three fell with a thud. Imo scooped them up from the grass.

'Ooh, how lovely. At this time of year!' Elfriede held the fruit up to her face to smell it.

'Do you have them at home, Ms von Fürstenburg?' asked Madeleine.

'Call me Elfriede, please,' said Elfriede. 'Otherwise I shall feel like my mother!'

Bea laughed and took an orange from Imo. 'These are English,' she said. 'Daddy's sister sends her stones and seeds as a treat.'

'It is a beautiful garden.'

'Mummy presses local plants in her herbarium,' said Gert. 'Then she sends the plants and seeds in tiny muslin bags to her friends back home in Germany and in England. Isn't that right, Bea?'

'Hmm,' said Bea creamily. She was walking just ahead of the pack and she led the group in a gentle turn until they were heading back up the hill again.

Gert and Madeleine wandered up the path, their steps in sync. Bea strolled beside Elfriede, pointing out this and that plant, this and that flower. 'I often get the names of the plants wrong, but Bea never does,' whispered Gert.

Madeleine laughed. 'I think it's a good thing. It makes you far more interesting.'

'Really?'

Imo yawned. 'I like the bits of the garden I can eat.'

Elfriede's mouth contorted in the beginnings of a yawn and she looked away to swallow it.

They had walked around the side of the house, past a croquet lawn and up to a garden enclosed by a picket fence. Madeleine could hear the creek running nearby.

'This is the kitchen garden.' Gert opened a gate in the fence, which sat under a little archway covered with glossy leaves.

Bea walked Elfriede up some of the small paths that stemmed from the gate. 'Rosemary,' Bea said, 'for lamb. Cumquats, for marmalade and—'

'For hurling like bombs.' Charlie picked up a cumquat and threw it at a sparrow on the fence. The sparrow got away.

Up the hill beyond the kitchen garden and picket fence was another little hook of garden. 'Mummy designed this,' said Imo. The hook garden had a tiny stone seat and a pond, which ran in a loose heart shape. It was almost completely hidden from the house.

'I love all the secret spots in this garden,' said Elfriede. 'It's so romantic.'

Charlie grabbed her stomach. 'That sort of talk makes me queasy.'

'Look at the fish!' Madeleine pointed to the thick, meaty carp that wove their way along the bottom of the pond. Some were speckled orange, white and black; others had mottled skin, splotchy like a dog's mange.

'That's my favourite.' Charlie pointed at a fish huddled under a lily pad, staying clear of the sun. It had a porous skin, purple-black like velvet.

Imo knelt down and wriggled her fingers in the water, whistling. '*Toow wooooo*. Look, you can touch their noses.' One of the big mottled fish, which had silver scales as big and shiny as coins, swam up to her fingers. The others followed in a braid of silver tails. Imo shrieked and pulled her hand out. Madeleine stared at the fish. Their bodies were at once grotesque and mesmerising.

'They are enormous,' said Elfriede. 'I've never seen them quite this big.'

'They have whiskers like dogs,' said Gert.

'You mean like rats,' said Madeleine.

The girls hovered around Elfriede. They knelt on the pond's mossy bank and let the wintry sun warm them.

'Aren't you uncomfortable?' asked Charlie. 'You can sit on the bench, you know. It is for adults.'

'Mummy would never curl up on the ground,' Gert commented, her voice brimming with admiration for Elfriede.

'Uncomfortable? This is heavenly.' Elfriede lay down and stretched out, long and lean; then she arched like a cat. 'I could sleep right here.' She rolled luxuriously over onto her side and reached an arm long. Just seeing that stretch made Madeleine ache to stretch too.

'Ah, but there's just one more thing I must do.' Elfriede stood up again. Madeleine watched as she slid her feet out of her shoes and dipped under her skirt to unclip her stockings. They fell to her ankles in two glossy clumps. Elfriede stepped out of them. 'That is much freer.' She grinned and sat back down, wriggling her toes before she lowered them into the pond. Carp scattered.

'Oooh, it's much colder than I'd expected!'

Madeleine stared at Elfriede's long toes. Seeing them was like sharing a secret. They were so white they looked green through the water.

'I don't think I've ever seen a grown-up's toes before,' said Charlie. 'A lady's.'

'Ladies have toes too,' said Gert.

'Do you often go with bare feet in Germany?' Charlie asked Elfriede.

Madeleine giggled. 'You'll see more than just a woman's toes when you go to Germany, Charlie. My mum says Germans are really into nudity – like as a political statement

127

or something – and that when she was a backpacker, every time she went to the park she saw big rosy bottoms sunbathing in rows.'

'*Madeleine.*'

Madeleine looked up. All four Williamson girls were staring at her, mouths open like those clowns you stuck balls into at Luna Park.

Elfriede blushed pink beneath her powder. 'I have never seen anyone naked in a park in Hamburg, Madeleine, but there are some Swedish baths being established in Berlin,' she said. 'I'm told they are somewhat progressive.'

'I want to fish with my toes too!' cried Imo, and within seconds both she and Charlie had kicked off their boots and dumped their feet in the pond.

'Well, it does look nice.' Bea drew her bony feet from her stockings. She inched her apron and dress up to her knees and lowered her feet into the water.

'Bea?' Gert, looking startled, followed suit, and so did Madeleine. The water was freezing, and it was sort of greasy, too. Actually, for all the fuss, it wasn't that pleasant at all.

Elfriede left her feet in the pond and lay back against the bank. The five girls copied, stretching their necks from left to right as Elfriede did to rid themselves of cricks. Madeleine could feel the cold of the moss beneath her dress.

Elfriede sighed, as content as a cat in cream. 'And so I think I know you all now. Your mother has told me. Bea is the beautiful one, Gert is the clever one, Charlie is the adventurous one, and with Imogen it's too early to know, but she's possibly the musical one, because she is always whistling!'

'Out of tune. Possibly the annoying one. Definitely the spoilt one,' whispered Gert. Madeleine smiled and scratched one foot with the other. It was only now that her feet had stopped hurting from the cold.

'Four girls, four flavours. Like ice-cream! Now, tell me, Bea . . .' Elfriede tapped Bea's knee and smiled, and Bea smiled back. There was an intensity in their locking smiles that excluded everybody else in the circle. Elfriede's eyes twinkled. 'Do you have a beau?'

Bea blushed. Her eyes darted from Gert to Imo to Charlie to Madeleine. 'No.'

'What?' Elfriede looked genuinely shocked. 'A girl as beautiful as you?'

Now Gert blushed. 'Bea's only seventeen,' she said, flicking her feet in the pond to create little splashes.

'Almost eighteen,' said Bea. 'And I have come out, but life is very dreary up here.'

'Well, we shall have to do something about that.' Elfriede tapped Bea's knee again. 'I had many beaux by your age. Only I suspect it's difficult to find a boy as handsome as your father. He has set the bar high.'

'Do you have a husband?' Imo bellowed over the top of Elfriede's ensuing laugh. Elfriede seemed to laugh more at her own jokes than she laughed at anybody else's.

'No.' Elfriede looked at Imo out of the corners of her eyes. 'Not at the moment. Do you mind if I smoke?'

The girls watched as Elfriede drew a long cigarette from a silver case. As she sucked in, her cheekbones became wedges.

'I didn't know that ladies smoked.' Gert cocked her head to the side. Elfriede drew back on her cigarette and the end flared red. 'Not even Aunt Hen.'

'Most don't,' said Elfriede a little smugly.

'You really shouldn't,' said Madeleine. 'Smoking causes lung cancer and stroke, and my grandfather died of emphysema because they gave him cigarettes in the war and he got hooked.'

Elfriede gave a startled cough, looked at her strangely for a moment, then drew in on her cigarette again. 'The Crimean War?'

Madeleine nodded, silently vowing to be more careful about what she said.

'What made you decide to journey so far, Elfriede?' asked Bea.

Elfriede blew smoke out through her nose like a dragon. 'I've been travelling for some time. After, well . . . my parents . . . I'm accompanying a cousin of my father's on a world tour. Next stop Sydney.'

'Oh,' the sisters all said, with varying levels of interest (Gert's intense, Bea's polite, Charlie's indifferent, Imo's non-existent).

'What's your father's cousin like?' asked Madeleine.

'Ancient. Straitlaced but perfectly friendly. I think my mother wanted that – the straitlaced bit.' Elfriede looked over Gert's hat and gave Bea an *I'll tell you later* wink.

'Bea's seventeen,' said Gert, 'but I'm twelve. Like Madeleine. Charlie and Imo are really the babies.'

'Beg your pardon, *Schatz*?'

Gert was dangling her legs a little bit away from the group. She and Madeleine were the furthest from Elfriede except for Charlie, who had just hopped up and was now skimming pebbles. Charlie didn't seem to care that Elfriede seemed to favour Bea. Madeleine could see that Gert did. Elfriede looked over at Gert and Madeleine and smiled a sunny afternoon smile through the smoke. It promised nothing.

The sound of a gong rang out across the yard. Elfriede started. 'What was that?'

'Nanny,' said Bea. 'The gong has to be loud so that the men can hear it. Two gongs for the servants and one for us. It's Nanny's code.'

'Our cousins had a gong in England, and so now Nanny's installed one here,' added Gert. 'Nanny's like that. Daddy says she's as English as Gentleman's Relish. She has been with our family for a jolly good part of Queen Victoria's reign. She was nanny to our cousins, and when they finally grew up Daddy said it was too good an opportunity to miss and that we must do anything we could to keep Nanny in the family. She's frightfully loyal, even if she hated the move. She said she expected Victoria to be more like a *proper colony* – with Mogul palaces, embroidered slippers and jewels. Daddy says that for all her strengths, Nanny is not terribly good at geography. Hen Pen says that just proves she shouldn't be teaching it, and that in England many of the governesses are so frightful that there is a tremendous push to educate *them*!'

'Gert, don't prattle,' said Bea. 'You are dull.'

The gong rang again – once – only this time from a different direction.

'Goodness,' said Elfriede. 'Does Nanny have an orchestra of gongs?'

'No, that's a lyrebird,' said Bea. 'Well, I think it is.'

'It must be in there,' said Gert, pointing at some bushes. 'Madeleine and I saw one the other day. Imo used to call them lie-birds because they fib all the time—'

'Gert, *don't* say that. You are mean.' Imo picked up a twig and pretended to inhale smoke from it.

The bell rang again, only this time from down near the house, not the bush.

'Which one was that?' Elfriede shook her head. 'I don't know whether it was the lie-bird or the gong, but it sounded like it was beaten with purpose. Ought you girls to go back? I don't want to be branded a bad influence.'

The fact that Elfriede seemed to be scared of Nanny too made Madeleine feel better. She pulled on her stockings, which kept catching on her damp feet.

Elfriede stood. 'Where's Charlie?' She took Imo's hand and linked her spare arm through Bea's.

'Oh, she's always disappearing,' grumbled Gert.

'Is she likely to be far?' Elfriede looked over her shoulders.

'We should find her. Nanny will be furious if she's missing again.' Nobody said anything. 'Nanny will be livid,'

Gert repeated, a little bit louder this time. There was still no response. 'Shall Madeleine and I find her, then?' asked Gert eventually.

'Oh, yes, do that please, darlings, will you? I do not want anybody offside, especially Nanny.'

Elfriede guided Bea back across the grass. She was holding Imo's hand. The gravel crunched as the trio of cousins stepped onto the path: two tall, one short. Madeleine watched as they walked down past the kitchen garden towards the front of the house, chattering and laughing, hat rims bumping. Not one of them looked back.

# The grotto

ert led Madeleine around the back of the house to check the garage, but there was no sign of Charlie, so they continued on around the other side of the house, across the drive and down past the side of the tennis court. Madeleine had to keep stopping to pull at her bodice, which was a bit like a rash – at best, uncomfortable; at worst, so maddening that she could think of nothing else.

'Are you okay?'

'It's just really itchy,' said Madeleine. 'I've had chicken pox that were comfier.'

'I can't believe we haven't done that yet. I promise that we shall sneak into Hen's room the next time she's out.'

Madeleine smiled. 'That would be super.'

The girls walked towards the broad, bow-shaped lake they had run past on Madeleine's first day and turned right onto the path that encircled it.

'It's ornamental,' said Gert. 'I'm not mad on the lake in winter – it can be so blowy on windy days.'

A breeze ripped across the lake as she spoke. Madeleine could see the wind in the surface of the water, which was thick and muddy like hot chocolate. The girls wandered past a little bone-coloured jetty, which had a tiny rowboat moored to it.

'Do you row?' asked Madeleine.

'Rarely. It's mainly for guests. Mummy's very nervous about the water.'

The lake had a tiny almost-island, which was connected to the shore by a ribbon of land hanging down its middle like that funny finger of flesh at the back of Madeleine's mouth.

'Can we go out on the island?'

'Sometimes. The land bridge tends to disappear in the spring rain, but it's been such a dry winter that it's secure at the moment. You haven't even seen the best bit yet – come and see the grotto; that's just down over there, another place Charlie likes to hide.'

Gert led Madeleine along the top of the lake and then down a path that headed past the empty tree and the small orchard they'd seen earlier.

The girls then veered off onto another, narrower path, this one hedged with thick, leafy plants no taller than their ankles and lines of brown stones identical to those in the fence. At its end, the path spiralled like a snailshell and opened into a cave.

'This,' said Gert, 'is the grotto.'

The grotto was like half an igloo, its walls made out of more of the heaped brown stone. It had a natural rock ceiling, which hung down low over a stone table and stools.

Most startlingly, every surface – walls, roof, floor, stools and table – was lined with a patchwork of photos, cards, shells and all manner of keepsakes, set in rows. Charlie stood on one of the stools, pasting a piece of paper onto the back wall. Millie was curled in a ball on the floor beneath her.

'Charlie! There you are,' said Gert.

'I wanted to include this.' Gert and Madeleine moved closer. The paper Charlie was pasting up was a photo of Elfriede, with a tiny signature of the photographer in its corner. Elfriede stared out at them, serene.

'Where did you get it?' asked Gert.

'Elfriede gave it to Mummy. I think it was intended for a frame, but I'm sure Mummy won't mind. I can always peel it off.'

Gert shook her head. 'Well, don't blame me if Mummy's cross.' The picture was already starting to pucker with the wet glue.

Madeleine thought of the endless pictures the kids in her class simply printed up at home. She looked about. The grotto seemed like a sort of three-dimensional scrapbook, where the girls stuck all the things that interested them or that they cared about.

Newspaper articles featured heavily:

*Plague! Over 60,000 rats killed in Sydney.*

*Hissing and stamping suffragists disrupt parliament!*

There were a few photos of the children, two in frames and two pasted up. Next to Elfriede was a newspaper article with a cartoon drawing of a woman. She was as muscly as a greyhound, with glasses, a hooked nose and a wonky, frizzy bun. She wore a tight dress and stockings that were baggy around her knees.

'Is that Aunt Hen?' asked Madeleine. 'What's she doing?'

'Campaigning. Mummy says it's a dreadful shame she's gone *that way*; that her father would be *horrified* to see her flopping about in tea dresses all day, and that all Aunt Hen's suffragist arguments are irrelevant anyway, as wives have been influencing their husbands and sons for years. Mummy says she feels like a queen, as all the servants – even Nanny – come under her. But I stuck Aunt Hen up anyway. She is family.' The paper was yellow from the gum Gert had used.

'Cook calls Aunt Hen the Mad Maiden Hen,' Charlie interjected. 'Says she's a right ma's mope. And Mummy's angry that Aunt Hen doesn't have a calling card. But Aunt Hen says that if people want to see her, they will. *I* say that her fingernails are often blacker than mine. I do like that.'

Charlie pulled at an unravelling thread on the hem of her sleeve.

'What do you think, Gert?' asked Madeleine.

'I think that Cook hates change almost as much as Nanny, which is very odd for the Irish. They're meant to be revolutionaries. Still, she makes good scones. I don't know, maybe Aunt Hen is a bit mad? And it is embarrassing for Daddy. There he is, trying to build a respectable new nation, helping to write all the documents, and she's waving banners on the steps of parliament trying to stop him.'

'She's not trying to stop him, though, is she?' said Madeleine. 'She's just making sure women are included. What seems mad to me is that women now *don't* have the vote. I mean, it's not like we're goldfish – we're future prime ministers, judges and governors-general.'

'Madeleine, you are terribly funny.' Charlie dipped her brush in the paste again.

Madeleine continued circling the small cave. There were dolls' shoes and a dried corsage (from Bea's season, Gert said), invitations and a few clippings of cartoons of the girls' father looking puffed up in his waistcoat and frowning at official functions.

'At night,' said Gert, 'you can wave a candle and all the little bits of mirror reflect the light, winking and twinkling. It's terribly exotic. Not our idea – Daddy read about it being done in India, where maharajas do it for their wives.'

Madeleine hadn't noticed the mirrors – but when she looked closer, she realised that there were fragments everywhere. 'It's incredible,' she said. 'All of it – I've never seen anything like it. Did you build it?'

'No, it was here before. We think it was built for prayer' – Charlie pointed to a niche on the far wall – 'but Daddy was happy for us to use it.'

Gert led Madeleine to the niche. It was filled with lines and lines of teeth.

'This is the very best bit!' Gert gloated. 'There are fifteen of them: all milk teeth, mainly, but one of Bea's grown-up molars is here, too. You can see the root.'

'Whose idea was *that*?'

'Mine!' Gert looked proud.

Charlie pulled out her notebook. 'Oh, I must have dropped my pencil back at the pond. Do you have one, Gert?'

'No – and go and fetch it. Daddy will be livid if you lose another.'

Charlie put her brush back in the paste bottle, which said *fish glue* on it. 'See you back at the house, then!' She ran off, the laces of her muddy boots flapping about her skinny, straight calves.

Madeleine rubbed her fingertip over the pointy end of an eyetooth. 'It's amazing,' she said again softly. 'I've been here, you know – in my time.'

'Have you really? With whom? It still exists in the future?' Gert asked excitedly. 'I'm thrilled. We've put so much work into it!'

Madeleine didn't have the heart to tell her it would be all littered with muddy Coke bottles by *Maddison 4 Kai*.

Suddenly an idea struck Madeleine the way brilliant ideas sometimes did – just shot from clear out of nowhere.

'*Gert*, I was at the grotto when I came back here. Maybe this is the link? Maybe, just maybe, we could bring Bea's shoes here, and maybe, just maybe, this will be like the TARDIS and take me home? The teeth might be the key to getting back!'

'Splendid idea!' Gert shook her head in agreement. 'Well, there can certainly be no harm in trying.'

'Let's get the shoes and do it right now!' Madeleine was filled with a wild and sudden hope.

The girls ran back past the lake and up the hill to the house, where Bea and Elfriede were sitting in cane chairs on the verandah. Their laughter was cut off by Nanny, who launched around the side of the house waving a gong stick, Imo at her side.

'Children, nursery tea will be served at five o'clock on the dot.' Madeleine's heart sank. So much for heading straight back to the grotto with the shoes. 'Miss Beatrice, you may dine later with the adults, of course. Miss Charlotte, *where* is your left boot?'

The girls spun around. Charlie was hobbling behind them, now in only one very grey stocking.

'How on earth did you end up behind us?' Madeleine exclaimed.

'Good evening, Miss von Fürstenburg.' Nanny nodded warmly at Elfriede and herded everybody inside.

Elfriede winked over her shoulder at Charlie. 'You shall have to tell me what you've done with that boot later.'

Elfriede was great, thought Madeleine. Really great.

Gert's demeanour had changed suddenly. She moped all the way up the stairs.

'What's the matter?' whispered Madeleine, alarmed, wondering if she'd figured out something wrong with their plan for the grotto.

'Nothing,' said Gert dully.

They climbed another three steps.

'It's just typical, really,' Gert blurted. 'It's always like this.'

'Like what?' Gert was being very cryptic, thought Madeleine.

'Haven't you noticed how Elfriede's favour is orbiting? First Imo was the favourite, which is always the case; then Bea, and now Charlie. Never me. No matter how hard I try, I am never the favourite.'

Madeleine *had* noticed. It was hard not to. There was something about Gert that you couldn't quite put your finger on, but that everyone sensed – something annoying. It was as if she were smelly or scratchy, when in fact she was neither.

'It's the same at school. The harder I try, the fewer friends I have. I never get invited to play tennis or lacrosse or to go to recitals. I don't understand it.'

'Well, you're my favourite,' said Madeleine.

Gert smiled at her – a deep, trusting smile. She linked her arm through Madeleine's and squeezed it. 'That's the most generous thing anyone has ever said to me.'

Madeleine squeezed back. Gert could be irritating, but she was also kind, very kind. For now, that seemed more important than anything.

# *Back to the grotto*

N anny poured water into an enamel tub in front of the shifting coals in the nursery fireplace that night, and Madeleine was treated to her first proper bath.

'Can't we have a bath in the bathroom?' whinged Gert. 'This is for babies.'

'Your mother would rather we left the bathroom for Elfriede,' said Nanny.

Madeleine had hated baths and showers as a kid, but she'd grown to quite like them lately, and while having her back scratched down by Nanny's rough cloth was a little less relaxing than anything she was accustomed to, she'd missed the warmth.

In bed in the dark afterwards, Madeleine could think of nothing but her own family. She thought of Teddy with his knees draped over the end of the couch, eating cheese on toast and playing chess on his laptop and scrabble on his phone with seventy-nine-year-old billionaires from Russia. She thought of her mum's goodnight kisses, with breath that smelled like the gum she chewed to stay awake while she studied, and her dad with his shaven, nuggety cyclist legs. She thought of Mum Crum and her house that smelt of swampy soup and plaster dust.

It didn't matter that everybody here was good and kind and that she was having fun. This homesickness was a real thing, an actual ache. Madeleine was surprised by its muscle. She turned into her pillow and started to cry.

'Madeleine,' whispered Gert. 'Are you all right?' She padded over and sat on the floor by Madeleine's bed. 'Please, Madeleine. Please don't cry. We shall get you home.'

'But *how?*' Madeleine asked. 'We couldn't even manage to get back to the grotto today, and I'm sure it won't work even if we do. I hate feeling so useless. I can never change anything. Not back home. Not here. I'm like a gumnut on the ocean, and I'm sick of it.'

'Don't you like it here?'

Madeleine sat up and looked at Gert. 'I had such a fun day. Elfriede is so sophisticated, and I've never had sisters – and the bath tonight was special here in the nursery, but it's only made me sadder. If I knew I were only here for a short stay it would be wonderful – but it's the not knowing how long I'm here for that makes it hard.'

Gert got up and sat on the edge of Madeleine's bed. She rubbed her shoulder. 'The grotto, then.' She thumped Madeleine on the back. 'Shall we try it now?'

'What?' Madeleine wiped her nose along the sleeve of her nightgown.

'We shall go tonight. It's a clear night, and it's not wet.'

'But we need Bea's dress slippers.'

'Wait here.'

Before Madeleine could stop her, Gert walked into Charlie and Imo's room. She returned moments later, the old sparkly shoes visible under her arm in the pink glow of the fire.

Madeleine smiled. Just seeing the shoes made her feel closer to home. It gave her something to hold onto.

Gert handed them to her. 'Mummy and Daddy have not yet retired for the evening, but we shall go later. I'll stay awake.'

Madeleine lay back on her pillow. 'Gert?'

'Mmmm?'

'Thank you.'

<hr>

Later that night, when nothing stirred, the girls sneaked down the skinny wooden servants' staircase in their nighties, boots in hand. The stairs were uncarpeted and as creaky as old-man knees; they were so small compared to the rest of the house that they looked like they were made for five-year-old kids or hobbits.

Gert held an unlit candle with a folded wick. The gas lamps were on downstairs, and the whole house had a sort of garlicky smell.

Madeleine put her hand over her mouth and nose. 'It stinks!'

'That's the gas,' whispered Gert as the girls crept down the butler's pantry and through the back door.

Outside, the girls pulled on their boots and stood still. The night sky was pinned with thousands of stars, but beyond the house the garden looked as black as pitch. The night was so cold and so silent that it had a smell and a density all its own.

Madeleine followed Gert along the gravel path down towards the lake and the grotto beyond. They stuck to the sides, picking their way silently through the bracken. The leaves of the flowers were black and shiny in the reflected candlelight. A pair of possums started fighting in a tree above the girls, hissing and belching. Gert hissed back, and they yelped and scuttled off.

Madeleine shivered in her nightie and wished she'd brought a shawl. *You know you've been in the olden days too long when you're wishing for a shawl rather than a parka,* she thought.

They reached the grotto more quickly than Madeleine had expected. It wasn't warm, but it felt warmer than outside because it smelt of earth and stone. Gert pulled a small silver box containing matches from her sleeve and lit her candle again. In the flickering light, the girls' breath was smoke. Gert waved the light around the little stone room and the mirror chips stuck to the wall winked back. It was beautiful but terrifying, thought Madeleine, staring right into a doll's eye gummed to the wall.

Madeleine held Bea's shoes out in front of her, one resting on each upturned palm, the silver sparkles dancing in the dim light.

'It must have been beautiful to watch these on Bea's feet,' she said to Gert.

Gert held her candle closer to the shoes. 'When she was presented she looked like a princess. We all sat downstairs, and she came floating down, with the longest train and three feathers on her head, and I . . . well, I thought of my own debut, and how I will never look like that no matter how beautiful my dress or slippers.'

'Yes, you will,' said Madeleine. 'It's amazing what they can do with make-up and lighting.'

'No, I won't,' said Gert, 'and sometimes that's really difficult.'

'But who cares, really? It's only part of the package. You've got a million other strengths,' said Madeleine. 'You're kind and brave, and I don't know any other kid who would spit back at possums in the middle of the night.'

'You sound like Aunt Hen. *Beauty is no thicker than my fingernail, and a lot less important. It's not Vida's beauty that makes her wonderful, Gertie; it's her nimble mind and her vim.*'

'Well, she's right,' said Madeleine.

'But I once overheard a lady at a school concert whisper to Miss Fawkner, *What a plain-looking thing that Williamson girl is. Common. Common. Common.* At school!'

The girls sat silently for a moment. Madeleine had to admit to herself that Gert, with her round, glistening face, did resemble Cook over a jam pan more than she would ever resemble any one of her sisters, and Madeleine could see that it was a grudge she bore like eczema. You just looked at

Gert and you knew that she'd be the type of girl who used too much glue and drew texta marks on top of each other so the colours all went a bit brown.

Madeleine kicked out at the stone bench. What could she say to Gert? That in Madeleine's time, a girl's passport on social media was a photogenic smile, and female sports stars couldn't even hope to earn an income from their sport unless they looked good in bathers on a calendar? That, on balance, things were worse in Gert's time, but that the people here were also more honest in the way they treated girls – more honest about what they believed mattered.

Gert sighed and said, 'Never mind. What if you put both Bea's slippers in one hand and place your other hand on the teeth?'

Madeleine was so grateful to be given some instructions – told what to do to try to make this situation better – that she felt weepy again. She made her way over to the row of teeth and did as Gert said. The girls stood side by side and waited patiently for something to happen.

Madeleine left her arm out even when it started to shake. She watched it trembling.

'Try singing,' said Gert. 'Perhaps we can sing you back?'

Madeleine tried to think of a song from her time, somewhat unsuccessfully.

'*Cally's Carpet Clean, squeaky clean, green clean,*' she sang.

Gert looked at her suspiciously. 'Is that really a song?'

'It's an advertisement,' whispered Madeleine. 'I couldn't think of anything else.'

'Green clean? What sort of clean is that? Try for another,' said Gert. 'Or think of home.'

Madeleine looked at the candle's flame until her vision went wobbly, and then she shut her eyes and dreamt of her mum's house and her dad's flat, and then of Mum Crum's house, just in case she needed to go back to the same spot she'd left from.

Gert eventually dropped down into a sitting position, her back against the wall. After a while, Madeleine did the same. 'My arm's too sore – I can't do it anymore.'

Gert gave her a look. The night shivered.

'Did you hear that? Shh!' Gert's eyes had widened. She and Madeleine both stayed stock still. There was the dull crunch of footsteps outside – heavy footsteps.

'Is it a zombie?' Madeleine held her breath.

Gert blew out the candle and the flame hissed. Madeleine could smell wax. There was the swish of plants, the creak of breaking branches and a muffled giggle.

The grotto was black. Gert took Madeleine's hand and squeezed it. A shadow loomed in the entrance.

'Holy frigging moly,' said Madeleine under her breath.

There was a pause that felt as long as the gap between thunder and lightning – as bristling and charged. Then Mr Williamson leant into the cave brandishing a candle. In the dim light he was all fairytale height and angles. His shadow was severe.

He held the candle towards the girls and his face flattened. 'Gertrude?' he said, surprised.

'Oh, Daddy, oh thank goodness it's you. I thought it was some sort of lake monster.'

'What on earth are you doing out of your bed at this hour? It is completely inappropriate to have you children wandering about the property at night. I shall speak to Nanny in the morning.'

A twig snapped.

'I'm sorry, Daddy. Please don't speak to Nanny. Please don't,' said Gert.

'Here, I will escort you back now. Straight to bed. I shan't tell your mother about this – her nerves are far too fragile at the moment – but if I ever catch you out of your bed at this hour again, Nanny will have something to say, of that I am quite sure.'

Gert grabbed Bea's shoes back from Madeleine.

'I trust you've not been indulging in your mother's nonsense, Gertrude,' said Mr Williamson, 'because I am cross enough already.'

'No, Daddy,' whispered Gert.

Madeleine felt dreadful. There was something so much worse about being told off by someone else's parent, and their failure in the grotto was monumental. The girls put their heads down and ran back along the path and through the watching garden to bed, cold and glum.

# The shrill hoyden

The next morning the lawn was lined with grey mist. The cold kept the adults in their beds for breakfast, so the girls were back in the gloomy room off the kitchen with Nanny.

Gert, Charlie, Imo and Madeleine sat swinging their boots under the table, eating with backs straight and napkins resting on their laps. Breakfast this morning was yet another bowl of congealed porridge, so thick it could almost be sculpted into balls.

Even if she could have sculpted her meal into balls without Nanny noticing and caning her or boxing her about the ears or whatever nannies did, though, Madeleine couldn't slip anything into her pocket like she did with her dinner at home when she didn't like it, because her clothes here didn't *have* pockets.

The bodice was also impossible. It had branded Madeleine, leaving red marks in the shape of Nike ticks under both arms. The tights still prickled, too, but at least when she was seated they didn't fall down.

To try to take her mind off all the discomfort, Madeleine

focused on Imo, who was sitting on a cushion on the chair opposite her. While she was no longer a baby, Imo was clearly the Williamsons' baby. She was like a calf, thought Madeleine, constantly at the cud. Every time Madeleine spotted Imo, she was eating or hovering about food. *As long as nothing gets between Imo and her food supply, she's happy*, Gert had said, and Madeleine imagined nothing ever would, because Imo was exactly the sort of child people wanted to pet.

Gert was not. Seeing the girls together at the table reminded Madeleine of her dad's buttons in the button jar. When Madeleine and Nandi divided the buttons up, they always fought over the gold button, the shiny red button with the embossed anchor, and the diamanté button, but nobody wanted to claim the plain white shirt buttons, which were always left blinking at the bottom of the jar. It may have been unkind, but if Gert were a button, she would definitely have come off a shirt. She was from a different button family entirely.

While they were eating, a ruckus started up in the hallway.

'Henrietta, what on earth are you doing? Here I am doing my darnedest to create a commonwealth while you're setting about bringing it down.' It was Mr Williamson's deep voice, macadamia-hard.

'Daddy,' Gert whispered.

Nanny got up and clicked the door shut. 'All siblings disagree sometimes, Miss Gertrude – you of all people ought to know that. And both your father and your aunt are entitled to a little privacy.'

Nanny shouldn't have bothered. Aunt Hen was no whisper-fighter. 'How dare you, Tom. I am not trying to bring down your commonwealth – I am trying to improve it. Just because you disagree with my views makes them neither irrelevant nor irrational.' Aunt Hen sounded strong.

'Well, perhaps you would find me more welcoming of your opinion and the opinions of your sex in general if you stopped embarrassing me. Strolling around any which way without a corset in front of my guests. Do you have any idea how powerful those gentlemen are? They are determining the very form this country will take, the powers and function of our own High Court in a manner that is palatable to London, and while they are doing so, nobody wants to see your wobbles. It's not impossible to hold those ghastly political views of yours and still look like a lady, Henrietta. Why can't you simply enjoy freedom at five p.m. with a loose gown and a cup of tea like every other self-respecting genteel woman in this colony, heaven forbid? Is this what those blue-stockings taught you at Oxford?'

Imo started to cry. Nanny looked at the older children, seeming unsettled. 'I'll take Miss Imogen upstairs to play in the nursery. You girls may stay here and finish your breakfast, but please be quiet.'

'What's Aunt Hen talking about?' whispered Madeleine as soon as Nanny had left the room. 'What happens at five p.m.?'

Charlie looked left, right, then left again. 'I'm going with Nanny too.'

More likely, thought Madeleine, she was going to sneak off – but Gert pretended not to notice as she slipped out.

'Women wear tea gowns without corsets – or in Aunt Hen's case, without a liberty bodice – to receive their friends,' Gert said. 'They're pretty – creamy and light. Aunt Hen gets around in a version of them most of the time.'

'Lucky Aunt Hen.' Madeleine shuffled in her seat.

Gert stood up quietly and re-opened the door.

Although they couldn't see Mr Williamson, they could see Aunt Hen, her face red and spitty. 'Freedom? You'd like to talk about freedom? A corset is a material indicator of the indignity women suffer. Have *you* tried to sit through a dinner strapped into one? Besides, there are swathes of medical evidence to suggest they are not hygienic. Freedom isn't only the right to breathe, however, Thomas. Freedom starts when a woman can not only obtain a degree, but may be admitted to the profession she's qualified to represent. You read law and you get to use your degree, every single day, but what happened to mine? Unlike you, I obtained firsts, and yet because I am a woman I was never actually awarded it. I then applied to sixty-seven jobs as a mere governess and didn't get one single situation.'

'If you wore a corset you might have had more chance. Who would want a lady like you around their children? And I use the term *lady* extremely loosely, but it does denote your sex, at least, factually. It would help if you kept civilised company. There are lots of lovely ladies around, ladies who don't have their noses in *The Dawn* or that frightful *Hens' Convention*.'

'Shut up, shut up, shut up. You pig. And how dare you criticise journals you haven't opened. I don't want to spend my days sitting around drinking brewed tea with a group of bored and, as a consequence, boring women. I am not going to allow my time to be pointless, and I have nothing but respect for Louisa Lawson's work with *The Dawn* – her commitment, her business nous, her intelligence and energy. She is doing her best to ensure that those girls in there – that *bright* little girl – will have every opportunity for which I have wanted.'

'Those girls have every opportunity – which *I* have provided for them: Gertrude's schooling; their toys; their clothing; this home and all the help we require to support it.'

Aunt Hen's voice was low and rigid. 'When I talk about suffrage, I am talking about extending the vote to *the help* – to the Annas and Cooks, and to the Percys too, Thomas – because if we are all governed by the same law, we should all have a say in determining it. *One people, one destiny*. You said it, dear brother.

'Well, *your* suggestions are preposterous. Any old juggins determining the laws? Those who *do* have the vote don't even turn out to the poll! You of all people know how conceptually difficult the law can be. And natives with the vote? You make me laugh. We have an obligation to protect *them* – and there are plenty of suffragists who support my view on this. Name one native in any of your suffrage societies. You can't! Besides, Percy would be on the streets if the church hadn't found him a position here. And he's so headstrong and erratic, nicking off for months at a time and refusing to go to certain places.'

Madeleine put down her fork. She had known her country's past was racist, but it was still a thump to her heart to hear it from the very mouth of someone tasked with forming the new country; someone with smart manners and a smart suit, a big house and big, busy words. She felt sick.

She heard the screech of chair legs on the polished floor. 'Percy goes back to his family – what little he has of it. Is it erratic for Elfriede to take a year-long sojourn to see her own family and the world? Aboriginal men *and* women can vote in South Australia, and do. They want change and, like me, they are trying to work within *your* system to effect it.'

'They can't really vote, Henrietta. They just can't *not* vote. It was sloppy drafting, giving every adult the vote. The quicker the laws are made consistent between the colonies, the easier things will be.'

'It was fine drafting, and quite intentional, Thomas. How I would love to follow in Mary Lee's footsteps.'

'Don't you even *think* of running for parliament. I will not countenance any further humiliation of this household. Of *my* household. Surely it is not too late for you to move on to bonnets and bairns?'

'Women have been campaigning and expressing an interest for too long for this to be considered a novelty. And anyway, why shouldn't we have women in parliament when we have a woman as our sovereign?'

'Queen Victoria does not believe in suffrage, Henrietta. And dammit, while you are under my roof, you *will* behave. I will not have those impressionable young ladies turned into shrill hoydens like their aunt.'

'You know exactly why I am under your roof, Thomas. My options are limited, but unlike my show-pony brother, I have discovered other ways to assist with the new commonwealth and make a difference – smaller, quieter ways. Just watch me.' And Aunt Hen picked up her case and walked out – taller, straighter, brighter and bolder, even without her corset.

Mr Williamson stomped into his study and slammed the door. He then swore and slapped what sounded like something heavy onto a desk or a table.

'Politics, politics, politics. It's all those two ever argue about,' said Gert. 'How on earth can they be related when their views are so different?'

'Maybe it's like religion,' said Madeleine. 'Mum Crum always says the gap between different religions, or even between being a believer or a non-believer, isn't nearly as big as people think. If people saw *that*, they wouldn't have to fight each other all the time. Maybe politics is just the same – at least your father and Aunt Hen have views and they are thinking about ideas.' *Even if your dad's would and should land him in jail in my time*, she thought.

'Your Mum Crum sounds very clever.'

'She is,' said Madeleine. 'And I miss her. Non-stop. Gert, do you think I'll *ever* get home? What on earth am I doing here? I've been wracking my brains.'

'I don't know why you're here or how you're here,' said Gert, 'but I'm very much enjoying your company. Holidays around here can be extremely dull.'

Madeleine sighed and smiled both at once. 'Well, if you can't get me back home, could we at least try for a looser bodice? All that talk of them has me squirming. When it comes to corsetry – and most other things, actually – I am Team Hen.' Madeleine pulled at her top. 'If I don't get this thing off soon, all my insides are going to squirt out like toothpaste.'

Gert giggled. 'We should do it now that Aunt Hen's stormed off. Nanny is with Imo, and all the grown-ups are sulking. Let's go!'

# Aunt Hen's (neat) nest

A unt Hen's room was tucked into the back of the second floor, in the wing beneath the servants' quarters.

It was a bare room – much barer than Madeleine had imagined, and wishbone dry. There was no carpet, only a small blue rug on the floor. A single bed, pulled tight and white, sat under a small window, and there was a wooden dresser in the corner with a mug, basin, little white porcelain pot and pair of spectacles on top of it.

The room seemed sparse and sad. The wind rattled the window in its sash.

'There's not much of Aunt Hen here,' Madeleine said. 'I'd imagined it messier, somehow. Louder. More bookish, I guess – more eccentric. What's that?' She pointed to a white pot with a hole in the top sitting on the dresser.

'A hair collector. To collect hair from brushes and re-use for pillows and such. Don't you have them?'

'No,' said Madeleine 'We just throw hair in the bin.'

'How wasteful,' said Gert.

Madeleine peeked under the bed. It was swept bald. 'It's not very . . . girly, is it?'

'Like Mummy's room, you mean? All pink cabbage roses? Not Aunt Hen. She gives whatever she has away.'

'But there's not even a cushion on the bed, or a place to write.'

'That's the way she seems to like it.'

Madeleine leant against the edge of the bed, uncomfortable as ever.

'Let's find you a bodice.' Gert pulled at one of the dresser drawers. It stuck, so she pulled again, and the drawer squealed. Inside, lying on top of a pile of neatly folded cotton, was a double picture frame hinged together in the middle. In the first frame was a photo of four children. Opposite was a photo of a little girl with a bob, who looked about six.

'Who's that?' Madeleine asked, just as it occurred to her who it was. Although the lips were pulled around gappy teeth, the face had an unmistakable hint of Christmas ham about it.

'It's me!' Gert puffed up a little, inflated to be singled out in anything other than a negative way. 'That's my old dolly, Molly McGolly. We had those pictures taken for Christmas. That's the perambulator Imo uses for Bob-Bear now.'

It was funny seeing Gert the old-fashioned girl as an even more old-fashioned little girl.

In the other photo, Bea looked exactly as one would expect – neat and pretty. Charlie was tiny but stern under an enormous bow, and Gert looked all lopsided, friendly but messy. In a pram was a baby in a white frilly dress, as bloated as a tick.

'Little Reggie,' sighed Gert. 'Look at those golden curls. I've never seen hair quite that yellow.'

'Reggie? Is that a boy?'

'He was one of the babies.' Gert put the photo back and shut the drawer and the conversation. She opened another drawer and lifted a fleecy bodice from a neatly folded pile of them. It had yellowed slightly but it smelt soapy.

'This is not very hygienic, is it?' said Madeleine.

Gert smiled. 'We'll give it a squirt with vinegar. It will be fine.'

'I'll smell like a jar of gherkins!'

'There are another three here. She probably doesn't even wear them all. Well, not around Daddy anyway.'

Gert laughed and then stopped short. The girls heard the *clack clack* of shoes coming up the stairs. Gert tucked the bodice into her pinafore and the girls fled the room, slamming the door behind them. They tore back along the hallway, eyes focused on the thin carpet runner, and banged straight into Aunt Hen heading towards her bedroom.

'Oops!' Aunt Hen put her arms out to steady Gert, and then she looked at both girls and smiled.

'Back already?' asked Madeleine.

'There is nothing like a walk to calm one down when one can do nothing to calm the views of others.' Aunt Hen winked as she pulled off her gloves.

'My mum feels the same way about running – she says it's better than any antidepressant.'

Aunt Hen squinted at her. 'You New South Welsh are quite a different breed altogether, aren't you? Are you having fun during your stay with us?'

'Oh, we are, thank you, Hen Pen,' Gert answered for Madeleine.

'Are you all right, dear?' Aunt Hen put the back of one hand to Gert's brow. Her nails were square and low, and the pads on her fingers were dirty, almost black. 'You look peaky.'

Gert stepped back. 'Fine, fine, thank you, but Nanny's expecting us in the nursery, so we'd best be off.' She turned and ran. Madeleine shrugged and followed.

'Gertie, you know how Nanny feels about running inside. Try not to get into any more trouble – I'm not sure I can bear it.'

'Stop worrying, Aunt Hen!'

'Not worrying, just Hen-pecking.'

The girls giggled as they ran up the stairs towards the nursery. At the top of the staircase, Gert stopped and looked at Madeleine, her face suddenly serious. 'You'd better be careful of your words, even around Aunt Hen, Madeleine.' Then she smiled again. 'That whole episode was too close for comfort.'

'No,' said Madeleine, taking the soft bodice from Gert's pinafore pocket and pulling at her own pinafore's ties. '*This* is too close for comfort! That was worth it. Well, this bit was.' Madeleine waved the bodice like a surrender flag. 'Quick, let's find somewhere I can get changed.'

Madeleine spent a much comfier afternoon playing 'dogs' with Imo in the playhouse while Gert and Charlie watched on and laughed. Even the rope around Madeleine's neck that Imo used for her collar and the constant need to bark and bounce on all fours was nothing compared to the pain of Bea's bodice.

As dusk hit, Nanny called the girls inside to prepare for nursery tea and bed. Mr Williamson must have heard them tumble in through the front door, because he came out of the study, sweeping Imo up and over his shoulder.

'Put me down, put me down, put me down, Daddeeeeee,' shrilled Imo. 'I'll tell Elfriede on you.' She kicked out, only just missing the stuffed lyrebird in the bell jar on the hall table.

'Daddy!' Charlie ran up to Mr Williamson and punched him on the arm.

'Ahh!' He pretended to double over. 'You're getting quite a strong hook, Charlie.'

'That's Master Charles Williamson to you,' teased Charlie, holding up her muscles like Popeye.

'If the federation should ever fail, at least we shall have you to protect us,' said Mr Williamson, smiling.

'Upstairs, girls.' Nanny bossed her way into the circle, throwing an apologetic look Mr Williamson's way. 'And what on earth have you done with Elfriede, Miss Imogen?' she asked. 'I haven't seen her all day.'

Mr Williamson tickled Imo's tummy. She squealed.

'Elfriede wasn't with us,' said Charlie. 'She decided to sit with Mummy, and that was hours ago.'

Colour had climbed up Mr Williamson's neck. He put Imo down and pulled on his watch chain, studying his fob watch and tucking it into his bottom pocket.

'Well then, I must be getting back to it.' He patted Imo loosely on the head.

'Can't we play, Daddy? Please?'

'Hmm? Not now, darling. It's far too late. Perhaps tomorrow.' He looked around, searching, as if he had left something – his shoes at the front door, perhaps, although he was hardly the sort of man to do that – then dipped his head and retreated to his study. A flatness settled over the party, as dull and airless as Boxing Day.

'He forgot to say goodnight,' whined Imo.

'Well, he's under considerable strain,' said Nanny. 'Upstairs, you lot.'

Later that night, however, Mr Williamson returned, bursting unexpectedly into the nursery and ruffling Charlie's hair. Nanny had been reading the girls a story called *Struwwelpeter*, the girls arranged about her feet on the rug, the light of the fire flickering around the room and the wallpaper making it feel extra snug, like the room was tucked up in a quilt.

'I knew you'd come back! You forgot to say goodnight!' Imo smiled.

Mr Williamson kissed her on the head and then raised his arms like a preacher in a pulpit. 'Excuse me, Nanny, children . . . I thought, if it's agreeable to Elfriede, we might have a picnic tomorrow. The weather should be fine again, and besides, it is my great pleasure to announce that we have something to celebrate.' He paused, and his dimples twinkled. 'I have just had word that Her Majesty shall sign the assent to federation. The bill has passed both houses; it's going ahead!'

'Bravo!' Gert sat right up on her knees and clapped. Charlie and Imo looked at her and joined in. Madeleine smiled. How amazing to be here in this very moment.

Even Nanny was moved to smile. 'That's jolly good news, Mr Williamson. Congratulations.'

'I thought we would take the motor and a carriage,' said Mr Williamson.

'May I drive with you, Daddy, may I?'

Mr Williamson looked at Gert. 'Yes, Gertrude, you may. The guests shall travel with me in the motor, and as Madeleine is your guest, you may accompany us. The others will follow in the carriage.'

'Yippeeeeee!' Gert sat straight up on her knees until she looked a little taller.

It was funny, thought Madeleine, how little people required to feel better about themselves. Gert needed to be singled out. She needed to feel special. Madeleine was pleased Mr Williamson had done that.

# *The sport of gentlemen*

The next morning, the sky was deep blue and everything had the feeling of crisp napkins.

The car – which was the black and shiny apparatus Madeleine had earlier taken for a carriage in the garage – didn't, to her credit, really look anything like a car at all; it was high like a carriage, only without the pincer bit for connecting a horse.

It had a metal frame, big red wheels with red spokes (a bit like a BMX), and two black seats facing each other. Mr Williamson and Elfriede's forward-facing seat was covered in dimpled leather, like a doctor's couch, while Madeleine, Gert and Imo's seat opposite was harder and more basic. If this were a modern car, thought Madeleine, the three girls would be pressed backwards against the windscreen like a toy on the dashboard – it felt very strange.

In front of Mr Williamson's seat was a funny steering column that looked like a nutcracker, and to his side was a horn so comically big it was like something a clown might squeeze.

'Are you sure you're all right?' Mr Williamson asked Elfriede.

'Ooh, yes!' said Elfriede. 'This is tremendous fun. Is it French?'

'It is,' said Mr Williamson. '*De Dion-Bouton voiturette.*' He'd said the last part in French that was so bad even Madeleine could tell.

'*Mon Dieu* – like my costume!' Elfriede winked at the girls across the picnic basket. She was wearing a long tan coat over her dress, with a wide-brimmed straw hat on her head. She looked like a movie star.

Mrs Williamson had headed off earlier in the carriage with Nanny, Anna, Bea and Charlie, to help set up.

The ride was bumpy and chaotic. Madeleine felt every single pothole through her bottom. They whipped along the rutted country road lined with tall thin gums that pressed in on them. Dust flew up into Madeleine's eyes and mouth.

'I can spy the river,' called Gert after half an hour. There ahead of them was a small clearing. Madeleine could see the water all treacly through the scrub. It was a clear tea colour, the knotted roots of the trees that lined it visible beneath the surface. The banks were lined with gritty sand and bleached stones.

Anna had set up a table under some thick gum trees, their trunks as saggy as elephant hide. She had covered the table with a large white cloth, which flapped in the breeze. Some pretty white flowers with yellow centres had been placed in a little glass bowl in the centre.

'Are the flowers really necessary, Anna?' Madeleine heard Nanny ask as they approached the site. 'Imogen will only spill them and spoil luncheon.'

'Actually I picked those, Nanny. I do like fresh flowers at the table. Even outside,' retorted Mrs Williamson. She sat in a chair in the sun facing the river, wearing a flat floral hat, trying to sew and hold a parasol at the same time.

Nanny squashed a little blood spider that was crawling onto the white cloth. 'Very jolly the flowers are, too, Mrs Williamson. I shall of course supervise Miss Imogen at the table.' She nodded at Anna, who was squatted by a picnic basket in the shade, rearranging a plate of cold joints. 'I am relieved to see Anna has at least had the good sense to keep the picnic in the shade *this time*.'

Nanny flicked some imaginary dirt off the front of her grey tunic and stalked down towards the river. Anna rewrapped a brown leg of lamb and bit her lip.

Charlie was down at the shore poking about in the shallows with a net, her boots off. She was trying to hold her skirts and the net, and they kept getting tangled. Her hem was wet and silty. Millie was next to her, fur stuck to her legs, making her little doggy legs look skinny and bent.

Seeing Charlie like that, fully dressed in the water, was like seeing kids in sunproof skivvies splashing at Bondi Beach, thought Madeleine. It might not have been sun smart, but as a kid there had been nothing better than swimming in just undies. There was a delicious freedom to be found at the beach, which had to do with the feeling of brine on your skin and sand in the Barbecue Shapes – not prim picnics at tables with linen. Homesickness flooded Madeleine like nausea.

To distract herself, Madeleine turned her attention to Mr Williamson, who was playing 'horsies' with Imo, crouched over and carting her backwards and forwards along the water's edge. Imo was kicking his sides with invisible spurs and cracking his back with a strip of limp weed. He reminded Madeleine of her own father when she was little. Every time Mr Williamson brayed, he looked back at Elfriede and Bea sitting on a sweet patch of green grass by the riverbed.

'Thomas? Elfriede? Would you care for some lemonade?' Mrs Williamson called.

'Lemonade? As well as cake? Isn't that butter upon bacon,' said Mr Williamson, cracking his dimples.

Elfriede laughed from the bank of the river, where she'd abandoned Bea to play catch with a ball. 'What a charming saying.' She threw the ball high in the air and then caught it.

'Thomas is very fond of idioms,' said Mrs Williamson. 'Would you care for some lemonade, Elfriede? Anna prepared it this morning, and it's bitter and delicious.'

'No, thank you,' called Elfriede.

'Oh,' said Mrs Williamson, putting down her glass. 'Well, what about a fort competition? Anyone care to join me? I do make a rather magnificent pebble fort.' She stood up and walked to the edge of the river and then back. 'There are some wonderful pebbles.' She was puffing a little. It took her breath a while to settle. 'Fort, Thomas?'

'I'd rather a game of ball,' said Mr Williamson. Imo slid down his back as he stood, and Elfriede threw a ball straight and firm at his chest. Mr Williamson caught it and tossed it to Gert, who missed. Millie ran after it, swiped it and took it to Charlie.

Elfriede laughed and ran after Charlie. She was, despite her cigarettes, a natural athlete, with an eye for a ball; she could probably read a game. She had pinned up her skirt to give her more freedom. Madeleine could see her arms, long and lean and muscular, and her strong, bony ankles. Gert stood to join in. Charlie scooped up the ball and threw it to Elfriede, who threw it to Gert. Gert smiled and held out her hands hopefully, but the ball flew past them, a good half metre away. Gert, sadly, was hopeless.

'I've never built a fort, but I love building sandcastles,' said Madeleine to Mrs Williamson.

But Mrs Williamson had retreated up the bank to a little chair placed precisely on a stretch of bright grass near the table, where she was sipping from a cloudy glass. She had brought her sitting room to the river, it seemed. She looked regal, presiding over the party. There were dark oblongs of sweat on the cotton under the arms of her frock.

'Come on, Madeleine,' called Gert. 'Do join in.'

Gert threw the ball wide to her, but Madeleine caught it; it made a satisfying *thwack* in her hands.

'You've done this before,' called Elfriede.

There was something deeply satiating about the weight and curve of a ball in her palm. It was only as she held the ball that Madeleine realised how much she had missed it. She threw it back to Elfriede, then ran down closer to the game. Wearing Hen's looser bodice, she could actually run, and if she breathed in she could feel a lovely gap between her clothes and her skin.

Mr Williamson had grabbed a cricket bat. They set up a game, and even Bea joined in. Madeleine hit and fielded, yelled and hooted. The wooden bat was a relic, but it felt wonderful to be up and active again; to sweat, to feel her body move, to feel how strong it was.

Bea left the game and went up to sit with her mother. Charlie was back with Millie on the muddy river banks, poking about with a stick. Millie yapped at any fish that darted too near.

'Charlie, not too far, the current can be strong,' said Mrs Williamson. Charlie ignored her.

Elfriede threw the ball to Gert and it nipped the tips of her fingers and then rolled off towards the water. Gert scrambled after it. Charlie picked up the ball and threw it hard, straight and fast to her father.

'Come back and play, Master Charles.'

'Thomas, don't encourage her,' said Mrs Williamson in a warning voice.

'Where *did* you learn to bat, Madeleine?' asked Mr Williamson. 'We could do with you on our team!'

'I have an older brother.'

Mr Williamson handed the bat to Charlie. 'You could play as well as Madeleine one day, with a little concentration.'

'Sadly, Daddy, I am the only boy in the family. There is therefore nobody to pester Master Charles for a game, and so not much point in learning how. Anyway, I like fishing, too.'

'Come on, Madeleine,' said Gert. 'Let's get some lemonade. Mummy looks so alone.'

Mrs Williamson had not moved, but she was no longer watching the cricket.

'Oh, don't take Madeleine from us, she's super.' Elfriede's eyes were bright from the exertion. 'I haven't done this much exercise since my last bike race.'

'I love bikes!' said Madeleine.

'I'm thirsty.' Gert pulled Madeleine up the bank. 'Don't draw attention to yourself,' she whispered. 'There are a few ladies' team, but no schoolgirl plays like that.' She stopped and punched Madeleine. 'Although I am quite proud.'

The girls made a beeline for the pitcher of lemonade, which had thin discs of lemon bobbing in it.

'You are a marvellous sportswoman, Madeleine,' Mrs Williamson said as they approached. 'I'm tired just looking at you. Do you ride?'

'Of course,' said Gert, pouring two full glasses, which slopped onto the cloth. She looked up to apologise, but Mrs Williamson was staring down the bank to Mr Williamson, who had Imo on his back again. Elfriede was throwing the ball and Mr Williamson was moving Imo so she could catch it. He looked so gangly that it was funny. Like a marionette.

Elfriede had taken off her shoes and was fielding the ball in bare feet; those long, bony feet.

'Isn't it fun having Elfriede here, Mummy?' said Gert. 'She has jollied things up a bit.'

'There's nothing quite like family,' said Mrs Williamson brightly. 'What about your family, Madeleine? Do you miss them?'

'Oh, yes,' said Madeleine. 'Of course, you've been so kind, but I do miss them. Mum . . . mmy, especially.' Madeleine's voice cracked and she turned away, her eyes full.

There was a squeal. Mr Williamson was dangling Imo above the river, upside down. Her skirts had flopped down over her head, and she was kicking and squawking. Under her hands, the river ran on, lapping its banks as it passed.

'That's enough, Thomas. That's enough. She can't swim,' said Mrs Williamson crossly.

'Oh, Bella,' said Elfriede, running up the bank. 'It's terribly amusing. She's the sweetest child.' Elfriede fiddled with a hook and eye on her skirt and the hem dropped. She sat beside her cousin and smiled back at Mr Williamson and Imo, laughing. 'What a beautiful family you have.'

Mrs Williamson tucked a piece of silver hair behind her ear. Her skin was still smooth and creamy, marked only by smile lines around her mouth, but her hair was as streaky as bacon. She had taken out a small hoop over which a piece of cotton was stretched and was sewing tiny stitches.

'The light here is perfect,' she said. 'I'm using white on white and it's horribly difficult. My eyes really aren't what they were.' Her thick fingers were remarkably agile despite being weighed down by rings. 'Do you do needlework, Elfriede?' she asked crisply.

'No, but even if I did, I could never do stitches as tiny as those.' Elfriede hugged her cousin. 'You are clever, Bella.'

Mrs Williamson smiled. 'Did you bring your sampler, Gert?' she asked.

'No, Mummy,' said Gert. 'Call us when luncheon's on. We're going to find a koala.'

Gert grabbed Madeleine's hand and they fled.

# To town

The car contingent of the picnic party arrived home late that afternoon, sandy, smelly and singing. Madeleine's feet were chalky-grey and itchy with river silt.

'Oh, it is lovely to see you all so happy,' said Aunt Hen, who was sitting in the drawing room with a sherry glass in her hand that looked like it was made from cut ice. She put her book down on the table as the girls all tumbled in. She was sitting back in her chair like Mr Williamson, rather than perched on its edge in the way Elfriede and Mrs Williamson sat.

'Where's Mummy?' asked Imo.

'She's up in her room,' said Aunt Hen, taking a sip from her glass. 'Now, tell me, what was your favourite part of the day? Did you catch a fish?'

'No, but I did catch the sun. I'm a bit burnt.' Gert rubbed her arm. The freckles on it looked even darker.

'At this time of year! Poor girl. Don't let Bella see it. She does bristle when you girls get too much sun. I shall arrange a cool milk compress to take the sting out.'

Madeleine picked up a children's book that had been left sitting open on the table.

'That's *Cole's Funny Picture Book*, and it is hilarious,' said Charlie. 'Hen Pen bought it for us.'

Madeleine sat down at the table and flicked through it. It was part newspaper, part riddles, part encyclopedia, part 'Cole's Patented Whipping Machine for Flogging Naughty Boys in School'. There didn't appear to be any young adult fiction here, she thought. What she would give for a copy of one of the novels she had taken completely for granted in the library back at school. She sat still, the thin pages unread before her.

Aunt Hen put down her glass. 'I have been thinking . . . I'd like to make you girls an offer. I have spoken to your father, Gertrude, and provided Nanny is amenable, I must go into town tomorrow morning – and I thought you and Madeleine might like to join me. We'll stay at Park Street and return Sunday morning.'

'Is Master Charles invited too?' Charlie looked over at Aunt Hen and smiled hopefully.

'I think two girls is probably enough for tomorrow, Charlie.'

'What about two girls and one boy?'

'Why don't we ask Nanny if you can come on your own special trip one day? I'm down there frequently enough, and I could certainly do with an escort.'

Charlie's eyes got wet and shiny.

'Of course, there is usually room for a strapping body-guard, but not tomorrow. I *will* need a big man like you, Master Williamson, when I go to the bank to remove the family jewels from the safe.'

Charlie giggled.

'We're planning to stop in at Jacksons,' Aunt Hen went on. 'Have a think about what sort of sweets we can bring you back, Charlie.'

'Edinburgh rock!' said Charlie. 'It's so soft and crumbly.'

'You are a man after my own heart.' Aunt Hen smiled. 'Now go and find Nanny, and let her know we will need to make sure these girls are packed tonight. We'll leave first thing in the morning.'

~~~

The next morning was cold and damp again. Nanny rugged Madeleine and Gert up in heavy serge dresses and double-breasted coats with shoulder capes and bundled them, plus their small shared case, to the front door.

'Please remember your coats, your gloves, your hats and your manners, and be sensible. Do not stray from Aunt Hen for a minute, and remember that different people have different rules, Miss Gertrude. When in doubt, my rules prevail.'

Despite the dress and the blue-grey coat, Madeleine felt lighter in her new, looser bodice; she didn't think she'd ever stop being grateful.

'Any chance we can follow Aunt Hen on the bodice front?' she whispered to Gert. 'I'd be happier to lose this thing altogether.'

'Madeleine, shhh! Nanny will never let us go if she hears you.'

Aunt Hen emerged from the shadows. 'Are you girls ready?'

They nodded in unison and she smiled, looking very pleased with herself, and led them to the car.

As Aunt Hen pulled out of the driveway, Madeleine said, 'You're the first woman I've seen drive.'

'It's great fun, and so much less temperamental than a horse!'

Aunt Hen turned the stick on top of the wheel and shifted the car up a gear. It clunked. She wore little cream-coloured mesh gloves with buttons.

'Besides, I think it's important to know how to do things oneself. Our class is so horribly dependent and incompetent. What if things change, if our skills become redundant? Needlepoint and piano-playing will not fight wars. What would *we* do if *we* had to fight the Boers?'

The gears clunked again.

'We'll drive to the station and then we can catch the train into the city. Someone will collect the car later.'

The train into town was a big black steam engine with carriages the colour of cream-of-beetroot soup. It hissed as it slowed at the tiny weatherboard station, and whistled with a blast of steam that shot across the platform.

'Just when I thought we were getting a break from Imo's whistling,' said Gert.

Aunt Hen followed the girls down the wooden aisle of the first-class carriage. It was divided into compartments, each with its own door.

'Not that one,' said Aunt Hen, shaking her head. 'It's smoking. The next one is for ladies.'

The girls opened the door to the next carriage and sat on blood-red seats that smelt as rich as a new football. An inspector came and punched their thick card tickets.

'I've never been in first-class anything!' said Madeleine. 'We certainly don't have a dedicated ladies' carriage.'

'Really?' said Aunt Hen. 'Does your grandmother travel second class? That's a superb idea – I'd never thought of doing that. There are even separate trains for working men on some lines, although catching one of those might be going too far. This is what I mean about questioning *all* our beliefs and the foundations that underpin them. It's so difficult to question things when they're part of the wallpaper. But I do love the idea, Madeleine – we can travel in second on the way back. If you girls are old enough to go to boarding school, you are quite old enough to travel with the working classes.'

The train whistled again and took off. Aunt Hen stood up and opened the window, and cool mountain air rushed in.

'Fresh ideas – just what we need.' Aunt Hen looked at Gert. 'Just don't tell your mother!'

Gert smiled. 'She would be very cross with you, wouldn't she?'

'Your mother has very firm ideas about girls and their role. My wish for you, dear Gertie, is that you be independent. That you live in a world where you are free to make choices.' She smiled sadly, and fell silent.

The train stopped at some stations longer than others, for toilet breaks built into the timetable. It shrieked as it pulled away from each station.

Madeleine relaxed and enjoyed looking out the window. As the train chugged on, the trees thinned out, and houses and roads sprouted. A yellow haze appeared above everything, like a bruise.

After a time Aunt Hen stood, smoothing loose curls behind her ears. 'We'll be pulling into the station shortly. Are you girls ready to go?'

When the train finally drew to a stop, they stepped down onto the platform. Aunt Hen left their cases with a porter, to be collected later on, and they made their way out of the station.

They were at the bottom of the city. The street consisted of an expansive band of earth. A tramline ran along its middle, the tram carriages all open-air, with no sides, no windows or doors. The street was crowded: on the stone footpath there were boys in caps selling hot nuts, and kids with newspapers and hoops, and women wearing big skirts. On the road were open horse-drawn carriages carrying barrels, and zippy one-person traps, and a man with a flag directing traffic. There were horses and carriage-wheels and puddles and shouts, and the hollow *clop clop* of horse-shoes on pressed dirt.

Aunt Hen walked crisply down the street. She looked just as determined but even more energetic than ever out here in town, bolstered by the chaos.

'Now listen up, girls. There are two things I always do when I'm in the city. First stop, journals!'

Aunt Hen took them to a soaring arcade cosy with armchairs and lined with books all the way up to its second storey. *Read for as Long as You like – Nobody Asked to Buy*, said a sign. The air was tinny with the circus sound of clockwork-music.

Aunt Hen barely seemed to notice the astonishing shop; all her focus was on picking up copies of journals: *Boomerang*, *The Dawn* and *The Woman's Voice*. 'These will give me ideas and your father some kindling.' She winked.

Madeleine looked down at one of the journals on display and stopped short. On the front cover was a grotesque caricature of a Chinese man with a plait. He wore a robe and smoked a long pipe. *He has the vote, but we women don't!* screamed the headline.

The racism was cruel and overt; Madeleine was shocked by it. 'Are they allowed to *print* that?' she asked, thinking she'd use that page – that whole magazine – for kindling.

'Of course,' said Aunt Hen brusquely.

'What about a copy of *Table Talk*?' Gert pointed to a great pile of magazines on a crate next to the counter.

'No, thank you!' Aunt Hen pulled out a purse. 'I do not need to fill my mind with details about who escorted whom to the races and in what fabric.'

*Honourable*, thought Madeleine. *And yet you don't kick up a fuss about a journal with a monstrous cartoon.*

Gert smiled and elbowed her aunt. 'Come on, Hen – *Table Talk* is for Bea, not you! She does like them.'

Aunt Hen sighed. 'All right. Even I am moved to pity about Bea, stuck up in the hills at her age with no invitations. I'd have eloped years ago. Just promise me neither of you will go anywhere near it.'

Aunt Hen tucked the copy of *Table Talk* under her arm, together with the other magazines. 'Righty-oh, girls. Next stop, Jacksons!'

Madeleine and Gert walked along the broad stone footpath behind Hen Pen, past a series of shopfronts. The footpath was lumpy, and the air was heavy with the peaty smell of horses. The dirt road was caked with horse dung. A teenager with a blank face and a filthy bag walked along scooping it up. People were shouting and yelling. It was wild and crazy, and a bit scary, really. Madeleine inched closer to Gert.

Aunt Hen paused in front of a shop with children's clothing in the window. There were two sailor suits displayed, both navy-blue and both for boys, with white piping around the square collars.

'That would become Master Charles,' said Hen.

'No,' said Gert and walked on. 'Nanny would never let her wear it.'

'But Gert, she'd love it,' said Madeleine. 'Don't be such a party pooper.'

'What a first-rate expression!' said Hen Pen. 'I might start to use that one.'

Gert looked around. 'I can never stop looking up!' she said. 'The buildings are so high, and they feel so much grander!' They were at the bottom of the city, only it wasn't any city Madeleine recognised. Madeleine didn't have the heart to tell Gert that it was nothing like the Melbourne she knew, with its sparkling highrises and thick trees. This was wide and flat and dusty – like Cook had had a good go at the place with her rolling pin.

They walked on. 'Look, there it is!' cried Gert, her voice fizzy. 'There's Jacksons.'

The shop at which Gert had pointed had a lovely window that bowed into the street, edged with brass. In it, a man stood at a marble counter kneading a large slab of something white and doughy. On the front was a sign: 'J.P. Jackson. Manufacturing Confectioner.'

'Is he a baker?' asked Madeleine.

'No! Nor a butcher nor a candlestick-maker. Watch!' cried Gert.

The man flicked the mound over and over with one leather-gloved hand. He moved quickly, tossing the great milky lump into the air. His meaty forearms, spattered with bright pink marks, were as thick as a pro wrestler's, busting from his rolled-up sleeves.

The man moved on to another mound on the counter, which was as shiny as glue and as green as mouthwash. He carried the mound to the back of the shop and began pulling and folding it over a nail on the wall – pulling down and flicking it over. He was strong but also graceful. The mass looked alive.

'What is it?' asked Madeleine, perplexed.

'Toffee! He's a sweet-maker.'

'That's so clever.' Madeleine had never seen anything like it. When she felt like sweets at home, she would walk to the nearest fluoro-lit 7-Eleven and buy a bar of chocolate, and sometimes a few straps of raspberry licorice from the plastic box on the counter, which would last for four years (and counting) without rotting if you left them in a drawer.

The man hacked pieces off the wrung toffee and moulded it into strips with his gloved hand. He ran his hands over the back of the strips, massaging them, smoothing the toffee down like Mum Crum sanding wood. When the toffee was in four neat logs, the man pulled out a long machete and diced each log like a TV chef slicing celery.

The girls walked into the shop, Aunt Hen behind them. It was sunny and lined on three of the four sides with tall shelves. The shelves were crammed with glass jars – long glass cylinders, filled to the brim with hard lollies in all sorts of shapes and sizes and colours. The room was fragrant with peppermint and pineapple and cherry.

A man with boggly eyes that looked constantly surprised smiled at Gert from his perch on a ladder halfway up one of the shelves. His shirt was as stripy as his peppermints. 'Good morning.'

'Please may I have sixpence worth of raspberry rock, and sixpence of brandy balls, and four chocolate cigars, and sixpence – actually, no, that's Charlie's favourite so perhaps one shilling's worth – of Edinburgh rock?' Gert rubbed her eyebrows as she studied the sweets.

The ladder the man stood on ran along the shelves on tracks. He was able to go up and down it, side to side, as Gert demanded more sweets, ladling the lollies into two large paper cones.

'Ummm,' said Gert, 'perhaps some—'

'That will do, won't it?' said Madeleine as the man reached for another paper cone. The first two packages were heavy and hard with sugar. Mum Crum's views on sugar as the enemy were difficult to shake.

'Here, allow me,' said Aunt Hen.

'That will be two shillings and sixpence,' the man said. He smiled at Aunt Hen and she handed him some coins.

'Please don't tell Nanny,' said Hen. 'I'm tiring of the displeasure.'

Back in the street, Aunt Hen hailed what she called a hansom cab (which was really a shiny black one-horse carriage with a driver in a bowler hat) and bundled the girls into it, jumping in after them.

'Once we have collected the cases, I wish to take you somewhere before Park Street.'

She looked at the girls closely.

'If you do accompany me, you must both promise that you will not breathe a word of it to anybody. If your father were to know, Gert, there would be serious consequences.'

'More serious than Nanny finding out about the sweets?'

Aunt Hen managed a sad sort of smile.

'I think that you are both bright, independent-thinking girls, and that if change is ever to be effected, it will start amongst the petticoats of mothers. Look at Vida – so active by age nineteen. Could that have happened in any other family? It certainly didn't happen in mine. I only got to read law because my parents had died and there was nobody to stop me.'

Aunt Hen was holding the edge of the seat to steady herself, and Madeleine could see her gripping it firmly through her gloves.

'If it hadn't have been for Cornelia Sorabji, I probably wouldn't have been there at all.'

'Cornelia who?' asked Madeleine.

'Every household will know that exceptional woman's name soon enough,' said Aunt Hen. 'Mark my words.' Then she called over her shoulder, 'Back to the station, and then on to Drummond Street, please.'

'Carlton?' asked the driver.

'Yes, please!' Aunt Hen called. She turned to Gert. 'So, you shan't tell your mother?'

'Pinky promise,' said Madeleine, holding out her little finger. Gert raised hers too.

'I like that,' said Aunt Hen.

The man cracked his whip and the sharp clap of horse hooves rang out as they pulled away from the kerb. Madeleine was in a hansom cab, a long way from Lyrebird Muse and even further from Mum Crum, heading somewhere she was not meant to be . . . She shivered deliciously. It was naughty, it was bold, and, she had to admit, it was very, very exciting.

# The secret

~~~~~

The hansom cab pulled up outside a row of tall, elegant grey homes.

'These seven houses were built by a wealthy merchant for his seven daughters,' said Aunt Hen. She swung a light leather case out of the cab. 'Could you wait here with our other cases, please?' she called up to the driver. He nodded, and Aunt Hen helped the girls to step down onto the kerb. She led the way off the main road, down a narrower, darker side street wet with mud.

The houses in the side street were collapsed against each other, joined cheek by jowl. There was a strip of water in a ditch down the centre of the road; it was brown and greasy and it stank. Kids with muddy feet, wearing pants hitched high and tied with string, stopped their skipping to watch the new arrivals. There was a woman peeling potatoes on a front verandah, the skins curling about her feet. There were lines of washing everywhere you looked. And there was the feeling that, whichever way you turned, people were staring. The girls stepped closer together.

'Is this a slum?' whispered Gert.

'Not quite,' murmured Aunt Hen between closed lips. 'But I do worry about disease, so try not to get too close to anyone.' She smiled out at the children around her and prodded away a chicken pecking near her feet. 'Good morning!'

Madeleine was suddenly aware that the three of them looked so clean, so creamy, so unpatched.

Aunt Hen stopped outside a small, squat house at the end of the street. The windows were milky, as the curtains had been drawn, and there was nothing and no one on the verandah. It looked blind.

Aunt Hen pulled a long brass key on a string around her neck out from beneath her dress. She unlocked the front door, which had four panels of plain red glass in it. Through the doorway Madeleine could see a long hallway, with unpolished floorboards and a fraying rug. Three doors ran off the hallway along the right-hand side, and the far end was blocked by a dusty curtain.

Aunt Hen motioned to the open door. 'Welcome!'

The girls stepped inside, hopping over a mass of letters that had been stuffed through the letter slot. The walls were plastered but bumpy, and the place smelt damp and airless. Aunt Hen swept the post to one side. 'Anna will go through that later.'

'It's the tiniest house I've ever seen,' said Gert.

'Tiny? Tiny depends entirely on how many people are crammed into a home – there are families with twelve children each in the slums, all sleeping in rows like biscuits in a tin. This is really very spacious.'

Aunt Hen walked past the first room on the right and into a second. It had dark lino laid out on the floor and it was lit by a small square window with a simple window seat built in beneath it. There was a barren fireplace in the middle of the far wall. The room was cold and smelt of stale smoke and industry. Madeleine pulled her coat closer around her.

To the left of the window, pushed against the wall, was a table, on top of which sat a big wooden crate filled with long metal pins, and a wooden box. Under the table was an open box with paper inside. In the centre of the room was a chunky machine made of dull, worn metal. It had a flat disc slightly bigger than a paper plate angled up towards the roof like a satellite, and a big smooth wheel on the side with a heart-shaped pedal. The floor beneath the machine was dented and covered in dark smears that had a deep sheen, like blood.

Gert pushed the machine's pedal and the wheel spun with a perfect mechanical elegance. The mouth of the machine opened, and out popped three rollers covered in hard, calloused rubber.

'Is it a spinning wheel?' Gert asked.

Aunt Hen shook her head. 'I'm hardly Rumpelstiltskin.'

'Is it . . . is it a time machine?' asked Madeleine, trying hard to sound casual.

'A time machine? Gosh no, but it *is* a machine. Do you really have no idea?'

Aunt Hen stood behind the apparatus, her foot cocked above the heart-shaped pedal. 'This, girls, is a voice.'

'A voice?' Gert tilted her head to the side and ran a finger along the metal.

'Don't touch, darling. These machines can be brutal if they're not used properly.'

Gert dropped her white-gloved hand, which was now looking smudgy and a bit navy blue.

'Think Johannes Gutenberg in Mainz, fourteen thirty-nine: the world's most glorious invention. It's a voice, a glorious voice, my darling girls. This is a printing press, and we are producing *The Hens' Convention*.'

'*You* produce *The Hens' Convention*?' cried Gert.

Aunt Hen nodded. 'The very one and the same Hen! I'm surprised you didn't guess.'

'Does Daddy know? He would *slaughter* you!'

'We publish under a *nom de plume*, obviously. That's why I asked you to promise not to breathe a word.'

Gert looked shocked, but she also looked, well, a bit proud – in awe, even. 'Tremendous title, Aunt Hen.'

'Why, thank you. I'm quite proud of it myself!'

'You really publish *The Hens' Convention*! How?'

'We do. I have a tiny team, and we all work hard to produce and distribute it. Even in London! I thought, *Well, if Louisa Lawson can manage it with very little means, I can do it too*, and this machine makes it so simple. I began by printing leaflets, but I found I wanted to do more.'

'But Hen Pen, it's so scandalous! It's wonderful!' Gert was smiling now. She turned to Madeleine. 'Daddy always called her Hen Pen because she was studious, sitting there with her pen in the inkpot. He has no idea how right he is!' Gert looked around. 'But who bought the press? Whose house is it?'

Aunt Hen smiled shyly. 'The house is mine, actually. My father left it to me – it was a part of his estate – and I've always drawn an income from it, but my expenses are met by the other properties he left me, and I realised that by ceasing to rent it out, I had my own workplace.'

'A room of one's own,' said Madeleine.

'Indeed! I like that.' Hen Pen nodded at her. 'And so I bought the press.'

'I don't think Grandpa would have expected you to do *this* with it!' Gert laughed.

Aunt Hen nodded. 'Instead of just reading about what needs to be done, instead of just identifying problems, I thought I could jolly well get off the sofa and actually *do* something! One can't change anything from the parlour!' Aunt Hen looked excited and proud and almost as surprised by her action as Gert was.

'How does it work?' asked Madeleine. 'Can we see a copy of the paper?'

'I have a typesetter who helps us. Every little letter has to be set in a line, sentence by sentence, so it takes a long time to print a page – and then we have to edit carefully, as there can be frightful inaccuracies. Look at this one: *Women Untie.*'

'*Untie?* What's it meant to be?' Gert tilted her head to the side.

Aunt Hen walked over to the table. She selected a range of small metal letters from the case, which she lined up on a wooden lip not unlike the one Madeleine lined her Scrabble words on at home.

'Women unite!' Hen declared when she was done. 'One little slip and a very different meaning!'

Madeleine thought of her computer at home. 'That took about three minutes to collate two words!' she exclaimed.

'It *is* a cumbersome process, but once it's set we can print hundreds of copies. All we have to do is smear the ink here' – Hen motioned to the plate – 'and then the rollers distribute it onto the press. Come and have a look.'

Aunt Hen led the girls out into the hallway and back towards the front door. She opened the door to the front room. Inside, there were piles of boxes on the floor, all lined up and labelled.

*Jan–March 1900.*

*July–Sep 1899.*

*April–June 1899.*

'So you bring your paper out four times a year, then?' asked Madeleine.

'We do. It takes us a while to get the articles together and edit them, and we are committed to a high standard of intellectual rigour, so quarterly is preferable. We're always working on the next edition while the latest one is circulating.'

Aunt Hen opened a box and pulled out a copy. It was lovely. The ink was irregular, and you could see where the roller had missed little bits. The metal letter squares had sometimes left square edges around the letters on the page.

*Hissing and stamping suffragists disrupt parliament!*
*Western Australia wins the vote!*

'It's amazing,' said Gert. 'Good show, Aunt Hen. I mean, it looks like a proper journal! There's even advertising!'

'We mainly sell copies via subscription, but the advertising assists. Tea, coffee, cocoa, typewriters: there are so many businesses that rely on women's custom.' Aunt Hen smiled. She looked younger and happier and so energetic.

'Identifying where change is needed is just the first step. Most of the work is acting on it. Just think, one bullet can start a war; one termite can bring down an entire house. And our current situation is outrageous. What is the point of securing education for women if we can't take out degrees? If we can't then work? Well, this way I *can* use all I learnt. I can read the cases, and we are effecting change. Moreover, my brother may shun me, but many of the men who are sitting MPs studied in England too, and they will listen to me. They will put down *their* newspapers when I wish to speak to them. We will be heard.'

'You will, you know,' said Madeleine. 'I really believe it.'

Hen Pen grinned back at her. 'Does your grandmother feel the same way, Madeleine? That piece of paper you gave me, I'm convinced it was part of the monster petition. I was still in England, but I'm told it took four women to carry the beast into parliament! They had over thirty thousand signatures, from right across the colony.'

Aunt Hen took off her jacket and pushed her sleeves up. Her arms were long and strong.

'Right, well, let's get these in here.'

Hen Pen clicked open the brass clasps on her empty leather case, and took the top off a box labelled *Apr–Jun 1900*. Inside were hundreds of printed pieces of paper.

'We can fold and staple them at Park Street; some are circulating already, but there is demand for another five hundred at least.'

Aunt Hen counted bundles of paper as she placed them in the case, her face puckered with concentration. Once she was finished, she picked up a large piece of fabric that had been tucked away between the two of the boxes of journals and spread it over the contents of her case.

'What's that?' asked Madeleine, taking one end. The house seemed to offer up endless discoveries.

'*The Hens' Convention* flag! Do you like it?' She shook it out. It was huge – about the size of a single doona cover. Printed on the front were three women dressed as old-fashioned soldiers, carrying enormous red shields and wearing brass helmets with bristly crests running along their tops like roosters' combs. Instead of swords, the women had fountain pens. Across the front, letters which had been cut from felt and stitched on read: *The Hens' Convention. Fighting for votes for women. Common wealth, common suffrage.*

'We use it for rallies, but it's torn. I can't have a soldier with a flapping shield – the symbolism is appalling.'

'I love the pens as swords,' said Madeleine. 'Always mightier. It's so clever.'

'Thank you! We'll take it with us to Park Street too, and stitch it back together tonight. Those skills your mother drills into you are not without their purpose! I'd like to get you girls back now, before it gets dark. This area can be precarious in the evening.'

Aunt Hen hauled up her now much heavier case and pushed it along the hallway in front of her with her boots. The bottom hinges scraped two tram tracks in the dust, but if Aunt Hen noticed she didn't care. Once they were outside, she locked the door with the brass key and tucked it back in under her dress. She then patted her chest twice, as if to check it was still there.

She smiled at the woman on the verandah of the house next door, who threw a big enamel tub of water out onto the street and looked at the ground.

'Do they know what you do in there?' asked Gert, reaching over to help Aunt Hen with her case.

Aunt Hen shook her head. 'I'm trying to help them, but they have no idea. I think they believe I'm of dubious repute.' Hen winked.

'Well, you are, according to Daddy!' said Gert. They all laughed.

'I do have one friend here – Agnes at number six.' Aunt Hen motioned towards the other end of the street. 'She keeps an eye on the house for me, but she's at her sister's today. Poor Agnes. She's frightfully busy with six small children and the washing she must take in to support them all. Her husband is a ne'er-do-well – one assumes he hits the bottle.

Agnes said that just because she doesn't have time to fight for the vote doesn't mean she doesn't see it as important. That has stuck with me.'

Hen Pen tucked an arm through Madeleine's and her other arm through Gert's, pulling them close.

'The cab will be waiting – come on, girls!'

The cab was indeed still waiting for them at the corner. The driver was eating a sandwich tucked inside a sheet of greasy paper. He poked what remained of it into a cloth bag. 'Where to now?' he asked.

'Twenty-four Park Street, South Yarra,' said Aunt Hen. 'Oh girls, I am bone weary.'

The driver helped her lift the case up onto the cab. 'What have you got in here? A third daughter?' He winked.

Aunt Hen smiled up at him.

The trio settled into the carriage and it drove them back towards the city centre.

They passed a tall, dark building as they entered the top end of the city. 'That's the gaol,' Aunt Hen commented. 'It was bigger than the cathedral at one stage. What does that say about a town?'

The carriage drove along a street and out over a bridge, then down a broad, dusty boulevard. Madeleine sank back against the hard leather seat and tried not to doze off.

The cab rattled along the road. The streets were not so hemmed in by houses here; rather, there were acres of parks as fresh as salads surrounding them, the birds in their trees cheeping as they settled down for the night.

The cab finally pulled up in front of a row of smooth white terraces with ironwork as fancy as any wedding cake. One of the terraces proudly displayed a brass number twenty-four in the centre of a very smart black door.

The door opened and there was Anna in her apron, smiling out into the dusky evening. 'Miss Gertrude and Miss Madeleine.'

'Anna!' both girls cried.

'Come in, come in. The fires are lit, and supper is almost ready. You must be exhausted after a day of travelling and touring.'

Madeleine walked up the bluestone stairs leading to the three-arched terrace and let Anna help her take off her coat. The hallway inside was carpeted with a runner tacked down on both sides. The strip of deep red carpet led to a staircase and continued on up, held in place on the stairs by horizontal brass rods. It was weird the way nobody actually carpeted to the edges, Madeleine thought. She could smell meat roasting.

Anna opened a door off the hallway onto a comfortable room with a fire burning in a tall marble fireplace. Above it, a painting of English-looking countryside was set in a golden frame, and lovely couches lined two of the walls.

'Sit down, my weary travellers,' said Aunt Hen, unpinning her hat.

The girls peeled off their gloves and unpinned their own hats.

Madeleine sank back against a solid cushion. Directly ahead of her, in the neat space between the large bay window and the return wall, was an oil painting of a woman with a brown coat and a curly striped feather in her hat.

'It's your mother!' said Madeleine, recalling it in the hall of the Muse in her own time. 'And the feather is a lyrebird's!'

'It is,' said Gert. 'Painted just after she met Daddy. I can never work out if she looks more like Bea or Imo. But she does look happy.'

'Gertie, where are the sweets? I'm starving,' said Aunt Hen.

'Before we dine?' Gert fished in her pinafore for a lumpy paper cone.

'Once one has broken one of society's rules, one discovers how very easy it is!' Aunt Hen leant over to rummage in the cone, then popped a brandy ball into her mouth. 'The longer you suck these, the smaller they get, but the shinier they get, too. That's how I'd like to live my life as I age – shrunken but dazzling! Anna, do join us!'

Anna came into the room. Her demeanor towards Aunt Hen was different here – she wasn't as shy as she was back at Lyrebird Muse. Aunt Hen offered her a cone of sweets and Anna took a red one. 'We've a lovely joint for dinner,' she said through the lolly.

'Yum! No nursery tea here,' said Gert.

'If you're old enough for suffrage, then you're certainly old enough for dinner with the grown-ups!' said Aunt Hen.

Gert beamed.

'You'll like it here,' said Anna to Madeleine 'We're not so stiff and starchy.'

Aunt Hen pressed one finger between her eyebrows. 'Anna, I am simply too tired to attend the meeting this evening. I still have an article to proofread, and my eyes are hurting.'

'What meeting?' asked Madeleine.

'One of the so-called monster meetings of the United Council for Woman's Suffrage, at the town hall. The council is a group that joins all the smaller groups fighting for the vote together. Do go for me, Anna, won't you? You can relay it all back to us tomorrow. And here.' She handed Anna some money. 'Make sure you take a hansom cab. This city is too drunken for young women out on their own.'

Anna smiled. 'Thank you, Miss Williamson. I'd love to attend.'

Aunt Hen looked at the girls. 'Anna and I have been having a number of discussions lately. Your father always assumes that women are represented by their husbands. Putting aside the fact that many husbands ignore their wives' opinions altogether, the fact remains that there are thousands of us who do not have husbands – thousands like Anna, in paid employment; thousands of widows, and deserted wives. These women are not represented by anyone. They need to have a say in the decisions affecting them.'

'Like my ma,' said Anna. 'Six kids, and a husband gone. That's the thing about men; they do seem to hop the twig early, especially the good ones.'

She smiled softly, picked up the discarded gloves and hats, and left the room.

'Does Anna go to all these meetings too?' Gert asked her aunt. 'I'd never have guessed.'

'Yes – and why not? In many ways, Anna lives with the problems of which I speak more acutely than you ever will.' Aunt Hen poked another humbug into her mouth. 'I saw Anna attending a debate once, back near the Muse, so I asked her if she might like to go along to a big one. She was very keen, so now I request her assistance at Park Street whenever I'm able. There's no need for me to attend every meeting personally – I certainly don't require conversion!'

The two girls and Aunt Hen sat with cold cheeks, sucking lollies by the fire, wrapped in sugar and the buzz of their shared secret, and Madeleine wondered who else was secretly on Hen's side.

# Same direction as the hair

A unt Hen and the girls boarded the train to return to Lyrebird Muse the following morning. They did travel in second class – in the very last carriage. Apart from being completely empty and substantially noisier, as it had hard wooden seats forming a semi-circle inside each carriage rather than compartments, it was not too unpleasant.

Aunt Hen and Gert had dark rings under their eyes, and Madeleine suspected that she herself did as well. All three had stayed up until well after Anna had returned from the meeting, folding and stapling *The Hens' Convention*. Once the magazines were stacked in their case like Weetbix in a box, the three had retired to bed, agreeing that Aunt Hen would just have to take the flag with her tomorrow to be repaired at the Muse. They'd had to get up very early to deposit the magazines back at the Drummond Street house, ready for distribution, before they'd left town.

A few stops past the city, the train drew in at a station. Smuts blew in through the ill-fitting train windows, and Aunt Hen stomped them with her boot. A Chinese couple boarded the carriage. The man wore a high white collar, waistcoat and smart tweed suit. The woman was dressed in a brown woollen dress, gathered at the wrists, with a square hat on her head. They were an elegant couple, thought Madeleine, smiling at them as they sat down nearby, neatly stacking three wooden crates filled with vegetables, fruit and bunches of herbs at their feet.

'What lovely apples!' said Madeleine, spotting a red cheek. 'I've barely seen a piece of fresh fruit since I got here. Why *don't* you eat the fruit in your garden?' she asked Gert. 'Those oranges looked so delicious, but I don't think I've seen them served.'

'Cook uses them,' says Gert. 'She makes marmalade with the citrus.'

'Fresh fruit is terrible for the digestion,' said Aunt Hen. 'I may take issue with Nanny on most topics, but we will never go to war over stewed apple; it is much gentler on the constitution.'

Aunt Hen looked at the couple and then looked away. They spoke quietly together in Chinese. Madeleine learnt Mandarin at school, but this Chinese sounded quite different and she couldn't understand them.

The woman reached into a bag and pulled out a woven bamboo basket. Inside were four plump white buns with perfect crosses slashed into their tops.

'Char siu bao!' said Madeleine.

The man smiled and offered the basket. 'Would you like a bun? My wife made them this morning.'

'Yum! Yes, please!' Madeleine took one and bit into the soft, white dough. Glossy sauce oozed out from the middle onto her fingers. The bun was warm and comforting and tasted like dinners in Chinatown with Teddy and her dad.

'Thank you! I'm Madeleine,' she said, trying to ignore the fact that Gert was staring at her. 'I love these buns.'

'I am James Chan,' said the man. He had broad cheekbones and a deep smile, with a gap between his teeth that made him look handsome. 'And this is my wife, Wong Ting Lei.' The woman nodded and smiled.

Aunt Hen was still looking out the window. Despite her earlier claim to want to travel with *the people*, in practice she sat in silence, staring at nothing and no one.

<hr />

The house, when they returned, was unusually calm. Bea sat by herself at the piano, flicking through music sheets. Charlie, Imo and Millie had gone for a ride with Nanny, and the other adults, including the servants, seemed to have dissolved in a puff.

'I'm going to read my new periodicals,' said Aunt Hen. Lugging her cases up the stairs towards her bedroom, she disappeared too.

'I am bored rigid,' said Bea, yawning. 'I shall have a little rest. Send Elfriede up if she ever gets home.'

'Aunt Hen bought you a copy of *Table Talk*,' said Madeleine.

Bea sat up. 'Oh, wonderful! That will revive me. I'll fetch it from her.'

'I might go for a walk,' said Madeleine. 'Stretch my legs.'

'Do you mind if I stay?' asked Gert. 'I'm tired.'

Madeleine was secretly relieved. They had reached that lovely stage of comfort with each other where they could be apart. Madeleine and Nandi were like that.

Madeleine shucked her hat and gloves, stashing them behind an urn outside the front door; then she headed straight down the front steps and started running. She hadn't expected country life to be so inactive. Playing cricket the other day had left Madeleine longing to play with Nandi and Teddy; to smash them. It had reminded her that she was Mum Crum's wriggly girl – a wriggly girl who loved to stretch and pound and run in nothing but shorts and a singlet.

Madeleine held up her skirt and ran, up through the bush, jumping over branches and pushing through bracken. She ran until she could hardly breathe, the sharp mountain air punching her lungs; ran until she could feel her muscles tough under her tights. Then she walked back down the hill, self-conscious but calm, hoping nobody had seen her. She could smell her sweat pushed up through the neck of her dress with each step. It may not have been ladylike, but she felt so alive.

Madeleine passed over the creek again and, not quite ready to return, walked the long way back, up around the house. Passing the stables, she discovered Percy brushing down a dumpy little pony, whistling as he worked. '*Toow wooooo.*'

She hadn't been in the stables before. Unlike her sisters, Gert didn't seem to be much of a horserider.

Bridles and saddles hung in a leathery line above a floor of smooth mud bricks. There was a long row of low doors, behind which horses and ponies snorted as they chewed on hay. Madeleine recognised a few of the chestnuts from the carriage-ride to the picnic. There was a mattress in the corner, a neatly folded blanket at its end. A book, a chipped enamel cup and an iron lamp sat beside it on the top of an upturned bucket.

Percy stopped whistling as she walked in. The pony he was brushing snorted, and steam burst out of its broad, wet nose into the cold air. It had short, pale-grey hair, mottled like the marble on the fireplace in the drawing room.

Percy held a brush flat in the palm of his hand; he pulled it along the side of the pony rhythmically.

'Shhh,' he said to the pony in his deep, calm voice. 'It's just Madeleine.'

The pony nickered.

'You whistle like Imo!' said Madeleine.

'I hope not,' he said. 'I'm in tune. And the truth is she whistles like me.' He smiled. 'I gave her a possum as a pet, which Nanny didn't let her keep, and taught her some language, which Nanny has forbidden. Then I taught her how to whistle. Nanny doesn't like that either, but it was more difficult for her to take away. The tune does seem to get under some people's skin.'

Madeleine laughed. 'One tiny grain of sand in a sock can cause a blister. I like that.'

Percy laughed too. His face looked different, happy. He pulled the brush across the pony's swollen tummy. 'Miss Charlotte and Miss Imogen have just had a ride. You feeling better than when you first arrived with us, then?'

'Yes, thank you,' said Madeleine. 'I was wondering where everyone was. We've been in town.'

Percy didn't respond, and suddenly Madeleine felt a bit silly. All she could hear was the breath of the pony and the beat of the brush. She wanted to tell Percy about the monster meeting and the printing press, and ask him what he thought of federation. 'Would you like to vote, same as Aunt Hen?' she asked quietly.

Percy shook his head, his face hardening. 'Not allowed to. They threw me off my home. Not black enough to stay with my people, too black to vote. Anyway, what's the point if nobody listens?'

Percy started pulling the brush across the pony's chest. The pony kicked out at him and he slapped it above the leg. 'Stop, you little bugger.' He turned to Madeleine. 'You want a turn with the brush?'

'Yes, please.' Madeleine smiled. Percy handed her the brush, and she ran it along the pony's heaving tummy.

'That's the way. That way,' said Percy. 'Same direction as the hair, and there's no trouble.'

He turned to pick up a tin bucket and opened a sack of oats. For a man who looked to be in his thirties, there was a slowness to his movements. And in the gaps of their conversation, in the silence, Madeleine could sense his hurt.

'Do you hate it here?' she asked softly.

Percy shrugged. 'At least I'm paid. Better than my last job. It was good at Coranderrk – not perfect, not always happy, but home. We worked; made it pay for itself. What did they do? Changed the law, threw us off for being "half-castes", left only fifteen men behind. Not enough to keep the station going. Not close.'

Madeleine shuddered.

'The Elders used to get us kids to help write all their letters. When they kicked us young blokes off, they took the writers from the speakers, crippled our lot so we can't talk to the authorities.' Percy shook his head and poured a cup of oats into the bucket.

Madeleine felt a wind rip through the stables. It came in through the gaps between the wooden walls. Thinking of Percy being thrown from his home made it difficult to breathe.

'We're a bit alike, aren't we, Percy?' she said, thinking of how she herself was stuck back in the past and couldn't do a thing to change it. 'Both away from our homes; both lost.'

Percy put down the bucket. 'No, miss. We're not. Not at all,' he said slowly. He took the brush from her hand. 'Go along, now – head back up to the house. It's cold in here.'

He tipped his dented hat at her and turned back to the pony, shaking his head.

Madeleine took a deep breath. 'Percy? Your whistle? It's great.'

She turned and ran.

# Sherry soiree

When Madeleine returned to the house, having only just remembered on her way inside to fish her hat and gloves back out of the urn in which they'd been parked, she was very glad she *had* remembered, for she found Nanny in the drawing room holding up Gert's hands.

'How ever did you get so filthy, Miss Gertrude Williamson? You can't traipse through town – of all places – with black fingers. What on earth is it?'

Gert shrugged, looking lost for words.

'Soot,' came a voice from within the drawing room. It was Aunt Hen, speaking quickly before *The Hens' Convention* could turn into *The Hens' Confession*. Gert looked relieved. 'From the train, I suspect. Upstairs and wash it off quickly now, darling – otherwise it will get everywhere.'

Nanny turned to examine Imo's pink little fingers.

Madeleine held her hands, back in their gloves, behind her back and out of sight as she took a seat. To her right, four tin soldiers were lined up on the arm of the couch, crouching, guns at the ready. Charlie bobbed up from behind them just as Gert came back into the room, making Madeleine start.

'Master Charles Williamson is thrilled to see you girls again.' She smiled. 'Did you bring back any sweets? I've been through your bags, but I couldn't find any.'

'Sweets?' cried Imo.

'Charlie!' Gert pulled the paper cones from her pinafore (where they seemed to have been stashed since their purchase) and handed them to her sister. The paper had lost its crunch. 'They're to share.'

'I know!'

Millie emerged from beneath the couch. She jumped up at Gert, barking, and then ran about the room in tight circles, chasing her own tail.

'I didn't mean share with *Millie*,' called Gert.

Millie raced back to Gert and stuck her sniffing nose right up Gert's skirt.

'At least some things never change,' said Madeleine, giggling, thinking of all the rude dogs in her life at home.

'Sweets for me too?' yelled Imo, jumping about in much the same way as Millie.

Charlie put a lolly in Imo's mouth and then her own. Millie stared at Charlie, head cocked.

Charlie took another lolly from the cone and pretended to throw it to the right. Millie tore off, yapping as she hurled herself at a small table while Imogen screamed.

'*Miss Charlotte!*' cried Nanny from the doorway. 'How often do I have to tell you that Millie is not allowed in the house?' Nanny then looked at Hen Pen. She couldn't say, *Why didn't you keep them in check?* but Madeleine could tell that she wanted to.

Madeleine squirmed in her seat. The room was too small for disapproval in that sort of measure – that quantity of disapproval required its own space.

Fortunately, Elfriede broke the moment by strolling into the room, a teacup and saucer in her hand. She took a seat in a chair beneath a fringed lamp. Nanny excused herself from the room.

Elfriede smiled. 'I have missed you. Did you have fun?' The girls nodded.

Elfriede took her teacup from the armchair to the piano, placing the saucer primly on the top.

'Bea!' she called loudly. 'The girls are back. Join me, Bea, do.'

Bea was at the doorway in an instant. 'We have been waiting for you, Elfriede! Where on earth were you?' She took a seat at the piano next to her cousin.

Aunt Hen watched them sitting together on the piano stool. 'What about Gertie?' she asked. 'She's playing *Minuet in G* extremely well now.'

'No, thank you,' said Gert, going to sit next to Aunt Hen on the couch and picking up Aunt Hen's periodical, flicking through the first pages.

Bea and Elfriede looked at each other, nodded, breathed in and began. The song rippled. Their four hands jumped up and down the keyboard, up and down, up and down, barely crossing one another. Elfriede was flushed, her eyes bigger and rounder and shinier than usual. The little teacup on top of the piano tinkled, hitting the saucer as the piano played.

There was an elegance to both of them – Bea and Elfriede. It wasn't just their fingers, it was the way their arms and their bodies moved too, in time with the music – Bea's less dramatically than Elfriede's, but still moving.

'Bravo!' Mr Williamson stood in the doorway. 'That was superb, truly superb. It brought me from my study!'

There was something very panto about Mr Williamson these last few days. His happiness seemed somehow exaggerated. He reminded Madeleine of her own father when he stood up and clapped extra loudly at her school plays – *Encore, encore!* – even if Madeleine was just an extra, and the orchestra was two bars in front of the choir, and the lead actor had conjunctivitis (which had happened once).

Mr Williamson moved over to the piano and placed a sharp elbow on it. 'What a shame I have a meeting this evening. I really can't move it. I tell you what, though, why don't we have a soiree tomorrow evening?'

'A soiree?' said Bea.

'Just the household. I shall have Bella organise it. No, actually, I'll ask her to invite some people along. Perhaps the Wilkinsons and the Purveses. I know society's quite thin around here at this time of year, but the Purveses may enjoy it.'

'Not tomorrow, darling, as I have my Friends of the Spirit World meeting, but later next week we could manage it.' Mrs Williamson stood at the room's other doorway. Her face was pink.

Mr Williamson raised an eyebrow. 'The only meeting I despise more than Hen's drawing-room meetings for women.'

'Well, I should be honoured to attend your Friends of the Spirit World meeting, Bella, and to partake in a soiree,' said Elfriede, standing. She picked up her cup of tea and returned to her armchair. '*Prost*,' she said all breathily, as if the piano playing had quite winded her. Her big nutmeg eyes stared up over the edge of the cup.

'Cheers,' said Aunt Hen and took a sip from her sherry, the little glass reminding Madeleine of cut ice or diamonds.

'I love to watch you have a sherry, Hen,' said Mr Williamson. 'Especially at this hour of the day. It reminds me that for all your faults – and they are numerous – you're at least not caught up with that frightful Women's Christian Temperance Union. Damned Americans. At least you are a suffragist who doesn't protest port.'

'Anything in moderation, Thomas,' said Aunt Hen.

'Will you be joining us for dinner this evening, dear?' asked Mrs Williamson looking at Mr Williamson. The *dear* was forced, stuck on the end of the question like a sticker on a car's bumper bar.

'Yes,' said Mr Williamson. 'I hadn't planned to, but why not. It's not every day one has family visiting all the way from Europe. Business can wait.'

'*Now* business can wait, can it?' asked Aunt Hen. She looked back to her book, eyebrows raised.

'Perhaps you ought to learn to play the piano as majestically as Elfriede and Bea, Henrietta. Now *that* would be a useful way to spend a lady's time.'

'So when will the soiree be, Daddy?' asked Bea. 'How about Wednesday?'

'Thursday. Thursday would suit,' said Mr Williamson. 'Can you manage that, Bella?'

Mrs Williamson twisted her wedding ring and nodded.

The soiree never happened, however, as the next morning, Mrs Williamson didn't rise from her bed.

# Steak-and-kidney life

꧁꧂

The next morning, Nanny allowed Madeleine and Gert, as 'the older girls', to take their breakfast in the morning room with the adults again. 'Manners,' she said, 'are terribly important, and breakfast is a wonderful way to test them.'

*It's just breakfast*, thought Madeleine, wondering how Nanny would take being handed a box of UP&GO on the way to school. Still, the room had a large, round table placed in a huge bay window overlooking the croquet lawn, so it was a bright and attractive place to eat. More attractive than, say, the backseat of Madeleine's mum's car.

Elfriede greeted Gert and Madeleine brightly as they entered the morning room, and then went back to chatting with Bea. Their voices were low and intimate, their conversation as tight as two fingers of a KitKat.

The two girls took a seat across the table from Mr Williamson. 'Good morning,' he said as he helped himself to a piece of toast from a silver rack in the middle of the table.

There was a tension about him, a stiffness. For all of his big gestures and floppy hair, he was a man of columns and angles. A moustache sat thickly on his upper lip, almost but not quite concealing a fine scar. He had a small mole high on his cheek beneath one eye. It was the sort of spot Madeleine expected to find on a woman – a woman like Elfriede; a spot as perfect and peaked as a chocolate chip.

'Is Bella coming down?' Aunt Hen looked up from the newspaper she was reading.

'I think Mrs Williamson is taking breakfast in her room,' said Anna.

Gert looked worried. Aunt Hen smiled at her. 'She'll join us later! It's her Friends of the Spirit World meeting this evening.'

'Oh, that will be sure to bring her down!' Gert grinned back at Hen.

'It's terribly fashionable at the moment in Europe too,' Elfriede interjected, breaking off her conversation with Bea momentarily to do so.

Elfriede was like Madeleine's mother, thought Madeleine – quite able to listen to two things at once.

'It's utter tosh,' said Mr Williamson with a succinct smile, which caused the scar near his moustache to stretch white.

'I find it quite interesting,' said Elfriede and smiled cheekily. 'Anyway, how does it work here?'

'Don't get involved, Elfriede,' said Mr Williamson. 'Those ladies never stop talking, ghastly mob of church bells that they are.'

'A medium comes to the house and tries to contact people who have *passed to the other side*,' explained Aunt Hen, ignoring her brother.

'It's trickery and wickedness to play on the feelings of bereaved parents,' said Mr Williamson crossly. 'Don't put me in a foul temper now, Hen.'

Mr Williamson's voice was snappy but his eyes were bright with something Madeleine couldn't quite name. He shot a look over the table towards Elfriede and Bea, who were once more locked in their own little huddle.

'It brings Bella comfort,' said Aunt Hen, pushing her glasses further up her nose. 'Besides, it's not just women; every politician seems to be doing it now, Thomas. Just look at your chum, Alfred Deakin. Perhaps I shall become a medium – it's a jolly good way to power!'

'Deakin always was a bit balmy on the crumpet with this sort of thing.' Mr Williamson took a bite of toast. 'He practises vegetarianism, too.' He smiled fondly.

'My mum's a vegetarian,' said Madeleine, and then wished she hadn't. The sentence hovered above the table like a fart.

Mr Williamson said, 'Well then,' and placed a curl of butter on the side of his plate. Only Aunt Hen smiled at Madeleine; then she went back to reading the paper. Her long fingers rubbed her left eyebrow while she concentrated.

Madeleine stared at the stretches of cutlery before her. She followed Gert's manners closely as the meal commenced, as she did at every meal, determined not to stumble this time. It was like a military procession, or even like the household itself: everything had a role, and everybody seemed to know the rules. Gert had said the adults' evening meal was even worse – held at the big table in the dining room, with an endless number of tiny courses, and an endless line of glasses, too. You needed a manual to get through a Victorian meal.

'So, Hen, anything in the good *Argus* this morning?' Mr Williamson said after a while.

'There is very little of interest covered in your paper, Thomas.'

'And what would you cover?'

Madeleine watched while Mr Williamson stirred his coffee, his fingers seeming too long for the spoon.

'When a husband dies and his wife discovers their children are to be left in the care of his sister rather than with their very own mother, I want proper analysis. When women are paid as little as one-third of the male wage, even where they may be the sole breadwinner for the family, I expect proper analysis. We women have tried to influence our men indirectly for centuries, but the laws are still unjust – and how can women not have occupied a single seat at any of your constitutional conventions?'

'Oh, Hen,' said Mr Williamson, 'you could make a stuffed bird laugh. Please, it is too early to talk about politics, even for me.' He went back to reading his own paper.

'Well, then don't ask, Thomas!'

'You are a woman – and I use that term loosely – who never takes the last piece of toast but must always have the last word.'

The two siblings went back to their respective papers in a sort of good-humoured truce.

Madeleine felt the napkin on her lap slide onto the floor. *Damn.* The napkins were laundered soap-smooth. She bent down to collect it. Across the table, beneath the embroidered folds of cloth, Elfriede's skirts were pressed hard against Mr Williamson's leg. Madeleine snapped back up to the table, a noise escaping her throat before she could snatch it back. Everybody stared.

'Are you all right, dear?' asked Aunt Hen.

'Yes, yes, excuse me,' Madeleine blustered. 'My tea went down the wrong way.' The lie felt oily in her mouth.

Gert slipped another soldier of buttered bread to Millie, who was fattening at her feet.

Madeleine stared at Elfriede through the parallel slices of toast on the rack in front of her. Elfriede was twisted away from Mr Williamson towards Bea, with whom she was still whispering. Sometimes she laughed much too loudly, throwing her head back until Madeleine could see the white points of her teeth. Next to her, Mr Williamson's eyes scanned lines in his newspaper, moving backwards and forwards across the print like wipers. Before them, their eggs sat whole and pearly on their plates. How could anybody guess that they were woven like a Christmas wreath under the table?

Madeleine studied the curls of orange peel suspended in the marmalade. She had always thought that as she grew up she'd come to understand more about the world, but she was coming to realise that the more she understood about life at Lyrebird Muse, the more she had to pretend not to. Life may have looked pie-perfect on the surface, but there was steak and kidney under the crust, and growing up here seemed to be about loading up your plate anyway.

Madeleine shook her head and looked over at Gert again. Gert was in turn eyeing the uneaten eggs, heaping her plate with spoonfuls of jam.

# *Secrets*

**W**hen they had finished breakfast, Nanny ushered
the children outside. 'It's grey, but it hasn't rained
since last night, and I'd like you all to get some fresh air.'
Fresh air was one of the things people seemed very keen on
in the olden days.

Someone had set up a series of white iron loops upside
down in the grass on the croquet lawn. The morning was
cold, and the lawn was damp with frost.

'Croquet!' cried Gert, picking up a square-tipped mallet.
'Come on, Madeleine, you'll enjoy this.'

Imo was crunching down the gravel path that formed the
eastern border of the lawn. *Step-hop, step-hop, step-hop* —
she was practising skipping, concentrating, her head on the
side. Charlie, as usual, had vanished; Nanny had gone off
to find her.

Madeleine picked up one of the heavy wooden mallets
and hit a ball with it. As it made contact, there was a lovely
deep crack.

'Like this,' said Gert, angling a mallet between her legs.
'You hit it like this.' She'd hitched her skirts up above her
knees.

Madeleine adjusted her grip and hit the ball again. This time, it shot right through one of the iron arches and rolled to a stop.

'Good show!' called Gert. 'That does take the egg.'

Madeleine laughed, and Imo laughed too. Her mouth gleamed filling-silver.

'Imo,' said Gert, 'what's in your mouth?'

'Nussing,' Imo replied, looking to the side. Her mouth was clearly full of something.

'Imo, what's in your mouth? Spit it out now.' Gert went over to her sister and held out her hand, and Imo spat a coin onto it. It was Madeleine's ten-cent piece. Madeleine dropped her mallet.

'Where did you get this?' demanded Gert.

'What is it? Is it from Daddy's collection?'

'You got it from the nursery, didn't you? Don't go near our things, Imo. This isn't yours. Now, where are the rest?'

'Elfriede says every decent lady has secrets.' Imo tilted her chin at Gert, but then she looked down and opened one closed fist, revealing a sticky collection of coins that she tipped into Gert's waiting hand.

'Miss Gertrude? What's going on? Is Miss Imogen all right?' Nanny had materialised on the edge of the crocket lawn, where she stood with her hands on her hips, as round as a sugar bowl.

Imo's eyes had begun to water, and her nose quivered.

'It's nothing, Nanny,' Gert said, pocketing the coins in her pinafore quick as lightning. 'Imo just had something in her mouth again.'

'Miss Imogen, come here, please. You can come inside and play with the doll's house in the nursery.' Nanny had on her cross face.

Imogen walked towards her, head hung, her hands holding onto her pinafore, and the two of them walked back up the stairs to the house.

'That was too close!' said Madeleine as soon as she and Gert were alone again.

'Tell me about it. Thank goodness she can't read yet – fortunately Nanny's a lousy teacher, and Imo is showing no aptitude as a student.'

'Here, give them to me.' Madeleine slipped the coins down the inside of one stocking. Her heart was beating hard. She'd left the coins with her clothes from home, which she'd taken from behind the doll's house the night of her arrival and hidden in the bottom of the cupboard in the nursery. Gert had stuffed the sparkly shoes in there as well after the midnight trip to the grotto. They had stupidly imagined these secret things would be safe there.

'I'll get rid of them, Gert,' she said. 'The coins – I'll toss them all in the well. It's too risky.'

Madeleine lined up a ball and hit it. It puddled off to the side, missing the iron arch.

'You can do better than that,' said Gert. 'I saw you play cricket.'

Madeleine stood up straight and leant on her stick. 'Gert,' she said. 'This can't go on. I'm going to get caught out, and I'm scared.'

'I know,' said Gert. 'That could have ended very badly. At least it was Imo and not Charlie who found the coins. Charlie might have blackmailed us.'

A slater wobbled across a stone beside Madeleine's boot. Madeleine pressed the tear ducts in the corner of each eye and breathed deeply.

'Don't cry,' said Gert, handing her a crumpled handkerchief. She hugged Madeleine, a soft, kind hug. 'I have an idea.'

Gert poked the slater with her boot. It contracted in a tight ball.

'What is it?' Madeleine just wanted to run and hide.

'Tonight is Mummy's Friends of the Spirit World meeting. You heard the grown-ups talking about it at breakfast. The meetings are held at a different person's home every month. Mummy hosts them once a year, and they're dreadfully important to her. She'll get to those meetings even if she's having a spell.'

Gert bit a fingernail.

'Spirits as in ghosts?' Madeleine asked.

'That's right. It's to do with the lost ones, I think.'

'What do you mean the lost ones?'

'The babies that died. Baby Robert, Baby Sebastian and Baby Reginald. Robert and Sebastian only lasted a few hours. They came after Bea. Little Reggie came after Charlie. He died when he was eleven months old, of measles – he was the baby in Hen Pen's photo.'

'You had three brothers and they *died*?'

Madeleine felt as if a little key had just been handed to her, unlocking some of Mrs Williamson's sadness. She wished she had focused on the baby in the photo a little longer, taken more of him in.

Gert shrugged. 'It happens,' she said softly. 'But Reggie was so tiny and soft and pink, and he had such chubby wrists. It's hard to let yourself love something that small when you know it could die. Even when I was six, I knew that. You push against it so you don't get hurt, but the hurts gets in anyway.'

Madeleine looked out into the middle distance. She could see the lake in the distance, pewter in the sunlight.

'And your mother's spirit group – what do they do?' she asked.

'A medium calls on spirits, and Mummy says she has actually held Reggie, felt his bonny weight – and she's smelt his baby hair, too; that delicious milky smell. Even Millie had that smell, when she was a puppy.'

'Have you been to a meeting before?'

'No. They're a group of just eight, mainly ladies. And I'm too young to go. Come on, let's put these in the well.'

Madeleine trailed after Gert as she set off. 'And your father doesn't go? How about Aunt Hen?'

'Daddy gets angry about it – usually much angrier than this morning. He says the meetings are hogwash, and he walks around reciting Browning's *Mr Sludge, "The Medium"*.

*'Then, it's so cruel easy! Oh, those tricks*
*'That can't be tricks, those feats by sleight of hand,*
*'Clearly no common conjuror's!—no indeed!*

'But Mummy's fascinated by it all. She hasn't spoken to the babies, because they couldn't speak when they went to Heaven, but Mrs White spoke to her late husband, who told her where he'd buried the family silver, and she had the gardener dig up the spot and low and behold, it was all there – still in its blue velvet bag, under the azaleas.'

'Why did he bury it?' Madeleine asked, confused. Mrs White sounded like she'd married a labrador.

Gert shrugged. 'I've no idea. They've always been a bit puzzling, the Whites.'

Madeleine stopped walking to roll a lemon on the grass with her foot. Its underside was green and furry. 'So . . . if the medium can talk to people from the past, do you think he or she can talk to people from the future, too?'

'She. I've certainly never heard of a male medium! But anyway, *yes*, that's exactly what I've been wondering. As well as, more importantly, whether she can take people from the future home.'

'I think we need to sneak into the meeting tonight and find out, don't you?'

Madeleine grinned and gave the lemon a good, hard kick. It shot off into the garden.

The girls walked on until they found themselves at the well with its old iron bucket. The water inside it was

Wizard-of-Oz green. Madeleine took the coins from her stocking.

Gert grabbed one and held it over the water. 'I was going to suggest cementing these to the grotto, but we can't possibly do that now. This is perfect. It's bottomless, and it's never cleaned.' She dropped it. The splash echoed about the mossy well chamber.

'Don't tell me it's never cleaned,' said Madeleine. 'We drink from it!' *Anyway, in years to come these coins will blend in with all the tourists' wish coins*, she thought.

Madeleine flipped the rest of the coins into the water. They split the surface and sank without a trace.

'At least my wax death mask won't be lined up on the shelf next to Ned Kelly's,' said Madeleine. 'I was worried I'd be hunted down as a witch if anybody found them.'

'We really must secure your passage home. Will you come to Mummy's meeting?'

Gert looked at Madeleine earnestly, and Madeleine smiled. 'It's worth a try. At this stage, anything is worth a try.'

A deep cough came from behind them, and girls both jumped. It was Percy, wearing a dark patched jacket, with a brown woollen sack knotted over his shoulder.

'You need to get Madeleine home? I need to get home too. So there is something we share now, Madeleine – I grant you that.'

'Percy!' Madeleine smiled with relief. She'd felt so stupid after the stables. 'Where are you off to?'

'I've handed in my notice.'

'Your notice?' said Gert. 'But . . . you've been with us for, well, forever. Does Daddy know?'

'Yes, Miss Gertrude. Your father does know.' Percy took off his hat and smiled. He face looked sunny and his eyes shone like polished stones.

'Why now, Percy?' asked Madeleine. 'Why after all this time?'

'Nothing's right. I want to be with my family.'

'I thought you were an orphan!' Gert almost shouted.

'I am. My Coranderrk family, Miss Gertrude. The people from where I grew up. They've all gone on to New South Wales, now – on to Cummeragunja. I want to be with my people. It's time.'

'But how will you get there? You can't have the fare for the train.' Gert looked worried.

'Walk!' Percy glanced down at his boots. The leather top of one had come away from the sole and his grey sock poked out.

'Are you mad? Do you have any idea how far it is to New South Wales?' Gert frowned.

'Thank you, Miss Gertrude, but I do. If our Ngurungaeta, William Barak, can walk a petition to Melbourne as an elderly man, I can make it to Cummera on these legs.'

Madeleine smiled. She felt light and free. 'Good luck!'

'Thank you, Miss Madeleine. To you too. I told Miss Imogen goodbye earlier, but will you farewell Miss Charlotte for me?'

'And Nanny? Shall we wish her farewell?' Gert asked Percy cheekily.

'No. There's no need, Miss Gertrude, no need for that at all.'

Percy winked as he put on his hat. Then he headed off down the drive, his footsteps crunching the gravel, whistling, '*Toow wooooo*,' as he walked.

# Coming, ready or not

That afternoon was as grey as the morning had been. Bored, Madeleine and Gert tiptoed into the drawing room, avoiding Nanny.

The dining room chairs had been brought in and were all facing a card table, which was covered with a cloth. Three photographs were placed upon it, each depicting a baby with hard black eyes. The first two showed Mrs Williamson nursing one baby and then another; in the third, yet another baby lay on a tiny chaise lounge, three little girls sitting behind it.

'Is that you?' asked Madeleine in a low voice.

'Yes,' said Gert weakly. 'Bea, Charlie, me and Reggie. That was taken just after he died.'

'He was *dead* in the photo? Why are his eyes open?'

'They paint them on. It's so we'll always remember him. Don't you do that?'

'No! We don't take photos of dead children. I'm not even sure it's legal. I suppose the other babies with your mum are Robert and . . .'

'Sebastian. Yes. Memento mori, they call them.'

Anna was at the back of the room, setting out the tea service on a credenza: two silver pans of fruit cake covered with a damp cloth, a milk jug and a sugar bowl.

'What time does it start tonight, Anna?' asked Gert loudly, heading towards the credenza, probably intending to help herself to a piece of cake. Madeleine followed, willing to travel any distance for Cook's cake.

'Not until after nursery tea, Miss Gertrude,' said Anna in a sterner voice than usual, 'but I'm anxious to have it all set up. It's dreadfully important to your mother. Please do stay out of the way – no meddling and *no* eating.'

Gert nodded and directed Madeleine to the side of the room.

'Where's the best place to hide tonight, do you think?' Madeleine whispered, looking about. For such a large space, there were remarkably few places to hide. 'It's all pretty exposed.'

'Behind the curtains,' said Gert.

'But won't we be visible from outside? What if your father walks by?'

Madeleine could just imagine Mr Williamson's reaction if he saw them spying. After the grotto, he would be likely to drag them out by their plaits.

'Not the curtains on the windows – the curtains under the window seat.'

Gert pointed towards the bay window, which nudged out onto the verandah behind it. This formed a little hexagonal nook, and an accompanying hexagonal seat was set beneath the windowpanes, looking rather like it had been cut with a Christmas cookie-cutter. A velvet curtain hung beneath the seat to the ground. Above were fattened cushions on which to sit and admire the view across the garden and down to the lake.

Just then, Nanny bossed her way into the room. 'Girls, outside! I'm not sure what you are thinking of, but do not loiter around the cake. Miss Imogen is in the playhouse, and Miss Charlotte is playing with Millie.'

Nanny ushered them out into the sunless afternoon. Charlie was on the verandah. She hurled a stick at Millie on the grass, and she, Gert and Madeleine watched as Millie sprinted off hare-quick to retrieve it, returned the stick faithfully, refused to hand it over and gnawed on it instead.

Charlie sighed. 'Come on, Gert and Madeleine, I think Millie's had enough of this game for now. She's rather like a wild man with a bone. Let's play hide-and-seek instead – it's so much better with more people. Besides, the other option is to play with Imo in the playhouse, and you know how bossy she is.'

Gert looked at Madeleine doubtfully, but Madeleine had some sympathy for Charlie. She remembered what it was like when Teddy and his friends had refused to play with her.

'Okay,' said Madeleine. 'But only if you'll be *it* first.'

Charlie sat down on the verandah floor with her back to the garden and began to count. Madeleine and Gert took one look at each other and ran.

'. . . fourteen, fifteen, sixteen, seventeen, eighteen . . .'

'Not quite so fast, Charlie!' yelled Gert over her shoulder. 'Or you'll need to count until a hundred at that pace.'

Although the garden no longer seemed as vast and mysterious as it had when Madeleine first arrived, she found it was still possible to look up and feel completely lost in parts of it. She followed Gert at first, then peeled off on her own.

'. . . twenty-four, twenty-five, twenty-six, twenty-seven . . .'

Madeleine crept around a tangle of bushes covered in pale sprays of waxen flowers, their deep-pink centres heavy with scent. *Daphne*. As she rounded one end of the bushes, Madeleine spotted a band of threadbare grass at her feet. Following it, she ducked under the daphne's canopy and found herself in a funnel of shiny foliage.

Madeleine crawled into the tunnel and lay propped on her elbows to rest. The light was splintered, green and peaceful through the boughs. It was a perfect hiding spot – she was almost completely concealed. Behind her, she heard a soft squeak, a breath, a sigh. Just as she turned to look, Gert and her petticoats came bumping inside.

Madeleine pressed her hands to her mouth to trap her giggles. Gert flapped her broad wrists towards Madeleine, motioning Madeleine onward. *It gets bigger*, she mouthed.

Madeleine wriggled forward. It was still too low to walk, so she crawled, the ground beneath her wet with composting leaves. She came to a bend, and beyond it a hollow space lined with low seats made from stone slabs covered with bright-green moss.

Madeleine stopped short. Her fingers gripped mulch. Gert, who had crawled up beside her, stopped too. Their eyes met. Neither of them breathed.

On a stone bench at the back of the hollow sat Elfriede and Mr Williamson. One arm was slung about the back of the bench behind Elfriede, hanging down behind her like the empty sleeve of a jacket. The other was harnessing her bare neck. Elfriede's fingers were looped in his braces, and their heads were bent in whispering kisses. The knees of his pants were scabby with broken pieces of bracken, and the little mole under his eye jiggled. Even in the filtered green light of the hollow, he glowed golden.

Madeleine didn't want to stare, to spy, but she couldn't look away. Her heart beat hard. Gert was crouched on all fours. She looked like she had been snap-frozen.

'*Schatz*? Is that how I say it?' Mr Williamson kissed Elfriede's forehead and bubbled kisses along her cheekbone. Madeleine thought she might vomit.

'Ah, Thomas, you tickle, your moustache,' tinkled Elfriede.

'. . . fifty-six . . . fifty-seven . . . fifty-eight . . . fifty-nine . . .' Charlie's numbers broke through the canopy as she came towards them.

Madeleine grabbed Gert and pushed backwards and backwards through the hooded bush, through snapped sticks and slimy moss, until she broke into the light, pulling Gert out behind her.

The two of them ran across the garden and into the empty tree. Safe within its walls, they huddled together, breathing in the smell of softened timber. Madeleine leant back and looked up the trunk at the sky, mute.

'. . . ninety-eight, ninety-nine, one hundred. *Coming-ready-or-not!*'

Madeleine bit her nail, trying to crush the memory of golden skin, that flop of hair and those kisses. She could taste daphne and compost on her finger.

She looked at Gert and tried to think of something to say, of something to make it better; but in the cool, quiet privacy of the empty tree, Gert was crying. She looked baggy and desperate and sad, and there was nothing that Madeleine could do.

# *Friends of the Spirit World*

The girls re-entered the house quietly just before nursery tea. The house felt heavy, and Madeleine found her breaths were still coming short and shallow.

Aunt Hen was writing at a little desk tucked away in one corner of the drawing room, dipping her pen into an inkwell set into the desktop. There was a pile of envelopes beside her.

'Are Mummy and Daddy in?' Gert didn't mention Elfriede.

'I assume so,' murmured Aunt Hen, sealing a letter with a great glob of deep-red wax and then pressing it with a round bronze seal. 'But you heard the gong. Wash your hands for nursery tea. With Bella's gathering on tonight, and Percy's departure, everyone's in a state.'

'Will he be all right, Aunt Hen?' Gert looked earnest.

'Percy? I should think so. He comes from a strong, political people. I think it was very brave of him to go.'

Soon afterwards, the girls sat around a meal of grey mutton in a pool of water and fat. It was all salty and overcooked. Dessert was a heavy, bland pudding. Like the curtains and the wallpaper in this house, there was just too much heaviness and not enough bok choy.

Madeleine and Gert moved silently on to the nursery after they'd eaten. It wasn't a comfy silence, a silence of friends – it was a slicing silence. A silence that seemed to divide the air between them.

Madeleine smoothed down her bedspread and sat on it. 'Can we still go tonight?' she asked. 'Do you mind?'

Gert didn't respond. Madeleine's eyes pinched. Fat tears rolled down her cheeks. *It's useless, it's useless. What the fig am I going to do?*

She didn't think she'd ever felt a loss this bruising and enormous. It was even bigger than the departure of her father all those years ago, for it was keeping him from her more definitively than any divorce ever could have – and not just him, but her mum, Teddy, Mum Crum, Nandi . . . everyone and everything.

While Madeleine was fairly sure the medium would not be able to whisk her back to the future, *perhaps* she could, and while there was a chance, even a very slim one, it was worth fighting for – but it was hard to explain to Gert why she needed to leave her and get home so desperately, especially when Gert was feeling so sad.

Madeleine climbed into her bed, her body leaden, defeated.

Some hours later, the nursery clock chimed. Just seconds later, the air was animated by the sound of hooves echoing about the garden like gunfire.

Madeleine went to the nursery's little window and looked down. Below her, carriages and cars rolled in, and women with hats as big as birthday cakes rolled out.

'We're going,' whispered Gert, standing beside Madeleine in bare feet.

'We're what?'

'I am *not* going to do nothing. I am *not* going to just sit up here and sulk. Daddy thinks Mummy's Friends of the Spirit World meetings are rubbish, and so *we* are going. It's the only thing to do. Blow it.'

Madeleine gave Gert a hug.

'Sorry,' Gert sniffed. 'I've been a monster.'

'Don't be silly – it's been a perfectly horrid day.'

'Perfectly horrid?' Gert smiled. 'What happened to *the worst ever*? You're starting to speak like one of us.'

Madeleine hugged her again.

'Now run!' hissed Gert. 'If we're going to do this, we've got to get under the window seat before Anna ushers the guests inside, or we'll have no chance.'

⟨⟨⟨⟨

The girls managed to skid down the servants' staircase and hurl themselves beneath the window seat's skirting just in the nick of time. The material was still swinging slightly as the first of the now hatless women entered the drawing room and helped themselves to cups of tea by the fireplace. From this position, the girls could see the side of the card table, which had been set up just in front of the window seat, as well as the lines of empty chairs to their right.

'How *do* they get hair to stay like that?' whispered Madeleine as she peered out into the room from beneath the skirting. The curled hair artfully heaped upon various women's heads looked like wigs.

'Tongs and irons,' Gert whispered back. 'And they bulk it up with horsehair pads.'

Mrs Williamson was there, in a dress the colour of cooked spinach, introducing Elfriede to the visitors.

'Oh, I am terribly interested,' Elfriede was saying in her singsong voice, 'and terribly grateful to be included. My darling cousin and her family have been so generous.'

Everyone was looking at her, fascinated, and Madeleine wondered if they'd be just as interested in a foreigner if she were ugly. She watched Elfriede — watched Elfriede pretend — for another few minutes; then she dropped the skirting back to the ground, erasing Elfriede from her sight. It was all such an *act*.

Beneath the window seat, the two girls could lie down quite comfortably on their tummies so long as they kept their knees bent, feet just brushing the back of the bench. Their heads were almost touching.

Gert lifted the skirt up a smidge again, then gripped Madeleine's hand and squeezed it. In the crack beneath the material and the floor, two square-toed shoes bloomed into view, the soles worn down deeply on each side. Maroon stockings caught on thin ankles. There was a snag in one, just above the tongue on one shoe, but the stocking hadn't run yet.

Next to the shoes, a carpet bag with a black leather handle dropped to the floor. Madeleine watched as two ropey hands pulled a rock, a candle, matches, salt in a little silver shaker, a flower, and a copy of the Bible without a spine from the bag, quickly and neatly. The fingers on the hands were threaded with rings, like quoits pegs.

Finally, Madeleine watched the ringed hand pull a large glass sphere about the size of a tennis ball from the bag.

'It's a crystal ball! This is classic stuff,' Madeleine whispered to Gert. Through the crystal, she had caught a wavering glimpse of the seats in front of the card table filling with guests, the whole view strangely shrunken through the ball.

*Teddy and Raj would love this*, Madeleine thought. They were obsessed with spirits. Teddy said that there really was such a thing as spirits, including spirits who communicated with their loved ones via their computers after they'd died – especially in America.

Madeleine angled her head so she could look upwards into the room. The clairvoyant's head was bandaged in what looked like cheap sari silk. She turned sideways towards her bag again, flashing pale-blue eyes as clear as glass with a striking dark-grey ring around each iris. She had no eyelashes, and her eyebrows were drawn in two lines of thin dark pencil just beneath her turban. Her skin was as dry and lined as a Cruskit cracker.

The woman had placed everything from the bag in a row on the table, alongside the memento mori photographs Anna had laid out earlier. She lit the candle with the exaggerated strike of a match.

Madeleine could hear the clipping sound of shoes on parquetry as the last of the guests took their spots. The woman sat down calmly in the chair that had been provided for her behind the card table, like a child with all the answers in the front row of a classroom.

There was an exchange of nods between the medium and a tall woman in the audience (bobbing bun and bobbing turban), and then the tall woman stepped up to the table too.

'Good evening, and welcome to the Friends of the Spirit World's monthly gathering. We are very grateful to our hostess, a most dedicated member, Mrs Isabelle Williamson, for providing us with such a gracious venue here at Lyrebird Muse this evening.'

The woman coughed. Her voice was school-prefect perfect, and it bumped around the crowded room politely. She nodded at Mrs Williamson and then angled her body towards the card table.

'We are most fortunate to have Madame Blanche du Boisier here as our guest of honour this evening.'

The woman pronounced *du Boisier* like she had a mouth full of bubblegum.

'For those not familiar with Madame du Boisier's work, she is a medium of some repute, who has had substantial success engaging spirits, and we are thrilled to welcome her to the Friends of the Spirit World for what I hope will be the first of many sessions with our little group.'

She coughed, and then continued.

'Now I understand that Mrs Williamson's charming cousin, Frau von Fürstenburg, and Mr Williamson's sister, Miss Henrietta Williamson, will take the places of Mr and Mrs Angus King, who are unfortunately unable to join us this evening. We are comfortable, however, that this will not disturb the sensitivity of our usual little gathering, and I do hope you have taken the opportunity to ask Frau von Fürstenburg about her own experiences of spiritualism on the Continent.'

The woman looked at Elfriede and smiled, as did everyone else in the room, nodding and murmuring at the happy timing of her visit.

The words washed over Madeleine like notices at a school assembly, until at last the maroon stockings of Madame Blanche du Boisier straightened as she stood.

'Good evening. I am hoping that we will have some form of manifestation from the spirit world this evening.'

Her voice was as soft and sticky as marshmallow.

'Remember that these manifestations come in many forms. I have been privileged, in the past, to experience smells, voices and even touch – indeed from the left-hand side, which is most common. Of course, a spirit may be present and yet remain unknown to us. There are signs, however. When a candle flame burns blue, or a dog is agitated, it is likely a ghost is present.'

'Where is Millie when you need her?' whispered Gert.

'I have lit this candle,' Madame du Boisier went on, 'to be our guide. I have also brought quartz, for in my experience I have found our spirit friends to be very responsive to this mineral. Are we all comfortable?'

Madame du Boisier paused.

'Please join hands with your neighbour, with the little finger of each hand touching that of the person on either side of you. In the centre of the table, we will place the crystal ball. We will place the quartz on the Bible, together with a lily – the flower of death – to beckon good spirits. We have placed the saltcellar here, as salt thrown into a candle flame will drive away spirits should we need to.'

The room swelled with gentle laughter, releasing tension like a skewer in a cake. Madame du Boisier stomped one square-toed shoe.

'Do not laugh. Do not speak. The dead cannot laugh, and it offends them.'

Her head had an actor's tilt to it. She held her nose up to the ceiling and sniffed. She then moved her arms right up above her ears, moving and moving her hands in a circular motion as she swayed from the knee like a serpent.

She stomped, her feet square on the floor again. 'We have a stranger in the room. I can feel a presence very strongly.' She reached out and waved her arms about the candle flame. It burnt bright and yellow.

Gert gripped Madeleine's hand.

'A stranger from a distant land. A land where the sun is veiled and communication is furious and altogether strange, and men may be seen in one form and again in another.'

Gert's fingernails bit into Madeleine's wrist.

*Oh man*, thought Madeleine. *It's coded like a riddle, but she knows about email. She knows about TV. Thank goodness. Can she get me back?*

Madame du Boisier sat back down in her seat with a thud – as if someone had pushed her.

'I sense this person. Yes, yes, I sense this person.'

She sat very tall in her seat now, and began thrashing her arms about again, breathing in and out over the crystal ball, her mouth hanging open.

'It is *you*.' She stood and pointed. 'You – you sir, *you* with the finger-moustache. Yes, I see it now. Born of the Raj.'

Another woman squealed. 'How did you know?'

Madame du Boisier stood again, taller with confidence. 'He is born of the Raj, serving our Queen and country. And yet despite his foreign birth, he seeks friendship here, and a new life.'

'Definitely not me,' whispered Madeleine.

'He has come to seek his wife, who was born here, and who died in childbirth. Tessa? Tessa, is it? I hear her now. Tessa, is it you?'

The medium's voice had become froggy. She held the crystal ball like a steering wheel and looked up at the chandelier. 'Tessa, Tessa, he's here and he hears you . . . Sir, she asks whether you love her still; whether you love the dear children.'

'Tess, oh my darling Tess! Can she hear me?' the man cried. He stood, clutching the ends of his grey waistcoat.

Madame du Boisier stopped still, her nose pointed towards the ceiling again. 'She has left, she has left, but now there is another – another spirit. A young spirit.'

'A baby? Is it Reggie? Reggie, is it you, darling boy?'

Madeleine peeped out at Mrs Williamson. Her arms were outstretched, reaching, her soft face desperate. But Madame du Boisier ignored her, concentrating. Her brow pleated, as if the thin skin had been stitched.

'No, no, it is not Reggie.'

Mrs Williamson sagged in her seat.

Madame du Boisier gripped the tablecloth. The little table beneath her hands quivered.

'*Maths in the nursery*,' she piped. Her voice was higher now, and her accent had changed; she sounded like a singsong child.

'*Maths in the nursery*.

'*Simple sums, simple sums*.

'*They lost three boys, but gained a girl*.'

Madeleine stopped breathing. *Lost three boys* – Baby Reggie, Baby Robert and Baby Sebastian. *Gained a girl*. Was it Madeleine? Was Madeleine the girl? What did it mean?

Madame du Boisier's chin sank down against her chest and her voice deepened.

'*The lyrebird calls.*

'*The lyrebird calls.*

'*Calls by troubled waters.*'

Madeleine leant right forward, poised to net every word.

Madame du Boisier paused, and the room filled with a saturated silence that stretched on for minutes. Then her voice started again, even deeper than before, gravelly now.

'*Eine Cousine heißt ihn in ihrem Haus willkommen. Sie kokettiert. Sie kokettiert und er lächelt.*'

'She spoke Dutch. Dutch, was it?' whispered one of the men.

'No, it was German,' said Mrs Williamson in a voice as thin as apple juice.

'Nobody has done that before,' said a woman with high hair. 'We had Latin once, but never German.'

'What does it mean?' asked a woman wearing a black ruffled skirt.

'We need Charlie,' Gert whispered to Madeleine.

But Mrs Williamson turned to look at Elfriede. She looked hard at her cousin, and then she spoke.

'*A cousin welcomed into their home. She cocked her hat at him. She cocked her hat and he smiled.*'

The audience murmured. Hen shook her head slowly, looking from Mrs Williamson to Elfriede. She patted the part of her gown where her key hung around her neck, a pat slack with sorrow.

'*Er hilft eine Nation aufzubauen, während seine Familie zerbricht,*' intoned the medium.

'What was that? What was that?'

'*He helps build a nation while his own family crumbles,*' said Mrs Williamson, more quietly still.

Madeleine's eyes darted to Elfriede. Her face was pulled. She looked angry.

The medium rustled her skirts beneath the card table. 'Shhh, shhh, do not interrupt the spirits, please.'

Elfriede stood. Her back was straight, her face pink.

'I am not sure of the purpose of this, but I seem to fall on the side of Mr Sludge and Mr Browning,' she said curtly. 'Excuse me.'

The girls heard the strong beat of her boots as she crossed the drawing room towards the door. Mrs Williamson watched her go. Her mouth was calm, but the wrinkles around her eyes were deep. The room was full of whispers, buoyant with scandal.

'Serves her right,' hissed Gert bitterly. 'I hope she's never invited anywhere ever again.'

Madeleine studied Madame du Boisier, who was now sitting still in her chair, her stockinged feet on the floor, her gaze on the candle.

Eventually, the tall woman who had introduced the medium stood up, clearing her throat. 'Hmph, hmph. Well, may I suggest that we all convene to the morning room for a small break to allow Madame du Boisier to recuperate before we recommence?'

Anna slipped in and began stacking the tea things onto a small wooden cart to move them into the morning room.

One of the guests swung the door behind her wide open, but nobody else moved from their chair. A cold breeze ripped through the room, and the candle was extinguished. Blanche du Boisier was still.

For a long moment, the girls didn't move either. And then Gert reached up to the underbelly of the window seat.

*Knock, knock, knock.*

The knocking echoed eerily through the seat.

'Oooooh!' The room took a collective breath.

'Tessa? Tessa, is that you?' Madame du Boisier spoke sharply. 'Answer me with a knock, Tessa, dear Tessa. Is that you?'

Gert knocked again. *Knock.*

Madeleine looked at Gert and laughed. She smashed her hands against her mouth. She couldn't believe Gert had the gall to carry this out.

'Tessa, was that a cry? Are you wounded?' The medium put her fingers to her turban as if tuning a radio. Under the window seat, Madeleine was shaking her own head violently at Gert.

The room was library silent.

'Quick, quick, the candle, the candle.' Madame du Boisier re-lit the candle with one short, sharp strike of a match. The wick flared and hissed, and the flame fell soft and waxy-yellow.

'Do you hear us?' asked Madame du Boisier, wistful now. 'I am no longer sensing anything.' She put her head in her hands.

The tall woman with the bun leapt to her feet yet again and rushed to the front. 'We shall adjourn to the morning room now. The tea is being served. Just let me know when you are ready to reconvene, Madame du Boisier.'

'Yes, yes, but I don't think we will be. I think it would be best if we retired for the evening. I am terribly tired. There were so many spirits this evening, and so much anger. It was worrisome.'

Blanche du Boisier stood to pack her instruments of telling back into her bag. The tall woman stood by helplessly.

'Go! Go!' Blanche du Boisier shooed the woman away. 'I am sorry. I have failed you. Another time, another time.'

Mrs Williamson was the first to move, dragging herself to the doorway, smiling a smile that was turned off on the inside, only her manners and her corset holding her together now. 'Thank you so much for coming. We must have another soon. Goodnight, goodnight.'

*Poor Bella*, the faces of the guests said. *How frightful. What a dreadful woman to come between her and her family! To think! Foreigners!*

The room, with its equal parts vitriol and pity, emptied more quickly than water at the end of a bath – *slurp* – as the guests and their birthday-cake hats fled.

Gert could no longer contain herself. 'Poor, poor darling Mummy.' She lifted the window-seat skirt and rolled out into the room. Madeleine was right behind her.

Blanche du Boisier whirled around. 'What were you doing there? Were you interfering?'

For a woman in fancy dress, holding a crystal in one hand and a copy of the Bible without a spine in the other, she was pretty snappy.

'Something was interfering – and in front of such a gathering! Perhaps it was *you*?' Madame Blanche du Boisier pointed straight at Madeleine, with her quartz crystal.

Madeleine stood forward. 'Perhaps . . . perhaps you are correct; perhaps I was interfering.'

Blanche du Boisier stood still. 'How?'

'I'm not sure, but that's why we tapped on the window seat – to give you credibility.'

'Are you querying my gift?'

'No, no, I'm terribly sorry,' said Madeleine.

Blanche du Boisier looked like she might explode. And then she did. 'Get out of here instantly, before I call your mother. Out of here *now*.'

She fixed both Madeleine and Gert with a stare as tight as the jaws of a pit bull terrier.

The girls turned heel and ran.

# *Tea for two*

~~~~~

The next morning, Gert was particularly ratty. 'Put that down,' she shouted when Madeleine picked up her hairbrush. Gert went to breakfast alone, which was held in the room off the kitchen since none of the grown-ups had risen yet. She then glowered into her porridge and barely ate a thing, ignoring Madeleine and her questions – simple queries about what they might do that day.

'Miss Gertrude, Miss Madeleine is your guest. Please be polite,' Nanny reprimanded her.

'Both guests and fish go off in three days,' said Gert under her breath.

'Now, Miss Gertrude, it's not like you to be so beastly. What is the matter?' Nanny put down her spoonful of porridge. 'Are you feeling unwell? I have a tonic upstairs that I can fetch.'

Gert shook her head.

Madeleine couldn't really be angry with Gert, though. She had to concede that she felt much the same way herself – tired and angry and sad. Nothing had happened to her after last night. Nothing. All that drama, and she was still very much *here*. As was Elfriede.

She decided to give Gert a little space, following Charlie rather than Gert out of the room once the children were excused, leaving Gert angrily kicking at the leg of the table.

'Let's fetch Millie,' said Charlie. 'I'm teaching her to be a gun dog.'

'What's a gun dog?' asked Madeleine, wondering if she'd ever get used to hearing words she couldn't even begin to work out the meaning for.

'A hunting dog. Daddy says we have left our run rather late with the training, but Millie's as smart as paint, so it's my great hope she can still be trained to be a pointer.'

~~~~

An hour later, Gert had thawed. She came to find Madeleine in the drawing room.

'Charlie, do take Millie outside. There are pheasants in the garden!' Once Charlie had left to find her slingshot, she turned to Madeleine. 'I've decided to have a tea party. You can come if you'd like to. Cook has made cake, and she said that we may have some.'

'How exciting,' said Madeleine, relieved that Gert's anger towards her had abated, although secretly wondering whether a tea party wasn't something even Charlie was a bit old for. In some ways it seemed the kids had longer childhoods here. It was like developing physically earlier made you grow up earlier, too, even if you didn't in fact want to. It was weird to think that back home Madeleine had friends the same age as Gert who wore short, tight skirts and high heels and kissed boys. At home, Madeleine had always felt quite young for her age; here, sometimes she felt old.

Madeleine followed Gert upstairs to the nursery regardless. 'Who will you invite?' she asked as Gert pulled a tiny rose tea set from a cupboard.

'Mummy and Daddy.'

'Oh.' Madeleine stopped. 'Is that a good idea?'

'Yes. You'll see,' said Gert. 'They'll love it. Besides, I've already delivered the invitations.'

Gert covered a small table in the nursery with a white cloth that had deft cross-stitches in different colours all around the hem, and organised the tea set prettily. The girls rushed down to the garden to pick a few sprigs of daphne, which Gert put in one of the rose teacups in the centre of the table. And then they waited. The petals were already starting to brown.

'Do you think they'll come?' Madeleine straightened a teacup so that it sat in the centre of its saucer, its little rose facing the nursery door.

'I'm sure they will,' said Gert. 'My invitations were on gold embossed card, in my very neatest letters. It's hard to ignore preparation as thoughtful as that.'

'I'll just nip out to the toilet,' said Madeleine.

'It's perfectly adequate to excuse yourself. How many times do I need to remind you?' hissed Gert.

Madeleine returned upstairs to find that Mrs Williamson had arrived. She was lumped on a small stool, her bottom spread over the edges like a toadstool. Madeleine took the seat opposite her, and she smiled at Madeleine vaguely but barely had the strength, it seemed, to lift the corners of her mouth. She was still in her nightgown.

'Mummy, your wrapper's dangling.' Gert pointed at a fold of Mrs Williamson's embroidered bathrobe, which had slumped onto the floor. Mrs Williamson looked at the ivory silk without reacting.

Mr Williamson walked through the door not long after. He looked at Mrs Williamson, blinked, pulled out his fob watch, clicked his tongue and started to turn around.

'Daddy!' Gert leapt up. 'Do come in and sit down.' And she ushered him firmly to a little chair, making it clear that there was not going to be a quick getaway – not without a massive scene, which would mean the getaway would be neither quick nor comfortable.

Gert sat her father down next to her mother in front of the little pink tea set and passed him a teacup with real tea in it. *That*, thought Madeleine, *is the advantage of playing with tea sets well into your double digits.* Gert was old enough to be trusted to use real tea in the cups, not plain water.

'Good morning, dear,' Mr Williamson muttered into the milk jug. His forehead was so shiny it looked like it would squeak if someone bumped it. He didn't greet Madeleine at all, as usual, and for once she was relieved.

Mrs Williamson was still. Her body barely registered Mr Williamson's presence.

'Do have a piece of mandarin cake, Mummy.' Gert handed her mother a tiny pink plate with a large segment of cake on it.

The plate seemed dwarfed by Mrs Williamson's dough-nutty hands. Her eyes were red and sparkly with tears. 'Well,' she said, 'isn't this jolly?' But there was nothing behind her smile; nothing but hurt.

Madeleine stared at the family clustered around the tiny tea set, and as she stared, the spaces between them seemed to expand. In the whole time she had been here, she had not once witnessed Mr and Mrs Williamson be anything other than courteous towards each other – it was always *Would you care for a devilled-egg sandwich* this, and *May I pass you the raspberry jam* that, regardless of what was going on. Even now, when things had reached crisis point. The polite pretence was exhausting.

Madeleine thought of her own parents' toxic fights before her mum had left her dad. Her mum spitting each syllable at her father; picking up the whole pot of meatballs and pausing, looking straight at Dad before the she dropped it. The crack as it hit the floor, the spray of the tomato juice on the wall and the meatballs banked up like road kill on the lino. Dad's caveman shouts, and the Robinsons leaving before dessert. Madeleine never wanted to go through that again, but at least in its own ugly way it had been honest. And it had had an end.

'Here's one for you too, Daddy,' said Gert as she handed her father a slice of cake. 'It's delicious, isn't it? Don't you think we should have parties together like this more often?'

Mr Williamson flipped Gert a quick, taut smile and popped the entire piece into his mouth. He swallowed without chewing or looking up from his plate, even though he must have known it was rude.

'Right then, I'd best be getting back to the study – I have some *very* important guests coming tomorrow, and we do have a Commonwealth to create! Thank you, Gertrude.' And he stood, bobbed his head and walked out of the nursery.

Mrs Williamson's cheeks had turned as pink as the saucers. Her slice of mandarin cake was hardening on its plate. Gert's attempt at matchmaking had been too awkward, too crude – and Madeleine didn't have a better idea. There was simply nothing the kids could do to fix this.

Mrs Williamson lifted herself up as if to rise and then slumped back onto her tiny seat. Madeleine stood and helped her to her feet.

'Thank you,' said Mrs Williamson, her voice chalky. She walked out of the room, wobbly on her feet. The seam along the back of her robe was visible, stretched white and exposed like ribs.

Madeleine started to stack the cups and saucers, but Gert just picked up a piece of cake and crammed it into her mouth. She picked up another, butter grease on her fingers. Madeleine stopped decanting the untouched tea back into the pot. 'Come on, Gert. Let's leave this behind. Let's go outside.'

Gert followed Madeleine wordlessly. It wasn't until they were almost at the door of the nursery that she asked, in a small voice, 'What will we play?'

'How about quoits?' said Madeleine.

'Quoits? Ooh, may I join in?' Elfriede had climbed the stairs like a cat, and was now fixing them both with a silky smile.

'No thank you, actually, Madeleine,' Gert said tightly. 'I have far too much tidying-up to do. Elfriede, we – that's Mummy, Daddy, Madeleine and I – just had a splendid tea party. It was so much fun. Mummy and Daddy laughed so hard that Mummy spurted water out of her mouth onto the tabletop, just like Imo.'

'Well,' said Elfriede, standing a little taller.

'Ooh, but elegantly, and how,' said Gert, looking up at her cousin. 'So elegantly. That's the thing about Mummy – at least, that's what Daddy says; she's even elegant when she's spurting water out of her mouth. Elegant, with a chiming laugh. Well, at least according to Daddy.'

Madeleine looked at Gert sadly.

'Well,' said Elfriede again, and tucked a curl behind her ear with a finger as long and slender as one of her cigarettes. 'Well, that does sound lovely. I shall try to find Bea, then, and see if she'll keep me company.'

'Oh, Bea's far too grown-up for quoits,' said Gert quickly. 'She won't even play croquet anymore.'

'I was going to ask her to accompany me on a walk.' Elfriede turned and left. Her scent hung hot on the air behind her, like a calling card.

Gert heaped the plates onto a tray while Madeleine swept up the crumbs on the tablecloth with her hand.

'Do you know what, Madeleine?' she said. 'Aunt Hen is about the only adult in this family who I like at all at the moment. I actually think she might be the only dependable one of the lot.'

# Red flag

'Stay away from your father. He has a number of gentlemen arriving for luncheon,' were the first words Nanny said to the children the next morning.

'And Mummy?' asked Gert sleepily.

Nanny's voice softened. 'She's taken another spell and she's resting.'

'Again?' Gert's voice sounded desperate. 'She seemed all right yesterday. We had tea.'

Nanny smiled her clipped smile. 'It's all right, Miss Gertrude. It's just her nerves. She'll be bright again in no time. She requires a little rest.'

'We'll take Mummy a tray then – Madeleine and me. I hate to think of her in there all alone.'

Nanny nodded. 'Have Cook include the bottle of Eno's Fruit Salts on the tray as well. It does seem to assist with these ailments.'

When the girls went downstairs and explained their request to Cook, she smiled and said, 'I'll put some of my cat's tongues on there. If anything will pull your ma out of a spell, it's some buttery cat's tongues.' She pulled a tin out onto a marble slab.

Gert sniffed appreciatively. 'We'll collect a nosegay from the kitchen garden, too.'

'Do flowers help?' asked Madeleine, stifling the urge to laugh at the word *nosegay*.

'No,' said Gert sadly.

'Jumping on her might? That always gets my dad out of bed.'

Gert shrugged. 'If she doesn't come down tomorrow, we can try it.'

Cook finished preparing the tray. 'There's the cat's tongues. I've dozens! Some for the church fair, and some for your father and his guests, but there's always more. Come back and fetch them after your breakfast.'

'Thank you!' Gert turned to Madeleine as she picked up the tray. 'Everybody is always so kind when this happens with Mummy.'

'Does it happen often?' asked Madeleine.

Gert pinched her lips together and nodded.

The girls carried the tray between them, walking carefully up the stairs to the second storey. Four closed doors came off the main hall.

'Shhh. This way.' Gert gestured at one of the doors. It was shut, no light coming from underneath it. The girls headed towards it, walking on the soft carpet that ran down the centre of the hallway, rather than on the wooden floorboards.

'Whose rooms are the other three?' whispered Madeleine.

'Bea's and a guest room. And that's Daddy's room there.'

'I thought you said your mum was in this room, though?' said Madeleine, confused.

'Yes,' said Gert. 'Mummy's room is here. Opposite Daddy's.'

'Oh,' said Madeleine.

'Mummy?' Gert knocked. There was no answer. The tray tipped slightly, and Madeleine heard tea slosh about in the silver pot.

'It's me, Gert. I'm with Madeleine.'

Silence.

Gert handed the tray to Madeleine and held her finger up. *Shhhhhh.*

'Mummy?' Gert pushed open the door. Inside, the room was dark, the curtains drawn like a cinema before the ads started. It smelt as musty as baked beans. The bedclothes were heaped together, and Mrs Williamson's big figure was lumped in with them, like a pile of dirty washing.

Gert took the tray and lowered it onto the bedside table. 'It's tea for you, Mummy. With fruit salts and some violets from the garden. We'll leave it here.'

Mrs Williamson didn't respond, and the girls left the room in a clotted silence.

~~~~~

After their own breakfast, Madeleine and Gert headed outside to try to escape the heavy atmosphere in the house.

They found Imo sitting on the verandah in her coat and hat, whistling Percy's song. '*Toow wooooo.*'

'Can't you whistle anything else?' snapped Gert. 'Percy's gone.'

Imo whistled his song louder.

'What are you doing out here, Imo?' asked Madeleine, trying to change the subject.

'Waiting for the carriages,' said Imo. 'And keeping out of the way.'

A series of carriages came rattling down the drive only minutes later. Inside them were men in hats and high-collared suits. They were all craning their necks to look over their shoulders, back towards the gate.

'What are they looking at?' asked Madeleine.

Nanny came out of the house. 'Come on, Miss Imogen, we'll go down to the post office for a walk. I'm hopeful we'll collect Miss Charlotte along the way. I could not find her anywhere in—'

Nanny let out an '*Oomph*' as Mr Williamson ran out the door and stumbled into her. His coat jacket flapped out behind him like an eagle's wings as he ran, down the steps and onto the drive, towards the approaching coaches . . . and past them, on towards the front gate.

'Look!' Gert pointed.

Madeleine looked up. The white federation flag, with its Union Jack in the corner and its blue cross and stars, flew boldly from one of the flagpoles by the gate. On the flagpole next to it, however – the one from which the Union Jack usually flew – Hen Pen's suffrage flag cracked in the breeze. The female soldiers on the flag jiggled madly, propelled by the breeze, their pen-swords jabbing.

Gert looked at Madeleine. Madeleine looked at Gert.

'Oh, *my*.' Nanny drew in a quick, hard breath.

Mr Williamson had reached the flagpole and was pulling at the rope that levered the flag up and down. He was so angry that he kept slipping.

Anna and Hen Pen ran through the front door and down towards the flagpole. The rest of the household followed suit – except for the men from the carriages, who stayed where they were on the front drive, staring.

Aunt Hen reached Mr Williamson first. Madeleine could see the veins in his neck, thick and blue, as he spun around to face her.

It was clear that Mr Williamson was trying to whisper, but his voice was fire and his hands shook.

'I tolerate you and your modern ways. I tolerate your moral looseness, your depravity, but I will *not* tolerate this. This time, you have gone one step too far. Do you have any idea who those men are? They are from all over the country. At least two are arch conservatives. The Union Jack was a statement that after federation our loyalty to the mother country will not change, but instead, you had the gall to fly *that* flag. Are you deliberately provoking me?'

'Thomas, I honestly did not—'

'Answer me this, Henrietta. Is that your flag? *Yes* or *no*?'

'But I didn't put it . . . I would never—'

'One simple question, Henrietta. Is this your flag?' His voice had become dangerously quiet.

The flag flapped at the bottom of the pole. The shields writhed, useless.

Aunt Hen nodded. 'Yes. Yes, Thomas, it is.'

Mr Williamson grabbed at the flag and tore it from the flagpole. The fabric ripped. 'I will not have you humiliate me. I will not have you and your ways sully these impressionable young ladies. Out of my house, Henrietta. Out of my house, now – just pack your bags and go.'

'T . . . Thomas,' stuttered Aunt Hen. 'Where? Don't be ridiculous. I have nowhere—'

He held up the flag. '*The Hens' Convention*? So you're behind that, too. What a fool I was not to have picked up on your clever little pun. What a gullible fool. Well, I will not suffer you and your ideas anymore. Pack your bags and be gone, with your brochures and your journals and your sashes and your flags and your ghastly ideas. Get out of my sight and off my properties, and that includes Park Street.'

Mr Williamson bundled the flag up in his arms and shoved it at Anna. 'Burn it. I shall be inside in a minute.'

'But Thomas, I . . .'

'You deserve the gutter. Just go, Henrietta. Go.'

'Thomas, don't make me, not from the girls. Thomas, *please*.'

Madeleine looked at her feet. It was galling to see Aunt Hen beg.

'*Go!*' Mr Williamson roared. It was a roar that was loud and primal and cut deep to Madeleine's marrow. A roar that hurled itself out across the property and bounced off the very mountain above.

'Nanny, take the girls up to the nursery, now.'

But Nanny and the girls were rooted in the gravel.

Aunt Hen turned then, and walked out the front gate. She left without a bag, without gloves, a hat or a coat. She put her head down, and she left without turning back.

# Owning up

**L**ater that afternoon, after the men had torn off in their carriages and the servants had cleaned up the lunch dishes and the adults had all retreated to their rooms like blue-tongue lizards in the cage back at school, Madeleine and Gert sneaked into Hen's room. It was cold and dark, but it always had been. Her little glasses were still on the dresser.

Gert picked them up. 'She won't even be able to read.' She shook her head and blinked. 'She won't really be in the gutter, will she?'

'I don't think so.' Madeleine took the glasses from Gert and put them back on the dresser. 'She can always go to Drummond Street. She keeps the key around her neck, remember? That house is awful, but it's safe and dry.'

Gert wiped at her eyes. 'I'd forgotten about Drummond Street. But even she said that street wasn't safe after dark.'

Charlie poked her head out from under the bed. 'She's not back then?' she asked timidly.

'Charlie! Don't be such a little stalker.' Madeleine smiled and shook her head. It was hard to be cross with

Charlie. 'I don't think she's coming back, though. Not today, at least.'

'I know you weren't there, Charlie, but Daddy was *beastly*,' said Gert. 'I've never seen him so angry.'

Charlie climbed out from under the bed. She beat the dust off her bottom and started to cry. 'I'm going to see Daddy now.'

'Charlie, I wouldn't. He was horrid. Anyway, he's not going to listen to you. He doesn't listen to any of us.'

Charlie took a deep breath. 'I will face it. Face it like a man.' She was gone in a flash. Madeleine and Gert followed.

Downstairs, Charlie stood at the door to her father's study. She had taken her brown dress from her knickers, and it was crumpled from the waist down. She looked tiny against the door, barely clearing the big brass doorhandle. She took a deep breath and knocked.

'Daddy, it's me. Charlie.'

'Hmmph.'

Charlie turned the doorknob.

'I'm working,' came Mr Williamson's cross voice.

'I know, Daddy, and I'm sorry, but this is important too.' Charlie took a deep breath and walked into the room.

Madeleine and Gert looked into the study from the doorway. Charlie stood before her father, who sat behind a big wooden desk topped in green leather. He was not alone – Elfriede sat in a burgundy armchair under a reading lamp, a small glass of sherry on a dark-red coffee table by her side.

'Daddy, I took the flag. I found it in Hen's room. I was

spying, and I shouldn't have been.' Charlie bit her lip. Mr Williamson stopped working and put down his pen.

'I saw the Roman soldiers and the word *fight* and I didn't even read it properly. I mean, I guess I knew, but I didn't want to cause that much trouble. I just thought it would be a bit of a tease. Like musical porridge, or pretending to wear knickerbockers. It was never Aunt Hen, Daddy, it was me, and I ought to be sent to the gutter instead.'

Mr Williamson looked at her seriously. 'You must not go through people's personal effects, Charlie, but you're not being sent away.'

Charlie burst into tears. 'I didn't mean to cause this much strife. I didn't mean for Hen to get into trouble.'

'You, dear Charlie, did not cause the trouble. Your aunt got herself into this mess all by herself. You only drew to my attention what I had long suspected.' He pulled at one sideburn.

'But please, Daddy. Aunt Hen is part of our family. Please. We don't even know where she is. There's been no word from her for hours. It's bitter outside. Mummy's in a spell. We *need* Aunt Hen.'

'It does seem a little much, Thomas,' Elfriede interjected.

Mr Williamson looked over at her and his eyes smoothed out.

'These views are very fashionable in Europe at the moment, in certain circles at least, and nothing has come of them. I find the groups all too Protestant for my taste! It's not such a threat, is it?'

Mr Williamson put his head in his hands and shook it. 'It was just . . . so awful. Did it have to happen while I had my colleagues here, for goodness sake?'

Elfriede smiled. 'Henrietta is family. Only you, Thomas, however, can decide.' And then she winked.

Mr Williamson was silent for a time. 'Charlie,' he said eventually, 'stop crying – and tuck your skirt back up into your drawers. You just don't look yourself unbreeched.' He shook his head. 'Hmm, I just know that I shall end up with nothing in the dresser but bluestockings.'

'They are not the criminal class,' said Elfriede. 'There are worse things in life.'

Mr Williamson checked his watch. 'Off you go now, Charlie,' he said. 'And close the door behind you.'

'Will you think about it, Daddy – about what Elfriede has said? Please?'

'Master Charles, I promise to do just that.'

# The lake

The next morning, Madeleine, Gert, Charlie and Imo were playing croquet on the lawn with Nanny. Bea sat on the verandah, a diary low on her lap. She ran her fountain pen over and over her fingers. Elfriede was curled in a chair some distance from Bea reading a novel, a large hat partially obscuring her face like a crescent moon.

'Do you want to join us, Bea?' called Madeleine. She felt a little sorry for her. Bea was still so unknowable. Because she didn't say much, it was hard to imagine how boring and lonely her life must be. There was no social media or phone, no school, no job; nothing to keep her in contact with anybody her own age. At least Madeleine had Gert.

'No, thank you,' Bea said in a constricted voice not like her usual smooth tone at all.

'She's still writing a list of prospective suitors; she's been doing it in consultation with Elfriede,' whispered Charlie. 'It's quite detailed – where she'd live with each fiancé, what his prospects are, whether Mummy knows his family. She's even been practising her married-name signature for each beau. No gentlemen ever call on her, even if she is beautiful; Elfriede thinks she'd be much better off in London.'

'One has three years to become betrothed after one's season. Bea had better get on with it or she'll end up a spinster like Aunt Hen,' said Gert blithely, swinging her mallet. 'Only without the brain. Such a shame.'

'Miss Gertrude, that was cruel,' said Nanny. 'I will, however, raise it with your mother again. Miss Beatrice does require appropriate company, and your mother's nerves really prevented Miss Beatrice from completing her season.'

The day was unusually warm. Madeleine closed her eyes and turned her face to the sun, and when she opened them again everything looked metallic, like bright steel.

Charlie was gone again. 'She's as quick as lightning,' said Madeleine.

'Charlie?' Gert took aim at another ball. 'Mummy says it's easier to keep track of time at the seaside than it is to keep track of Charlie!'

Madeleine laughed and looked around, only to find herself looking at Elfriede curiously instead, not for the first time that day. Elfriede had stood up for Hen Pen yesterday, when nobody else was going to. Madeleine hadn't expected that.

'Imo!' Mr Williamson stepped outside and held out his arms.

Imo flew along the grass and up onto the verandah, throwing herself at him. 'Daddy!'

Mr Williamson lifted her up and spun her around, laughing, her arms clasped tightly around his neck.

'Do watch out for your father, Miss Imogen, dear – he's not a toy,' called Nanny.

'It's perfectly satisfactory, Nanny. Actually, I was going to take a walk – perhaps Imo would like to accompany me? I thought we could sail the toy boat at the lake. I have to head back into town tomorrow.'

'That's an excellent idea,' said Nanny. 'I shall fetch it now.'

Nanny returned swiftly, a large wooden toy boat with a real fabric sail tucked under her arm.

'There's no need for you to join us, Nanny,' said Mr Williamson.

'Are you certain?' Nanny looked puzzled.

'Yes, she's no trouble. Elfriede has offered to accompany us.'

'Oh.'

Nanny looked put out, but her place had been made quite clear by the only person in the house she could not bully down.

'Well, I shall go and find Miss Charlotte, then.' Nanny's eyes went up to the top storey of the house. She's no doubt causing some sort of trouble.'

She handed the boat to Mr Williamson and turned back.

Gert looked at Madeleine and shouted, 'Daddy, Daddy, may we come too? I'd love to sail the boat.'

Nanny paused mid-step to listen.

'No, Gertrude, I think Nanny has something planned for you girls already. Nanny?'

There was a faintly perceptible shift in the tilt of Nanny's head. She turned to face the girls. 'That's right, Gertrude and Madeleine. I require help to hunt down Charlie, and then I thought we'd sort through the toys for the church fair. I know it's dull, but we must select some to donate.'

'Could we start with the toy boat?' Gert dragged her boots through the grass hard enough to leave an earthy track behind her.

Mr Williamson took off towards the lake before anyone could stop him. Elfriede put down her novel and took Imo's hand, pulling Imo along until they had caught up with Mr Williamson.

Nanny looked uncomfortable. 'Mr Williamson? Mr Williamson!' she called, stepping down off the verandah and onto the drive.

Mr Williamson turned around.

'She can't swim yet.'

He squinted. 'Excuse me, Nanny?'

'Miss Imogen can't swim yet.' Nanny was blushing.

Mr Williamson's face darkened like a rip, becoming still and murky. 'I'm well aware of that, Nanny. There will be no swimming. We are simply going to float the boat.'

'Oh dear,' said Nanny quietly.

Madeleine watched the trio's retreating backs. Mr Williamson and Elfriede were a measured distance apart. Imo skipped just ahead of them, whistling Percy's song. It really was a beautiful morning. The breeze was cool, the sun was still shining, and the sky was now clear and deep and blue. It felt like springtime.

Bea stomped across the verandah and Chopin erupted from the piano inside, dark and broken, the notes spewing across the lawn.

Nanny patted Gert's slumped back. 'Shoulders straight, Miss Gertrude. Now . . . Miss Charlotte or toys?' she asked, as kindly as Nanny could.

Gert sighed deeply. 'Charlie, I suppose.'

'Very well, then.' Nanny removed her hat and headed towards the house. She stopped. 'And girls? Do try the lake. Miss Charlie is often there.'

The girls watched Nanny walk inside.

'Did she just suggest we go down to the pond, ignoring your father's *express* instructions?' asked Madeleine.

'How dare she take off with him like that? How dare she? She's a guest. *Mummy's* guest.' Gert kicked at the grass.

'She did try to help with Aunt Hen,' said Madeleine.

'Well, Hen Pen's not back, is she?' Gert kicked the grass again and a clump of earth flew up. 'Anyway . . . Nanny's right. Charlie is most likely down near the lake. So let's go.'

The girls took the back path to the grotto then passed the empty tree and crossed the lower lawn towards the camellias, approaching the lake from below. The path was crisp with gumnuts and gravel.

'If we hide behind the bushes, we should be able to spy on them,' said Gert.

The girls peeked through the dark green leaves, spotting the trio instantly. They had chosen a spot on the water's edge close to the land bridge. Mr Williamson and Elfriede were sitting on the bank, lumped together far more closely than was necessary, talking and laughing, while Imo played nearby in the shallows. She had taken off her boots and was dragging the boat through the water. The lake was as brown and muddy as caramel. The wind had picked up a little, and the boat's sails were flapping in the breeze, agitated, setting Madeleine's teeth on edge.

'I loved that boat. Daddy gave it to Charlie, but we all loved it.' Gert watched on sadly. Her voice was damp.

*Arrrc, arrrc.* Two white cockies flew across the sky, fighting – throwing themselves at each other, squawking and dipping into an in-flight tussle. Their crowing was loud; it rang out across the water. Elfriede pointed and laughed.

Gert knocked an elbow sharply into Madeleine's ribs. 'She's gone. *Madeleine*, where's Imo? *She's gone.*'

Madeleine's head snapped back to the spot where Imo had been playing. It was empty. But Imo's whistle rang out across the water, coming from somewhere in the garden beyond Mr Williamson and Elfriede.

'*Toow wooooo.*'

'Has she headed back up towards the house? Alone?' Madeleine asked uncertainly.

'No, that's not her. It can't be. She'd never have got so far in such little time.' Gert charged through the camellias and sprinted along the shore towards her father, and then straight into the lake in her boots.

'Daddy, Daddy. Imo's gone. She's gone.'

'Gertrude? Rubbish! I can hear her whistling. Imo? Imogen? Where are you?'

'*Toow wooooo.*'

From the garden, the whistle came again – Imo's sweet, merry whistle.

'Imogen, this is not amusing. Come here at once.' Mr Williamson pulled at his fob watch. Both he and Elfriede were on their feet now, staring into the shrub beyond the path. The garden near the lake was wilder and less contained than the garden closer to the house.

Madeleine stood rooted to the spot. Her breath was thin. She willed Imogen to come whistling through the trees.

'*Toow wooooo.*'

'Imogen?'

Charlie burst from a rhododendron shrub. 'It's not Imo, Daddy – it's the lyrebird. I just saw it. I promise.' Her dress was covered in curled brown leaves and bits of undergrowth.

Madeleine ripped off her pinafore, the buttons popping like a series of burps, and ran. Tucking her dress into her knickers like Charlie, she kicked at her boots, pulling at the laces, trying to hurl them off as she ran, but the harder she pulled, the tighter they became on her feet. The flapping sound of the boat's sails now rang from the garden.

'A lyrebird. Damn folly. I'll shoot them all.' Mr Williamson ran for the shore. He reached it just before Madeleine did.

'She's there, right there,' Charlie yelled. Imogen's flannel petticoat was just visible in the shallows, like a floating dishcloth.

Elfriede shrieked. Behind her, the cockatoos shrieked too, higher and higher, screaming.

The wind blew, turning the leaves. Everything glistened in the sunlight.

'*Ach du meine Güte*, I'll get help. *Ach du meine Güte*.' She sprinted for the path back to the house. Charlie ran after Elfriede, overtaking her before they'd reached the end of the lake. 'I'll get a doctor,' she yelled.

Mr Williamson pulled Imo from the water, a tiny figure within a translucent bundle of cotton. He pulled Imo's dress from her face and hugged her to his chest, rocking her. 'She's all right, she's all right,' he kept saying.

Madeleine ran to him. 'Is she breathing?'

Imo coughed a deep, phlegmy cough, water pouring from her mouth. She opened her eyes and grinned. Her wet hair hung long and completely straight. The gaps in her teeth looked bigger and fleshier than usual. 'Madeleine.'

'Oh, Imo!' cried Madeleine, and she realised she was crying. 'Here, how many fingers am I holding up?'

'Three.'

'Clever girl!' Madeleine laughed. But then she blinked.

*Three . . . Three girls. In her dream. Back at Mum Crum's. There were three girls. Three.*

Madeleine felt time pause. The world, her world, hesitated. She turned her head, slowly, static in her ears; she turned her head against the buzz, back towards Gert. But Gert had gone. The lake was completely still.

'Gert!' Madeleine screamed. She stumbled back towards the water and ran straight in.

'Madeleine!' Mr Williamson shouted behind her. 'What are you doing? There's been more near-tragedy here this morning than in ancient Greece.'

'Gert. Gert's gone under too.' Madeleine's voice sounded far away in her own ears.

'Gert. Gertie,' Imogen cried, her voice crackly.

There wasn't so much as a bubble to show where Gert had been swallowed, only the flapping toy boat, marking the spot like an *X*. Madeleine waded into the water until it was up to her chest, and then she dived under.

The water was so dark and cloudy that she couldn't see a thing. It was thick and silty like soup, filled with bits that hit her face. She felt along the bottom as she swam, running her hands through the mud, trying not to think of what they might find. Her boots dragged her down. She thought about nippers training, where they'd made her fall into the pool in her pyjamas and then swim back to the side. Nothing could prepare a girl for being in real clothes, real heavy clothes, at the bottom of a lake.

Madeleine went up for air, gasping. The water came up to her chin now. She wiped at her eyes and tried to re-establish her bearings. The bottom undulated. She took a step forward, and fell into a hole. *Oh dammit*. Gert had been about here. *Oh, Gert.*

Madeleine kicked up to the surface, took a deep breath, and went under again. The water was colder here, but slightly clearer, brown as tea. Light filtered down in lines. Madeleine looked around her wildly, and there, on the bottom, about two metres away, was Gert in a $V$, both her arms and feet in the air. Her pale face was turned up towards Madeleine, eyes closed, mouth slack, her hair reaching up towards the light.

Madeleine didn't go up to the surface again to draw breath; she just pushed down through the water, pushing and pushing against it, grabbing Gert by the chest. She started to pull her up towards the sky, but she had to stop to readjust her grip. Gert started sinking, her petticoats floating like kelp.

Madeleine reached down through the water as she kicked. She caught Gert's apron and heaved her towards her. She was leaden in the water, much bulkier than she'd ever seemed on land and as slippery as a fish. Madeleine gripped Gert under her arms and pulled her up; she pulled her up with all the strength she had, kicking and kicking and kicking. When she broke through the silvered surface of the lake, Madeleine gasped, the pressure releasing from her lungs. She turned onto her side, looped one arm beneath Gert's arms, and began side-kicking to the water's edge in a scramble of limbs and gravel, wet cotton and mud. It felt nothing like the sleek movements the Bondi lifesavers had demonstrated for her; it felt more like a fistfight in a schoolyard.

Mr Williamson helped Madeleine to drag Gert up onto

the bank. Her dress and face were caked in mud and sticks, her body limp.

'Call an ambulance, call an ambulance,' cried Madeleine.

'The cart only operates in Ballarat,' Mr Williamson yelled back. Then he knelt over Gert and stroked her hair. 'Gertie?' he whispered. Imo peered from behind his shoulder, her eyes huge and bruised.

'Or a doctor. We need Doctor Purves,' snapped Madeleine, pushing his hand out of the way. It was shocking that a man so important could be so helpless.

Madeleine wiped a piece of weed from the corner of Gert's mouth. The skin around her eyelids was cold and grey.

Madeleine turned Gert's head to the side to clear the airways, and water gushed out of her mouth. Then Madeleine tipped back Gert's head and listened for her breath. There was silence. She listened and felt for her pulse: her heart was still beating faintly through her pinafore.

Madeleine lifted Gert's chin, put one hand on her forehead, and blew into her mouth as she'd been taught, watching as Gert's chest rose. It was satisfying and terrifying. She could think of nothing but filling Gert's chest with her breath.

Madeleine counted and then breathed into Gert again; counted and then breathed. She blew as deeply as she dared, filling Gert's lungs with all the hope she could muster.

Gert coughed, and brown water bubbled up out of her mouth and nostrils. She laboured, wheezing as she tried to draw breath, froth streaming from her nose. She coughed and then vomited. Madeleine turned her onto her side and she spluttered and choked, more brown water spewing from her mouth. She shivered violently, her face mushroom-white.

'It's okay, Gert. I'm here. You're going to be okay.' Madeleine looked down at her hand, the hand rubbing Gert's back; it was trembling. Everything stank of bile. Madeleine started to cry. Gert's eyes were now shut.

'It's going to be all right. It's going to be all right.' Madeleine gripped her friend tight.

Aunt Hen exploded down the path. Millie bounded beside her. 'Oh Gert, oh, oh, Gertrude.' She knelt beside the girls and Mr Williamson and stroked Gert's face.

Gert opened her eyes, smiled, and then coughed. 'My throat's sore,' she croaked.

'That will be the vomit; it will go shortly,' said Madeleine. 'We'll get you some water.'

'That's the last thing I want,' whispered Gert.

'It really is you – you're back!' laughed Madeleine. A massive smile broke out on her face. 'And you're back too, Aunt Hen.'

'Yes. Thomas sent Anna to find me.' She looked at her brother. 'I'm a little battered, to be frank. I haven't slept since I left yesterday, and I missed you all dreadfully.' She leant further over her niece and hugged her.

'We fished her out in the nick of time,' said Madeleine, squeezing water from her ponytail.

'Thank heavens. Oh, how perfectly dreadful.' Aunt Hen took off her shawl and wrapped Gert as tightly as a packet of fish and chips.

The veins in Gert's skin shone blue. Millie snuffled about her legs and licked them, and then settled down close beside her.

There was a thud from the path. Madeleine looked up. Charlie, Nanny, Elfriede, Bea and Mrs Williamson all ran down together. Mrs Williamson was still in her nightdress, the hem dark with mud.

'Gert's okay,' said Madeleine loudly, trying to reassure them.

'Imo,' gasped Mrs Williamson. 'Thank goodness – but Imo?'

'She's perfect.' Madeleine nodded to Imo with her head; she was squatting just beside Madeleine, the sleeve of her dress hard against the wet arm of her father's suit.

In all the drama of Gert, Madeleine had forgotten about Imo's mishap. It was a bit like someone enquiring after a grazed knee when there had been an amputation. Madeleine felt exhausted.

'Imo darling, my poor, soggy darling.'

Mrs Williamson held out a blanket for Imo. Nanny wrapped Imo in it and lifted her up for Mrs Williamson. Imo's face peeked out of a small triangle of green fabric; she looked a bit like a stuffed olive. 'Madeleine saved Gert!' Imo chirped. 'Madeleine *saved* her! She breathed her back again.'

'I just grabbed her from the bottom of the lake,' said Madeleine, suddenly realising that for all she knew, the CPR she'd just performed had not even been invented yet.

'She fished her out of the water,' said Mr Williamson. 'Swam down and hauled Gert out. We are just so fortunate we had such a competent swimmer on hand.'

Nanny knelt to hand another blanket to Gert, tucking it tightly around her shoulders. She gave them a rub before she handed a blanket to Madeleine too.

'Come up to the house now, everybody,' said Mrs Williamson. 'We'll get the girls off to bed and I shall have Anna bring in camomile tea and toast. I sent a servant to fetch Doctor Purves – he shall hopefully be here shortly.'

There was a lightness to her voice now. She was in charge. Mrs Williamson was back, looking after her family, directing people.

Gert smiled up at Madeleine. 'I love Mummy like this.'

'Thomas.' Mrs Williamson's voice cut through the air, sharp now. 'I am going to send word to Frau Lüers. It's time Elfriede departed for Sydney.'

Mr Williamson nodded. He lifted Gert into the air, her feet dangling from his arms. Madeleine walked behind them. Mrs Williamson handed Imo to Nanny and put one arm about Madeleine's cloaked shoulders.

Madeleine couldn't stop shivering. She could still taste mud in her mouth, and her hands stank of vomit, but she felt a freedom and a lightness and a pride that was almost dizzying in its warmth, and she could not recall another moment when she had felt so well, so strong, so useful.

Aunt Hen came close. 'Thank you so much, Madeleine. Thank you so much,' she whispered. 'We are so lucky to have you.'

Mrs Williamson rubbed Madeleine's hair with a blanket she was carrying. 'It's getting a curl, Madeleine!' she exclaimed.

The group trooped back to the house together, some wet and goosepimply, some with collars unbuttoned and the fug of stress about them. It was only when they were cradling warm cups of tea in the morning room that Madeleine heard the rattle of carriage wheels. Mrs Williamson looked at Mr Williamson and shook her head: Elfriede had gone.

# A doll and goodbye

That afternoon, after Doctor Purves had come to examine Gert and Imo, and Mrs Williamson had gone through a few litres of tea, Charlie harnessed the pony trap and then she and Imo ran it backwards and forwards over the lower lawn until the pony had kicked up thick clods of grass and Mr Williamson came bellowing from the house telling them to stop.

Madeleine and Gert watched from a tartan rug they'd laid out nearby, both lying on their tummies, the sun warm on their backs. Madeleine felt completely safe and comfortable – the way she'd felt as a little kid some mornings when she'd been allowed to snuggle in between her mum and dad in their bed.

She picked at a jagged thumbnail; it had caught right down low where the white met the pink. 'I must have snagged myself on the bottom of the lake.' She peeled the nail off; it came away like an orange skin. 'Here you go, Gert – a keepsake. You can stick this on the grotto wall.'

Gert scrunched her nose and rolled over.

'It's funny, isn't it? A tooth's acceptable on a wall – there's something sort of fairy-like about it – but a fingernail is disgusting!' Madeleine laughed and flicked the nail into the grass.

Bea was sitting on the edge of their rug and their conversation, sewing tiny crosses on a small, round frame. She looked up from under her hat. She'd rarely addressed Madeleine before now, but so much fuss had been made about Madeleine today that even Bea was moved to interest.

'I've always thought the same thing of hair. All those things they do with it – it's sort of ghoulish. Mummy has that mourning locket, which has a little curl of her own mother's hair plaited behind the glass.'

'May I have the scissors, Bea?' asked Gert.

Bea passed Gert a tiny pair of scissors shaped like a crane.

'Here.' Gert motioned at Madeleine's hair. 'Do you mind?'

'Of course not,' said Madeleine, and she heard the graze of a snip.

Bea passed Gert some aqua tapestry thread, and Gert bound it around the hair, leaving the thread a little grubby. 'I'll stick it to the grotto wall.'

'Let me get some of yours too.' Madeleine cut a little piece of Gert's hair from the bottom of her plait. The ends were dry and bushy and sprang every which way, but they glowed almost red in the light. She bound it in some red thread Bea had passed over for the purpose. 'Now we can stick yours up too.'

Madeleine manipulated the scissors and watched the little crane open and close its beak. When she thought about it, it wasn't so much strange what these times, these Victorian times, didn't have so much as what they *did* have. Apart from the internet and TV, the groundwork for almost everything Madeleine knew was already laid: trains, high buildings, sweets, cars, scissors, even feminism. It was all there, just old-fashioned.

Madeleine handed the scissors back to Bea. There were so many things – like scissors, and pins, and needles and thread – that had already been invented by anonymous people, and had already given the world a shape she recognised. Did she not know the name for the inventor of scissors because it had been a woman? Or were scissors something that had always been there, passed along an endless chain from generation to generation? Surely the invention of scissors was every bit as much a revolution as the invention of Gutenberg's printing press, and yet no single person was celebrated.

Madeleine rolled onto her back and stared up at the sky. She had obviously spent too much time around Aunt Hen.

They heard a crunch of gravel. 'Is that another lyrebird playing tricks,' said Madeleine, 'or is someone coming?'

Bea laughed. 'Daddy will shoot them all now.'

'What? Shoot them really?' asked Madeleine. 'Aren't they native?'

'No,' said Bea. 'Not in this area. They're fashionable. Daddy heard about them and thought they sounded fun. So he bought some. And they are fun, if a little deceitful. They liked it here, too – they've thrived. Even Millie doesn't bother them.'

A native bird that wasn't actually native. Madeleine was still mulling this over when a shadow above her blocked out the sun.

'Good afternoon, girls.' Aunt Hen stood above her, holding a large box wrapped in brown paper. 'This was left in the hall for you.'

Charlie and Imo had abandoned the pony trap and run over. 'For which one of us? Who is it addressed to?' asked Charlie.

'*To whom is it addressed*. All of you. *The Misses Beatrice, Gertrude, Charlotte and Imogen Williamson.*'

Aunt Hen handed the parcel to Gert. Millie bounced up on her hind legs, trying to have a look.

'It's written in her beautiful copperplate,' said Bea, and she was right – it was beautiful writing, even managing to make the word *Gertrude* look quite elegant.

'But who is it *from*?' asked Imo, jumping about like Millie.

'Take it back to the house,' said Bea imperiously.

'Oh, come, Bea, don't be such a party pooper!' said Aunt Hen and winked. 'Imo, you'll no doubt have to open the package to reveal the sender, although, like Bea, I am well able to guess who it might be. Everybody deals with life and its limitations in their own particular way, girls. I only hope you'll choose your own paths wisely.'

Madeleine watched Aunt Hen stride away, her steps short and nippy. She was a quick walker, Aunt Hen – a quick walker, a quick talker and a quick thinker.

Gert ripped the package open, to reveal a box and a note. 'It's from her – Elfriede,' she said, as spitty as a cat, handing the package too fast to Bea, who passed it straight back. There was something of the hot potato about that package.

In the end, Bea put the present on her lap, leant back in her chair and sighed. 'I'm not sure I have the strength to deal with this just yet.'

'I do!' said Charlie. 'Master Charles loves presents. What does the letter say?'

'Just one sentence. *Girls, I am so very sorry.* As if a childish present like this can ever make amends.' Bea's face had reddened.

'Has Elfriede really gone?' asked Imo.

'I hope so,' said Charlie. 'Now come on, Bea, pass me the box. Regardless of what she was like, it is exciting to get our very own package . . . I'd like to see what it contains.'

Bea stood up and handed the box to Charlie. The girls bunched tightly around it in a circle – all except Madeleine, who flipped over on the grass to lie on her back. The sun was warm on her neck and tummy. Sun! Man, she did miss Sydney's sun. The gong rang out across the lawns, calling the staff to tea.

Madeleine heard the rustle of packaging, the bleat of a doll – *Mama, Mama* – and a thud as Charlie dropped the box to the ground at their feet in surprise.

'But she's just so beautiful,' said Imo.

'Her costume really is quite elegant,' said Bea resentfully.

'Is that real ermine on her bonnet?' asked Charlie, sighing.

'*Er-min*, not *er-meen*,' corrected Bea. 'But yes, I suppose it is.'

There was a long silence then, eventually punctured by a sniffling sound.

'Gert,' said Bea softly. 'There's no need to cry.'

Madeleine opened her eyes. She watched as Gert bent to retrieve the doll in one hand and the box it had come out of in the other.

'Damn foreign cousins,' Gert yelled and threw the box hard across the lawn. It spun all the way into some white azaleas. The girls watched as the flowers swallowed it whole.

Then Gert stood up, running her finger over the doll's skirt. 'It's silk velvet.'

*Mama. Mama*, said the doll.

'Oh, stop that wailing, will you?'

Gert held the doll up and looked it straight in the eye. Then she handed it to Imo.

'Imo, you might as well have her. She is beautiful. Cold and hard the whole way through, but definitely beautiful. Anyway, that's just the way she was made.'

'Just for me? Really?' Imo squeaked. Gert nodded.

'That's a grand idea,' said Bea.

'*I* don't want her.' Charlie did a cartwheel.

Gert laughed out loud. She looked up into the sky and yelled, 'DAMN ELFRIEDE VON FRÜMPENBERG; DAMN EVERYTHING.'

Bea, Charlie and Imo watched on, mouths slack. Then they started to giggle.

Gert laughed again. She spun across the grass with her arms out, spinning and spinning, spinning like a top, petti-coats blurring.

Madeleine closed her eyes. The muscles in her shoulder were still sore from the lake, and she was sleepy, so very sleepy. Imo was whistling Percy's song again. And it was funny, Madeleine could have sworn she heard Elfriede's high-pitched, musical laugh coming from somewhere high above the tree canopy . . .

'Beat you to the playhouse,' yelled Gert. 'Madeleine?'

Madeleine heard the girls take off across the lawn. She imagined the streak of flying hats, skirts and boots.

'Madeleine?'

'Hmmm.' Madeleine was so sleepy she could barely muster the energy to answer.

'Madeleine?'

'I'm fine, thanks. I've seen the playhouse plenty of times,' she giggled from under her hat. She felt too thick and lazy to move. 'And do you know what? I know you love the playhouse and dolls – well, most of them – but me? I'm too old for dolls. There, I said it.'

'Too old for dolls? Possibly. But you're certainly too young to be snoozing in parks all by yourself in the middle of winter, young lady. Even in the country.'

Madeleine sat up. Mum Crum stood above her, frowning, a deep *N* formed between her eyebrows.

'Mum Crum, Mum Crum. *Ohmigod!*' Madeleine yelled.

She leapt up and spun, taking in her surroundings. The fence was back: there it was in the distance, and the barbecue, and the old metal slide. She took a breath. There was the long line of tall soldier-oaks – and Madeleine could smell hay, lanolin and rust.

'Oh, thank goodness. I thought I'd never try your seven-root-vegetable juice again.'

Madeleine threw her arms around her bony little grandmother. Mum Crum gave Madeleine a quick, sharp hug. It was glorious.

'Mum Cruuuum!'

'Calm down, darling,' said Mum Crum, linking her arm through Madeleine's. 'You only went to the Muse. I know that new volunteer is unbearable, but I didn't expect you to be this excited. I got less of a welcome at the airport.'

Mum Crum looked at Madeleine and the skin around her eyes crinkled. 'What have you got on? Are they having a costume day? Sovereign Hill does that sometimes!'

'I didn't really have a choice,' said Madeleine.

'Rubbish,' Mum Crum snapped. 'There is always a choice, but fancy dress' – she pushed Madeleine's hair off her forehead – 'is a fun one.'

Madeleine smiled at her grandmother. 'Do you know what, Mum Crum? There might always be a choice, but sometimes the consequences can be seriously unfair.'

'Oh Moo, I don't mind what choices you make, darling, but I would prefer it if you'd keep me informed. If I lost you, your mother would never forgive me. Next time, I'll let you take your phone. Didn't I learn *that* the hard way!'

She gave Madeleine another hug, and Madeleine let her. There really was no better feeling in the entire world than when someone was happy to see you.

# *Joining the dots*

**M**um Crum lay on the floor of Madeleine's room pulling her leg over her head while Madeleine packed her bags. 'I love yoga, Maddy Moo,' she declared. 'That's the key to long-lasting youth – flexibility.'

The droopy tattoo on her ankle stretched and sank as Mum Crum moved her legs.

'What does the tattoo mean, Mum Crum?'

Her grandmother laughed. 'Nothing. Absolutely nothing. I chose a tomato because it has no meaning. I simply wanted to do something outlandish, a reckless celebration, and it was pretty outrageous. But don't you even think about getting one.'

'What did your parents say?'

'My mother had listened in on a phone call I'd made to a friend of mine, so it came as no surprise to her.' Mum Crum pressed her palms together. 'I was a rebel – just like your mum. The only thing *she* could do to get up my nose was drop out of uni and get married, and so she did. It just about killed me.'

Madeleine stopped packing and threw a pair of socks at her grandmother. She was going back to Sydney tomorrow.

'Ow!' Mum Crum rubbed her head in mock pain. 'I'll show you a photo of Mummy, if you'd like.'

Mum Crum disappeared for a few minutes, then returned carrying two old silver photo frames. She handed the first one over to Madeleine to inspect.

The picture showed a couple sitting on a beach. The man was in a short-sleeved shirt; he had a square, dimpled chin and he was sucking on a pipe. The woman had long, shiny limbs and was wearing navy bathers. She looked strong and smiley.

'Mummy was an excellent swimmer,' said Mum Crum. 'She must have been about fifty there. She looks pretty astounding for somebody who'd had six children. I was the last child, and the only girl.'

'Six children!' Madeleine frowned. 'There's something sort of familiar about her.'

'Well, she *is* my mother,' said Mum Crum with a laugh. 'I looked quite like her when I was younger. Look, here she is as a girl.'

Mum Crum sat down next to Madeleine so that they could inspect the second photograph together. It was a picture of four girls, and although they were teenagers, there was absolutely no doubt who they were: the Williamson sisters.

Mum Crum pointed to Charlie in the photo. 'You see? That's Mummy there.'

Madeleine choked. 'That's your *mother*? *Charlie* is your mum?'

Mum Crum nodded. 'Charlotte, really, but they called her Charlie, and great fun she was, too. Now there's a connection – you know they lived at the Muse for a while.'

'*What?*'

'Oh Maddie, I've told you that at least a thousand times . . . They sold most of the property when Mummy was a girl – subdivided the land, kept a few smaller blocks like this one as investments, and the family moved back to Melbourne. This area was terribly social in summer but completely isolated in winter. Coincidentally, Mummy met Daddy up here years later, at a cricket match.'

'Charlie *married?*'

'Why yes,' said Mum Crum, looking surprised at Madeleine's reaction.

'A boy?'

'Well, she married a man. I just showed you Daddy. Mummy was just like you, Maddy Moo – very sporty. She ended up playing cricket for Victoria.'

'You could do that back then, as a girl? That's amazing!'

'I didn't know you were so interested in family history.' Mum Crum wiped her finger across the frame of the old photo.

'Neither did I, really,' Madeleine admitted, 'but it's a bit more interesting than family present. Nobody in my family does *anything*.'

'Your mum's studying for her infectious diseases exams. That's interesting. If people keep refusing to vaccinate their kids we're going to start—'

'Losing babies.' Madeleine ached as she thought about Mrs Williamson and her outstretched hands reaching for Baby Reggie at the séance.

'Exactly. And as for me, well, if I didn't need to get this place done up for the next tenant then you'd never have sanded my old cupboard and you'd never have found those shoes! And doesn't it look wonderful!'

Madeleine looked at the cupboard. It was as brawny as a bouncer at a bank. She walked over to it, opened the door and sniffed: mothballs. The secret compartment on the right-hand side was still open.

Madeleine ran her fingers left along the shelf. 'The left drawer doesn't go all the way to the end either, but there's no finger groove here like there is on the right.' She looked back at Mum Crum. 'Do you have a knife? There could easily be a compartment under this side too.'

'Do you think so?' exclaimed Mum Crum. 'Let's see if we can jimmy it!'

Mum Crum retrieved a butter knife from the kitchen, and Madeleine angled the metal blade down the side of the board. She levered it upwards. The board creaked and then popped open.

'It does!' Madeleine plunged her hand down into the second secret compartment and pulled out a cream cardboard box.

'It's not as fancy as the last one,' said Mum Crum. 'Perhaps not worth showing to the Muse this time.'

Madeleine pulled off the lid. 'That's fortunate. The last one took me much further than I'd anticipated.'

Inside the box, laid out on a square of blue felt, was a silver locket. The lid of the locket was slightly dented, and the initials *G.M.W.* were etched on the front.

Madeleine picked it up. The locket was smooth and opened like a book; inside were spots for two photos. From the left-hand disc, Aunt Hen stared out, her bun lopsided and her chin tilted, intelligent and fierce. Tucked behind the glass of the other frame was a tight curl of honey-coloured hair, bound in faded aqua thread.

Madeleine ran her fingers over the initials again. 'Gertrude Mary Williamson,' she said. 'They called her Gert.'

'They did! She was my aunt. What on earth is that doing in there? I was very sad when she died. We were close.'

*Died.* Madeleine started.

'Not until she was in her eighties,' said Mum Crum gently, noting her reaction. 'But that's old age for you. We all go at some stage.'

Mum Crum took the locket and hung it around Madeleine's neck. 'You can have it, darling. It looks pretty, and I'm hardly going to wear it.'

'Really?' Madeleine smiled and opened the locket again.

'I wonder whose hair that is.' Mum Crum ran a finger over the little curl under the glass. 'Mummy's, perhaps.' She held the locket up to Madeleine's face. 'Snap! It's exactly your colour!'

Madeleine smiled and snibbed the locket shut. Her hands were quivering. 'Thank you. I'd love to keep it.'

'Good,' said Mum Crum, smiling back at her. 'Old Aunt Gert was the illegitimate daughter of the suffragist Henrietta Williamson. She was adopted by Henrietta's older brother, Sir Thomas Williamson – my grandfather. He played some role in federation – not as big a role as he liked to think, Mummy always said, but he did go on to become a judge.'

'Gert was illegitimate?' Madeleine couldn't quite get her mouth around the words.

'Don't look so surprised, darling,' laughed Mum Crum. 'People had babies outside marriage back then too, you know. It was just not spoken of . . . not spoken of at all. The families tended to absorb the children.'

'So . . . who was Gert's father?' Madeleine swallowed.

'They're not certain. *Latere semper patere, quod latuit diu.*'

'What? Come on, Mum Crum. Don't go all Latin on me now.'

'*Leave in concealment what has long been concealed.* Should be on the family coat of arms. Henrietta was very young – no more than eighteen. Gert lived with Granddaddy's family but never really fitted in. She read law at Oxford later, like her mum.'

'Aunt Hen? I mean . . . Henrietta?'

'That's right. After she studied, Aunt Gert returned here and campaigned for illegitimate children. *Don't blame the child* stuff, which is completely taken for granted now, but it was pretty revolutionary at the time. It was her life's work. She used all her legal contacts for lobbying – some of those men became quite powerful in the end. I don't think she was ever a girl of her own time, but she was a dab hand on the property market.'

'Is that where you get it from?'

'I'm just continuing the family tradition.' Mum Crum laughed. 'It was Aunt Gert who left all that property to me. She never married. It's been important for me to give back, Moo. Property has become so expensive, and even rent is impossible for many people these days; that's why I set up the trust.' She knocked on the walls of the little house. 'These houses were never mine to start with. It feels fair.'

'Did Gert know who her mum was?'

'Of course,' said Mum Crum. 'But not until she was an adult. Her mother never knew *she* knew, mind. It must have been horrible for Henrietta, always resented, always judged.'

Madeleine's head was whirling. Everything suddenly made sense. So that was why Aunt Hen had stuck around; why she had always been hovering on the edges: *Thomas, don't make me, not from the girls. Thomas,* please.

*How awful*, thought Madeleine, contemplating the enormity of Aunt Hen's loss: present, but only ever an observer; watching the disfavour bestowed upon her own child, but powerless to do anything about it.

Mum Crum pulled the felt out of the cardboard box. 'Maddy, look!' She drew out a tiny black leather case that had been hidden beneath the felt. Inside the case nestled a thin ring, made of white gold, with two locked hands across its top. Each hand had a tiny ring on one of its fingers, one a little emerald chip and the other a small amethyst.

'Purple and green – the colours of emancipation. It's a suffrage ring!' said Mum Crum. 'I bet it belonged to Henrietta.'

Madeleine slipped the ring onto her index finger. 'If it did, she didn't wear it in nineteen hundred.'

'How could you possibly know that, darling?' asked Mum Crum. 'Anyway, I don't think they had the suffrage colours until later than that.'

'Really?'

'Different leagues used different colours. These ones came from England. *White for purity in public as well as private life; purple for dignity and self-respect; and green for hope and new life.* Old Aunt Gert had a poster about it in her kitchen.'

Madeleine gazed at the ring on her finger, the little hands clasped strong in solidarity.

'Emily Wilding Davison, an Englishwoman, ran in front of the King's horse at a derby carrying flags in these very colours under her coat, you know,' said Mum Crum. 'She ran in front of a horse . . . and died for the vote.' Mum Crum looked thoughtful. 'We didn't have to be so extreme here, as we got the vote sooner. Maybe that's why there's still so much for us to improve.'

'What do you mean?' asked Madeleine.

'As my mother used to say, everyone thought Australian women got the vote early because we were a young country with our own rules, like New Zealand, which just got in before us – but really it was messier than that. In Western Australia, men gave women the vote only when they thought women were more likely to keep them in power. And we weren't so quick anyway – the great majority of Aboriginal people couldn't vote in Australian elections until the sixties. Criminal.'

Madeleine studied the cardboard box; it was shallower than it should have been. She peered more closely, and then lifted up a thin board that had been dividing the top of the box from the bottom. Beneath lay thirty little compartments, filled with small metal letters and punctuation marks on long pins, all jumbled up like a box of assorted chocolates.

'Letterpress blocks!' said Madeleine. 'From the printer!'

'So they are, clever girl,' said Mum Crum. 'Aren't they terrific?'

It felt so strange but also glorious, sharing this with her grandmother. Like trading lunches over a century.

'Didn't your mother have other sisters?' Madeleine asked.

'Two – Imogen and Beatrice. Beatrice married an earl and went to live in England. That's the fancy side of the family. Imogen was a nurse in World War One, and then came home and married. Mummy always said she baked a mean teacake.'

Madeleine smiled. 'And what about Elfriede?' she said, although she was almost too scared to ask. 'Was there an Elfriede in the family?'

'Not in the family, darling, but it is the name of this cottage. How did you know to ask that?'

Madeleine frowned. 'But this is Elf Cottage.'

'Elf-*riede*. Go and have a look at the front – I just haven't finished painting the name yet. We always called it Elf Cottage as kids too. There was some sort of kerfuffle about it and Mummy never used its full name. Ahh, there is so much to do! Let's borrow a ladder later today and finish painting outside.'

'Okay,' said Madeleine wondering what on earth that meant. Had Mr Williamson named the cottage after Elfriede? Out of sentimentality? Had Elfriede come back? She'd probably never know.

Madeleine looked at herself in the small mirror above the fireplace. 'I'm going to have a shower before we start painting. I feel grotty.' One hundred years' worth of dust was sitting in her pores.

Mum Crum hugged Madeleine and rubbed her arm. 'Feel those muscles! I do love a strong, capable body.' She ran her fingers up Madeleine's back and through her hair, and then smiled. 'Your hair's starting to get a curl to it. My curls only kicked in at fourteen, and now look at them!'

Mum Crum left the room, her frizzy Maggi Noodle ponytail puffing out behind her.

After her shower, Madeleine sat on the couch in the sitting room with the box of letters on her lap and her laptop by her side. She ran the sharp alphabet pins through her fingers. Gert and Aunt Hen would never have guessed just how easy publishing would become – proper books printed out just one copy at a time; endless blogs about endless subjects and news sites online; everything broadcast on social media and shot all over the world. Anyone could do it. Even a school-girl like Tavi Gevinson.

Madeleine lined some of the letters up on a cushion.

Anyone could have a voice.

The thing about effecting change, thought Madeleine, was that you got used to being able to achieve some things by working hard – hitting the middle stump in cricket once you'd bowled enough balls, for example. Only then you realised that there were also things you could never change.

You might never manage to make your parents drink each other in over the tops of their teacups; never get them to kiss in the shadows of a hidden hollow, or even get them to simply look at each other nicely and say hello. And if you got jammed in the past, you mightn't always be able to get back, no matter how many clairvoyants were around.

But there *were* things you could change: little changes, little bits at a time. Like Aunt Hen and her magazine. Or Percy and his whistle. As Mum Crum had said, you always had a choice, and suddenly Madeleine could see that this choice had never been so easy.

Madeleine wouldn't be able to control the whole world, but there were things of her own that she could change. And she would.

Madeleine pulled out her laptop and started an email to Nandi.

Would you like to start a blog? A sports blog for girls . . . *Wriggly Girls*? We can ask questions like: Why isn't Ellyse Perry a household name; who else plays *two* sports at a world-class level? How can we get more women's sport on TV? How can we ever be any good if we have to spend all our practice time working at Bunnings to pay the gas bill? I'm going to start writing my first post now! If you join me, we'll finally have an actual use for all those Wisden cricket stats we've memorised.

She hit 'send', put down her laptop and grinned. Behind her, the juicer whizzed – solid, spinachy, certain. She was back with Mum Crum, and somehow she'd muddle through.

## Wriggly Girls!

Ninety-five per cent of change was in the actual *doing*. Madeleine would not just be a gumnut on the sea; she'd have her shot at doing something, changing something, something of her own.

With Nandi.

And all from the couch.

# *Acknowledgements*

The acknowledgements for my books always seem to run almost as long as the novels themselves, but there is a team behind any work, particularly an historical one. With love and thanks to the following people:

- Lisa Gorton, Elizabeth Glickfeld, Alice Kelly, Christine Hinwood, Andrew McDonald, Rebecca Lim and Fiona Wood, who read the full manuscript at various stages and provided encouragement and astute feedback.
- Sofie Laguna, who, despite her work and parenting commitments, read the novel quickly and provided such a generous and utterly joyful pull-quote.
- Clare Renner, Olga Lorenzo and my co-students at RMIT, who provided feedback on sections of the novel in the very early days.
- Antoni Jach and his wonderful Master Class II, which gave me confidence at the very time I was bogged in twins and had abandoned all hope.
- The Australia Council for the Arts, and Readings Foundation – thank you for your support as I wrote this.
- Pippa Masson, Fiona Inglis, Marie Campbell and also Bella Pearson, who loved the idea for this story from the outset and made me think it could work.

- Elise Jones, Eva Mills and Hilary Reynolds at Allen & Unwin, for the extraordinary attention you give, for the complete investment you have and for your willingness to be brutal with a red pen. There is no gilding, and I am always exceptionally grateful for your professionalism, intelligence and honesty.

The decision to write an Aboriginal character, particularly a nineteenth-century Aboriginal male, was not a decision I took lightly, but in a novel that deals with suffrage I believed, and still believe, the greater error would have been to exclude the Aboriginal part of the suffrage narrative. In making that decision, I am exceptionally grateful for the help I have had from a number of people, including:

- Aunty Joy Murphy and the Wandoon Estate Aboriginal Corporation, for their permission to reference cultural material in the story – and for so generously taking the time to consider this work.
- Lisa Fuller, for her specific advice on the novel, which was always smart, always nuanced, and for being so very giving with her time.
- Yolanda Walker-Finette and her mum, Esmai Manahan, for their speedy, ever-patient and thoughtful answers to my questions.
- Coranderrk, where I was privileged to attend the performance of the La Mama play *Coranderrk: We Will Show the Country* by Giordano Nanni and Andrea James on country on a perfect February evening in 2016.
- Dr Felicity Jensz, who introduced me to Coranderrk and suggested that with its history of political agitation, it might just be the perfect place for the character of Percy to have been raised.

In addition, thanks to the following professionals who also gave their time so generously to assist with this novel. Any mistakes are mine. Thanks to:

- Dr Andrew Hurley and Dr Shelley Marshall for their help with some historical fact-finding.
- My sister-in-law, Eva Lüers, for help with the German.
- The Gisborne Mount Macedon Historical Society Inc.
- Mrs Janet Davies and the PLC Melbourne Archive; your assistance is gratefully acknowledged.
- Gabrielle Wang and Rebecca Lim, together with the Museum of Chinese Australian History in Melbourne, for their illuminating discussions and information on Chinese early settlement in Australia.
- Dominic and Marie Romeo, authors of *The Constant Renovators*, for their help on historical homes in the Mount Macedon area.
- The State Library of Victoria, not only for giving me access to its collection but also for advice on the binding of periodicals and small presses.
- Mark Bau, for his expertise on Victorian trains and railway timetables.
- Celine Kiernan, for her help with Cook's Irish slang.
- Ruby Alpitsis and Gabriel Chan, who have set the soundtrack to this novel and, together with Annabel Orr, provided good counsel and medical information.
- Nandi Segbedzi, for her specific help on the Nandi character in this novel, and darling Gilbert, just because.
- Meg Dalling, with whom I first started thinking about women's suffrage and its implications for democracy as we undertook our honours legal thesis; and all the other

strong women with whom we went through university, bloody feminists all.

This novel has taken so long to write, and I undertook a considerable amount of research over the years as I tried to work out what the story would be. This is in no way a conclusive bibliography, but I would like to acknowledge the following works that have informed this novel and might be of interest to those readers seeking further information:

- *Woman Suffrage in Australia: A Gift or a Struggle?*, by Audrey Oldfield, Cambridge University Press, 1992.
- *Utopia Girls: How Women Won the Vote*, a documentary directed by Jasmin Tarasin, produced by Lucy McClaren and Alex West, written by Dr Clare Wright and Alex West, Renegade Films, 2011.
- Coranderrk website, **coranderrk.com**.
- *Coranderrk, We Will Show the Country*, by Giordano Nanni and Andrea James, Aboriginal Studies Press, 2013.
- Minutes of Evidence website, **www.minutesofevidence. com.au**, for further information on Coranderrk.
- 'Guidelines for the Ethical Publishing of Aboriginal and Torres Strait Islander Authors and Research from Those Communities', Aboriginal Studies Press, Australian Institute of Aboriginal and Torres Strait Islander Studies (AIATSIS), 2015, **aiatsis.gov.au/sites/default/files/docs/ asp/ethical-publishing-guidelines.pdf**.
- AIATSIS's 'My Voice for My Country' online exhibition, **aiatsis.gov.au/myvoicemycountry** – for a history of Indigenous suffrage in Australia.
- Australian Electoral Commission website, **www.aec.gov.au–**

© Australian Electoral Commission 2016, for some useful resources and background on suffrage.

- *The Constitution: The Document that Created the Nation*, by Scott Brodie, Trocadero Publishing, 2011.
- 'Marvellous Mimic' clip from David Attenborough's *The Life of Birds* series, **www.bbc.co.uk/nature/life/ Superb_Lyrebird#p004hgk8**, for a brief introduction to the wonderful performances of the appropriately named superb lyrebird.

To my grandmother, Nen, who is a wonderful story-teller and who taught me that the most important gift you can give a child to help them cope with life's curveballs is a sense of humour.

To my mum, who had Joyce Stevens's 'Because We're Women' on a poster next to the stove and who has provided meals, kid-sitting and historical feedback on this novel. And to my dad, who tolerated it.

To Peter, Ben, Madeleine, George and Edgar, who, to be perfectly frank, prevented me from writing this novel for so long, but in the end did everything they could to support me. With love and thanks.

Finally, as a writer, I am first and foremost a reader. I would therefore like to acknowledge the children's writers who have come before me, particularly Ruth Park, whose extraordinary novel *Playing Beatie Bow* continues to haunt readers today. This work, together with a number of other time-slip novels, gave me a love of history and my child-hood a feeling of infinite possibility.

# About the author

Kim Kane was born in London in a bed bequeathed by Wordsworth for '. . . a writer, a dancer or a poet'. Despite this auspicious beginning, she went on to practise law. Her picture book *Family Forest* was shortlisted for the Children's Book Council of Australia (CBCA) Awards, and *The Vegetable Ark* and *Esther's Rainbow* were both CBCA Notable Books. Her junior fiction novel *Pip: The Story of Olive* won the Barbara Ramsden Award and was short-listed for the Australian Book Industry Awards (ABIA) and Speech Pathology Australia Book of the Year Awards. Kim's young adult thriller *Cry Blue Murder*, co-written with Marion Roberts, was shortlisted for the Inky Awards and the Davitt Awards and was highly commended in the Western Australian Premier's Book Awards. She has also written a junior fiction series called Ginger Green, Play Date Queen. Kim lives with her family in Melbourne. She writes whenever and wherever she can.